MINUS FIFTY BELOW

by

Ronnie Sarkin

Other books by Ronnie Sarkin

The Maya Trilogy:

Condor's Eye

Kismet

Maya

Tau the Talking Lion

Galaxy Destroyer

Rippling Time

PREFACE

Why write about an impending ice age when the world is grappling with accelerating global warming? In my journey through life, I've never been content with superficial explanations. I've always sought to probe deeper, uncovering hidden truths often shrouded by misleading narratives. Are we wrong to assume that global warming will continue unchecked? This novel questions that assumption, offering serious justifications for considering an alternative future.

I've long admired authors like Malcolm Gladwell, who masterfully challenge conventional thinking. His recent book 'Talking to Strangers' demonstrates how often we misinterpret people and events, exposing the flawed reasoning behind our assumptions. Similarly, 'Minus Fifty Below' confronts the widespread belief in a never-ending global warming trend, suggesting that this trajectory might lead to an entirely different climatic event.

Another source of inspiration is Yuval Noah Harari, whose books Sapiens, Homo Deus, and 21 Lessons for the 21st Century are thought-provoking explorations of humanity's past, present, and future. Harari's insistence on questioning widely accepted "truths" resonates with my own belief: that we must continue to dig deeper and not accept anything at face value.

This mindset became especially relevant during the Covid-19 pandemic, a time rife with unsubstantiated theories, conspiracy theories, false narratives, and general misinformation. It taught us to view even seemingly credible information with skepticism, as hidden agendas often distort the truth. Cynicism about a possible ice age is central to the themes explored in Minus Fifty Below.

In the 1960s and seventies, books like Rachel Carson's Silent Spring, Herman Kahn's Thinking About the Unthinkable, The Doomsday Book by Gordon Rattray Taylor, and The Limits to Growth by the Club of Rome all sounded early alarms about humanity's destructive path. Their warnings were terrifying, but it took decades for the concept of even global warming to gain widespread acceptance. Now, we face an even graver question: Are we already at the tipping point, with apocalyptic consequences looming? The younger generation, burdened with the legacy of environmental destruction, voices the loudest cries for change. Yet, those in power remain entrenched in old ways, still reluctant and hesitant to embrace the transformative measures urgently needed.

The Covid-19 pandemic offered a glimpse of how quickly nature can regenerate, but at an enormous cost with ruined economies, widespread hardship, and untold suffering. The inertia to sustain our current economic momentum perpetuates outdated practices, even as the need for a new paradigm becomes increasingly urgent. Without significant change, we and even more so, our children and grandchildren will bear the consequences of humanity's blind march toward destruction.

In the 1970s, I was captivated by apocalyptic survival novels like Larry Niven and Jerry Pournelle's Lucifer's Hammer. In March 2017, a lecture presented in Toronto offered a chilling perspective: Global warming doesn't lead to a barren, Mars-like wasteland. It could trigger an ice age instead. The warming northern hemisphere traditional cold winters that have contained the Polar Vortex is showing a breakdown with storms of increasing intensity leaking out southward from the North Pole. Is this the signal for the onset of such a dramatic shift? This novel, Minus Fifty Below, explores the events leading to and following this cataclysmic transformation in Earth's climate. Though fictional, the story is grounded in scientific and technical detail, making it as realistic as it is gripping. Will it prove to be fact or fiction? Predictions suggest the answer could arrive within less than a decade.

The goal of this book isn't to incite panic or predict doomsday. Instead, it aims to raise awareness, providing readers with insights into what might happen and what to watch for. If the climate does shift, you'll be better prepared for the possible outcomes. And if global warming continues, let's hope your region does not become an arid wasteland. Either way, the message is clear: Significant climate change is on the horizon, no matter where you live.

August 2020,
Plettenberg Bay,
Western Cape,
South Africa.

KEY PEOPLE

Don & Fran's family:

Don Whitely – Fran's husband

Fran Whitely (née Brandt) - Don's wife

Sean – first son. David – second son.

Jake & Mary Whitely – Don's parents

Robert & Sybil Brandt – Fran's parents

Delaney Street neighbors:

Enrique and Gabriela Rodriguez

Evan and Lily Thomson

Jacob and Hannah Aaron

James and Amelia Jones

Javier and Adriana Garcia

Logan and Isabelle Smith

Lucas and Evelyn Robertson

Mason and Harper Anderson

Michael and Ella Levy

Miguel and Beatriz Hernandez

Noah and Charlotte Miller

Oliver and Sophia Williams

Simon O'Connell and Emma Taylor

William and Olivia Johnson

Intruders:

Bill Wheatley and brother-in-law David Saunders

CONTENTS

PART 1

Messenger texts

during the

Covid-19 virus pandemic

between

Fran Brandt

and

Don Whitely

Chapter 1   CHAOS THEORY

> What happens to a human being in Wuhan
> has a reflection on the entire planet....
> men and women are moving towards a new normal.
> They don't want to go back to old normality.
> The virus invited us to design a new future.
> **- Isabel Allende on the Covid-19 pandemic**

Don:

Chaos Theory states that in underlying dynamic states of disorder there can be physical laws that could predict what will happen because of small changes. The classic example is how a butterfly flapping its wings in China could cause a hurricane in Texas.

Fran:

Please stick to English as I do not understand Chinese - lol. Maybe as an engineer, you understand whatever that means but I don't.

Don:

No, I do not really understand it either. I feel like I am reading the story of *The Emperor's New Clothes* by agreeing that they are probably extremely important laws. In looking at the world today with the Covid-19 lockdown, it all seems to be too disorganized chaos for anything to be predictable.

Fran:

Not a butterfly's wings but something much smaller in China. This Wuhan virus has caused an unquantifiable disruption to not merely Texas but the whole world. Could it have been predicted? In 2015 Bill Gates on a TED talk predicted that the world is exposed to a serious virus incident and we were as totally unprepared then as we still are five years later with this virus pandemic. Add to this the many Sci-Fi movies, books, TV shows and serious comments like Bill Gates' about a possible deadly viral attack on humankind, the world cannot plead ignorance or be surprised.

Don:

It is all very well knowing these things on an intellectual level but when it becomes reality, I personally am quite freaked out. Even if I hold my breath when someone walks passed, the passer-by's breath could still contaminate me. Anything like a door handle, elevator button or supermarket food packaging could infect me. And then what? Will I be someone who simply produces antibodies without becoming symptomatic; one of the less than 2% who become severely ill; or perhaps one of the 0.04% in the fatal category? Canadian stats are lower than the world averages, but there is still risk and who wants to be a statistic?

Fran:

The media is feeding us fear and with everyone locked down in quarantine, we have more time to indulge in Internet searches resulting in widespread terror caused by reading about these horrors. There are all these conspiracy theories circulating that the pandemic was orchestrated. Fake news exacerbates it further. I am sure that we are amongst the billions who lie awake at night worrying. Looking out of the apartment at the quiet streets in the middle of a working day feels like the planet's pause button has been pressed.

Don:

The eerie sight of dead streets reminds me of the terrifying movie *On the Beach* that was released at the end of 1959, based on the book by Neville Shute. This US Navy submarine surfaces in San Francisco Bay after a nuclear world war when everyone who was not killed by atomic bomb blasts died from radiation fallout. The sights of deserted streets on the movie screen through the green color of the submarine's periscope was surreal and frightening then, and our deserted streets are as scary now.

Fran:

Remember at the time of On the Beach, the world was living under a nuclear Cold War threat between the US and Russia. Confrontations like the Cuban Crisis represented a different world threat to this one. But what have we learnt if we simply moved on from nuclear confrontation then to an escaped virus now from a germ warfare laboratory? And what will be the next crisis for humankind? Do you think people have learned anything about whether our values have become more wholesome or need major revision?

Don:

I do think we have learnt something since the pandemic started. There are all sorts of Internet based messages claiming how indirectly the Corona virus is the best thing that could have happened to humankind. We have been on an express train with unstoppable momentum rushing to work, back home, gym, socializing, shopping, travelling, eating out and just being distracted from the more moral values of earlier times.

Fran:

This is reminiscent of Brendon Fraser in the film *Blast From the Past* which typified the contrast between values in the nineteen sixties to how the US had evolved over thirty years. His parents had quarantined themselves in a nuclear fallout shelter during the Cuban Missile Crisis, had a child while underground – Brendon – and thirty years later when the radiation would have subsided sufficiently, sent him up to the surface to see what was left of the world. No post-apocalyptic nuclear war zone but a thriving Los Angeles that had evolved or perhaps devolved according to the film's mixed messages. Brendon relies on nineteen sixties values that his parents taught him to navigate around in this future world and finds they are totally inappropriate for the harsher nineteen nineties.

Don:

I saw the movie too and found the contrasting values and ethics between the two periods on which this supposed comedy was based to be contradictory. To me it represented the tragic loss of the more descent values that I feel we had in the past rather than laugh at Brendon's out-of-date morals. Extrapolating from the nineteen nineties to now, I feel this decline in wholesome principles has continued to deteriorate.

Fran:

Is this why there has been such an extreme event on the planet? Is there some type of correction taking place? Is this a mystically driven event to awaken humanity to how we have been losing our way? At least you share many of my sentiments and beliefs and wonder what you think of this possibility?

Don:

Because of the wakeup call from Covid, I hope to change irrespective of how or why there has been a worldwide lockdown of people's lives. But I feel that many if not most people will return to their old ways when the virus threat passes and not use this event as an opportunity to reflect on personal ethics and lifestyle to implement any fundamental changes.

Fran:

Yes, instead they will want to return to the comfort of the familiar rather than embrace any significant lifestyle adjustments. As disheartening as this may seem, change in society, other than through war or some other disaster, is slow and can take generations - although the pace of change has been speeding up in recent times. But we are fundamentally resistant to adapting to changes in life.

Don:

I think you will like this quote by Franz Kafka:

We are born,

We leave childhood without knowing what youth is,

we marry without knowing what it is to be married,

we enter old age; we don't know what we're heading for.

In that sense, man's world is the planet of inexperience.

Fran:

Astute and observant. It seems I have uncovered a philosophical engineer? To me the quote indicates how most people are forced to change as they grow older without planning or anticipating what the next phase of their life may inflict on them. We move out of being youngsters into teenagers with no knowledge of what it will be like. Understandably so, being too young. As we approach adulthood, we are enticed by the thought of the apparent freedom we perceive adults to have. But we know nothing of what it will be like to be a young adult after leaving school and have all sorts of responsibilities thrust upon us. We get married, have children, they leave home, we become grandparents, and we are therefore constantly moving into new stages of inexperience as Kafka describes. Few people try to anticipate life while the majority mainly endure whatever changes are thrust upon them. What do you think of this similar quote about change by William Somerset-Maughn?

We are not the same persons this year as last;

nor are those we love.

It is a happy chance if we, changing,

continue to love a changed person.

Don:

My first thought is that we still need to love ourselves despite any life pressures that have forced us to change. If you do not love yourself, you cannot really love anyone else.

Fran:

True, but I need to change the subject as all this philosophical discussion is quite hectic and too much to absorb. To change (pun) the current topic, what do you do for exercise while stuck at home?

Don:

Katas.

Fran:

Should I know what that is? Maybe a typo or an unexpected predictive text change?

Don:

Just giving you a trivia test. They are forms or movement routines in karate. What do you do for exercise?

Fran:

Sivananda yoga.

Don:

Similar test for me? What is it all about?

Fran:

It is a form of spiritual yoga that includes asanas or postures and other exercises on the purely physical side. But it is a holistic approach to life that also embodies breathing techniques, relaxation, diet, positive thinking. and meditation.

Why did you take up karate? How long have you been doing it? And are you involved in any other activities?

Don:

A high school friend asked me to join him to do karate and we continued at university. We then joined the police reservists where we did completely different training. I also played various sports at school, especially football.

Fran:

I suppose you did the usual police things like firearms, unarmed combat and plenty of admin, laws and stuff.

Don:

Pretty much that. But with work commitments, I have cycled down my involvement and time I am able to spend as a reservist. The original excitement has also waned somewhat.

Fran:

And on the philosophical side, what do you subscribe to?

Don:

What happened to the respite from serious thinking that you wanted? To answer your question, as someone who was born with a drive to seek the *whats, whys and hows* of life, my initial research was into religions, philosophies, and people's thoughts and experiences. But there were so many contradictions and conflicting theories, all purporting to be the truth, that I was forced to look elsewhere. It was therefore inevitable that my searching would drift to the mystical and finally into channeled teachings where I finally found uniformity.

While waiting for Fran's reply, Don thought 'Am I making progress with Fran? She is maintaining our messenger chats. But is it because she is bored or interested in me? What are your hot buttons Fran? If I can focus on them, that should enhance my status and chances with you. Are any of these revelations of what I believe in and like doing attracting you or scaring you off? I do need to be honest about who I am so I cannot be accused of ever having been false. While our careers are so different, we still seem to have a lot in common. I hope lockdown eventually becomes something great for me with you rather than a heartbreaking loss if this all fizzles out.'

Fran:

Does that mean all these sources are saying the same or similar things? That stretches the realms of possibility!

Don:

Yes, as bizarre, or impossible as these esoteric teachings may be for the infinite number of differing explanations about life and how it works, these sources finally have a consistency, integrity and plausibility for me. Their predictions and explanations have proven to be dependably accurate over years of following them. Also, they do not contradict each other.

Fran:

So, who or what are these sources? You said they are channeled sources. From across the veil? The other side? And what exactly does that mean?

Don:

The thread goes: There is a God, we have a soul, it survives death and goes to `the other side' of the *veil* as some call it. When we die, whatever or whoever is over there can communicate with those of us here who are open to it. From that or those dimensions, they have access to higher knowledge so their teachings and information is not the conjecture of us humans with all our limitations and prejudices. They are therefore far more valid than our mere mortal suppositions and postulations. They also have no need to impart anything but the truth adding to the veracity of their teachings.

Fran:

I had to re-read that a few times as these few words are overloaded with many concepts and ideas. Before I even try asking any questions, I would rather go on and let us see where that takes you or us.

Don:

I am relieved you still seem to be interested and have not aborted our communications. To continue then, if one accepts this soul theory and wants to seek information from the other side of the veil, there is so much available. The rate it is now coming through to us is overwhelming and impossible to keep up with. It removes many myths and adds clarity to events that we invariably look at superficially without access to these hidden facts.

Fran:

Okay. I presume you have found *higher* reasons for the Covid-19 virus outbreak and then you are going to tell me of some big event that you have become aware of that may change civilization as we know it? Actually, if it is scary, do I want to know?

Don:

Well do you really want to know? Should I answer your question?

Before replying, Fran thought: 'Should I be surprised that my stereotype idea and bias of who and what I based you as being just another engineer is so wrong? Sure, you are hot physically, but you also have all these other dimensions to you. Plus, a big plus, you are quite sensitive and not all head. Where is this going? And I nearly never bothered to reply to your first message. Lucky I was bored when your first message came in and I was soon hooked. Maybe I got lucky with someone like you Mr. Don Whitely.'

Chapter 2

PROPHESIES

> "A legend can just as well be founded
> in the future as in the past."
> "It's called a *prophecy*," Urruah said.
> "You may have heard of the concept."
> **- Diane Duane, The Book of Night with Moon**

Don:

So, do you really want to know what may be coming? Do you want an answer to your question?

Fran:

Hmmm. I suppose so. Ignorance would then be a disadvantage if something serious happens and I could have been prepared. Or I could say that I would then be better prepared to accommodate inevitable change that may be forced onto me. Let us up the ante and hit me with your wildcard.

Don:

How about an ice age in ten to fifteen years from now?

Fran:

Seriously? With all this global warming taking place are you suggesting an imminent ice age? These messages are becoming increasingly off-the-wall! Describe this highly implausible ice age scenario as you think it may happen.

Don:

Consider the Polar Vortex storms that are becoming more frequent and severe over the past few years. Imagine a storm hitting us in Toronto with temperatures averaging fifty degrees below zero for a month. Utility supplies such as electricity and gas would fail. Emergency services would be unable to reach you. If you do not have a fireplace or stove that could burn your wooden furniture - which are currently banned because of pollution - you will freeze to death.

Fran:

But all our CO_2 emissions from fossil fuels have been causing global warming. How can you suddenly go from overheating the planet to freezing it so quickly? Traditional climate cycles have been much slower in moving from one phase to the other.

Don:

Cycles are being accelerated because we have never had so many people on the planet before, generating enormous excesses of CO_2 and methane, which are the main culprits causing global warming.

Fran:

You therefore agree that current pollution is causing global warming, not an ice age. Yet you want to jump from the one dominant climate to the opposite so quickly?

Don:

It is a technical explanation, not merely conjecture. For example, the Gulf Stream ocean current takes warm waters from Florida up towards Iceland. To replenish the volume of water moving away from Florida, there is a current of cold arctic water that returns from the North Atlantic to Florida.

Fran:

This is the heat pump that warms Iceland and cools Florida. I know about the Gulf Stream.

Don:

The returning water, being colder is denser and is a current lying below the warm one. But with global warming the ice is melting and running into the sea, salt water is being diluted with the enormous freshwater melt and being less dense than salty sea water, the colder water does not sink to form the lower current layer. Historically this disruption to the heat pump has precipitated freezing winters as the cold is not carried back to the warmer regions closer to the equator to maintain the present heat balance on the planet. And a recent study reported that the Gulf Stream is at its weakest in a thousand years.

Fran:

I read that with melting ice there are more dark, rocky areas appearing at the South Pole to absorb more of the sun's heat rather than snow and ice to reflect it back into space. Although heating can cause droughts, one suggestion is that increased cloud cover through more evaporation from overheating would also reflect the sun's heat and of course light back into space. That would also cause cooling. But how does this heating trend impact Polar Vortex storms?

Don:

Our cold winters somehow contain this vortex to remain circulating around the polar region. But without the normal winter cold, this containment breaks down and freezing arctic storms have started breaking out of the region in certain places, spilling southward. Look at this early spring snowstorm in Texas where electricity failed, and people were burning cardboard boxes to survive the cold. Texas is far south showing how far a forceful Polar Vortex storm can reach and it has happened in a season when then weather should be warming. Of course, with all these theories and conflicting possibilities, will there be net overheating or freezing?

Fran:

You tell me?

Don:

That is why I resort to channeled sources of information

It is not subject to conjecture and speculation but is based on some or other *higher plan*. And my one source says the ice age cometh.

Fran:

If you believe that, what are you doing about it?

Don:

There is too much to consider with no simple answers to easily form a survival strategy going forward. For example, if I wanted to relocate to somewhere warmer, how cold will the planet be as maybe even the equator will be much colder. Looking at a globe of the earth, the only countries on the equator where one can speak English are Kenya, Tanzania, and Uganda in East Africa.

Fran:

Easier for one person to relocate but what about a family or an extended family? What would you do there? Would they let you in unless you emigrate now, well before another global crisis with a possible rush of people to warmer climes?

Don:

That is only one option and you already can see the many factors that one needs to consider.

The next important question is what an ice age would do to our food production capability?

Fran:

If it becomes too cold, it becomes a great opportunity for warmer countries to increase their agricultural output to feed North America, Europe and other Northern Hemisphere countries.

Don: In theory yes but these are Third World countries.

They are without the resources, infrastructure, and ability to ramp up food production by many orders of magnitude, especially in a short period of time.

Fran:

Well, I am sure First World countries will not sit back and just pray. My God, colonialism could be repeated. First World countries would have to literally take them over so agriculture and food processing could be elevated to the efficiency levels currently experienced back home. This sounds freakier than the Corona virus pandemic!

Don:

Irrespective of what Western governments decide to do, if we choose to remain in our countries, our homes need to be reengineered to survive such cold. Did you read John Vaillant's book The Tiger about how people and the Siberian tiger live in temperatures of -40⁰C below zero?

Fran:

No but to survive those temperatures we would need suitable accommodation and not what we currently have.

Don:

In 1976 there was the coldest winter in North America creating an oil shortage, people had no heating and were freezing to death in their homes. I met a couple who lived in Hoopeston, Illinois who told me they bought arctic survival gear including a specialized tent and camped in their living room to try and survive the bitter cold in their apartment with no oil for heating. The coming ice age will be far worse.

Fran: If this topic continues, I am going to have a panic attack.

You seem to have given it plenty of thought and I want to know what you finally decide to do. But I am not sure I want to hear it as this is making me feel vulnerable and scared. What happens if there is a collapse of essential services and survivors have nowhere to shop, replenish supplies and obtain other vital commodities like medicine, or even a wood or coal stove? There could be anarchy and a collapse of civilization, never mind services. This is reminiscent of a science fiction book called Lucifer's Hammer with his mallet striking the planet. I must admit, I am quite freaked out.

Chapter 3   IGLOO DESIGN

> A candle is enough to warm up
> the igloo in an icy region.
> Why is a human heart so
> cold having a warm blood?
> **- Hemashkwethya KS**

Don:

Now I feel guilty about broaching this subject.

Fran:

As I said, even if it is unpleasant information, I must surely be better off knowing about an impending ice age than pleading ignorance is bliss after it hits us. If I do succumb to your belief, I will need to adjust to this new paradigm, albeit quite frightening. How are you acclimating to this new climate possibility and how are you considering ways to survive?

Don:

It is quite weird that I read a variety of doomsday books and watched many science fiction films about such scenarios without specifically seeking them out. None were enjoyable or reassuring but were quite realistic about whatever apocalyptic event they were depicting. This made me aware of what can happen and gave me an indication of what would be necessary for survival. Now with my engineering training, I therefore feel I would be able to adapt proactively.

Fran:

Why do you think you were exposed to this unusual genre? From some other level I suppose you feel you were led to it. Your karma? Tell me more.

Don:

Ignoring the possible necessity to arm oneself and become proficient in using firearms for protection from desperate people, our houses need to be designed to have minimal heat loss and store enough fuel and food to last a winter with long storms. Coal is better than oil or wood but so much heat goes straight up the chimney making fossil fuel fires extremely inefficient. Anyway, since it is a dirty fuel, coal stoves are illegal here.

Fran:

Igloos are thick and I suppose they contain some of the heat that the occupants generate. What do we need to have the same heat containment abilities of an igloo in a house? I am sure you are aware of the recommendation to have a candle and matches in a car during winter for heat and light if it breaks down. Some people have free standing fireplaces in their homes, so the chimney is inside the house up to the roof. The pipe then gives off additional heat to the stove.

Don:

That does recover more heat but most still goes out the chimney. I think if one has a basement, the combustion heater should be there. The smoke should go through pipes in the floor between the basement and living areas before being vented.

Fran:

That sounds dangerous. I am sure it would have been done long ago if there was no risk of carbon monoxide and carbon dioxide leaking into the house.

Don:

Refrigeration uses noxious gas and they run inside people's kitchens without anyone even thinking about being gassed. Many hobs, ovens and fireplaces use gas in the house. Today we have detectors for gas leaks, which can be installed for additional safety. Ducting smoke safely through floors and out is technologically quite easy but adds to the cost of a house.

Fran: Another added expense would be to increase the insulation.

That includes thicker polyurethane foam between the outer walls and maybe triple glazing of windows.

Don:

There are too many considerations to start covering all of them now. I have started some research and a specialized house would need to be built from the basement up. It would then have all the requirements necessary by using various technologies to create a self-sufficient dwelling able to withstand a long and extremely cold winter. Obviously, this would cost much more than a conventional home of the same size but if it has a livable environment to survive long, incredibly harsh storms, it would be money well spent.

Fran:

Changing the subject back to your ice age, we covered physical challenges but what about the psychological ones like we are enduring now under this voluntary Covid lockdown period? Have you considered those aspects?

Don:

Only superficially. My thoughts generally about an impending ice age have not been obsessive and all consuming. I am not sure what I can do about it right now and therefore it sits in the background receiving occasional attention. What are your initial thoughts about an ice age lockdown?

Fran:

Scary if it is a possibility as even during this less austere lockdown, I am lonely.

Don:

You know what I feel about you and what my solution to your loneliness problem would be.

Delaying her response, Fran thought about how she should answer. 'I made myself wide open to that reply by admitting I am lonely. What did I think? Was it my unconscious mind that prompted it? That means at some deeper level, it must think a relationship with Don would be a good thing for me. I suppose I can always back out if it does not work. But it does feel right. Well, nothing ventured …'

Fran:

So, would you be happy to take our relationship to the next level?

Don:

That must be a rhetorical question because you know the answer.

Fran thought: 'Last chance before I get involved with this man. He is a fine man. Yes I want to.'

Fran:

You know why I have not responded to your physical and emotional approaches before?

Don:

I have too many theories to even start offering any of them, especially as I would not like to say anything that is way off target.

Fran:

I have a simple philosophy. I need to *get someone into my head before I let them into my bed.* Our communications now during lockdown have enabled me to get to know you better to the point where I really like you.

Don:

Suddenly lockdown looks great.

To be locked up or down with you is something I fantasized about, never expecting it to become a reality. Can I suggest my place as it is bigger and has a small garden that helps break the feeling of being imprisoned? And I will come and pick you up.

Fran:

You are assuming I would say yes. Is it your ploy to steamroller me? But let me not play games and say yes, I would prefer your place as I can do yoga in your garden and retreat back to my cave if it does not work out.

Don:

You will find me so attentive, considerate, sensitive, and amenable that I would never give you cause to consider escape.

Fran:

I am relying on that. Give me about two hours to pack and close my place. You will need to disconnect my automobile battery. Remind me to switch off the geyser and leave a small light on.

PART 2

Preparing for the unthinkable.

Chapter 4   MY NEW HOME

Love turns a house into a home.
- We Heart It.

Fran was halfway through packing perishables from her refrigerator into a cooler bag, choosing from her wardrobe what to pack including toiletries, yoga mat, electronics and other *bits and bobs*. She realized that she needed more than the two hours she had asked for, then noticed how she was dressed.

'Oh no! I have been locked down for too long. Look at me dressed in sloppy tracksuit pants, a yoga tank top and I did not even realize it. Don cannot pick me up so casually dressed. I need to look good, no great for our first meeting and even an hour now would be too short for me to get ready properly. What to wear? My denim mini skirt with a tight T-shirt perhaps. Don must be six inches taller than me so heels would be good, but I think that would be ridiculous. High cork heel sandals? I hate those. Okay flat sandals with thongs. What make-up? Just mascara and lipstick. Which perfume? Maybe Jo Malone Pear and Freesia? No, Wild Bluebell. It's the one that is supposed to represent liveliness and suggest fun.'

Don arrived promptly at Fran after two hours. She opened the door, stood on her toes to give him a hello peck on the lips. With a broad smile she watched him gawking at her, drinking in a sight that reinforced the passionate feelings he had already felt for her. Her deep brown eyes with matching colored, gentle wavy hair, pert nose and glowing smile showing a perfect array of white teeth. Beautifully picture perfect! She took his hand and led him into her apartment. "Welcome to my world. I assume your place has more space otherwise we can revise our decision and stay here."

Looking at her inviting, open plan area's soft feminine touch with tasty, modern decor he replied "Thanks for the reciprocal offer. But if you decide to retreat and we are staying here, you will have to move to my place and leave me here in yours. I prefer the original suggestion and am looking forward to your energy buzzing about in my place."

"Sounds most inviting. Grab my suitcase on my bed and let us get going."

Don was not surprised to see Fran's pillows, cushions, soft, cuddly toys and throw neatly arranged around her bed. Her soft, congenial personality extended to her furnishings, creating a feeling of a warm ambiance. "What else besides this suitcase?" he asked.

"This wheely, my handbag and some things by the door." Fran was not surprised to see that Don drove a Toyota Rav4 Prime. In his future world, a hybrid car would be essential, and this SUV was both appealing and functional on and off road. He put her things in the trunk and shortly after heading off, Fran shouted to Don "Stop. Back-up. Quickly." As he reversed, she said "I am sure I saw someone trying to break into that closed computer store in the side road. He looked like he was fiddling at a backdoor entrance."

Don reversed back to the crossroad where he saw someone disappearing into the store's side door, pulling it closed behind him. "Lock the car door when I get out, climb across to the driver's street and leave the engine idling in case you need to drive away quickly if someone rushes out and wants to commandeer the vehicle. Call 911 and ask for urgent police assistance." As he climbed out, he grabbed a pair of handcuffs in his car door and in a moment was running down the street while pushing the cuffs into his back pocket. Don moved towards the door warily. Thoughts rushed through his head while assessing how best to proceed:

'Door slightly ajar for a quick escape but sufficiently closed not to attract attention.'

Don carefully entered, scanning the environment as he slowly moved forward, ears listening for telltale signs.

'A back passage and fortunately quite dark. Empty boxes. I am going to lay a few out at random in case he bolts as it could slow or trip him up if he tries to bolt. I am also going to close the door properly as another delaying tactic.'

He moved quickly hearing muffled sounds coming from deeper inside.

'Lucky there are display shelves in rows to give me cover. Can I see him from here?' as he came to the end of the passage in the rear of the shop. 'There he is. Hmm, cutting security cables to laptops so he can steal them. Caucasian in his twenties, light brown hair, grey sweater with hood, black sneakers with white rims, faded blue jeans with tear on left knee ...'

Don moved to the isle before the one where the thief was working and quickly crouch-walked quietly to the far end so he would be close to the intruder. Don stepped around the gondola shelves almost on the man and declared loudly "Police. Hands behind your head and turn around slowly." The thief twisted around with a shocked look while slowly raising his hands, stared at Don and seeing he was alone and not in uniform, launched himself at Don in a tackle. In the limited isle space, Don sidestepped as much as he could and raising his arm, did a forearm block onto his assailant's neck causing him to stumble. But as his arms were still open to grab Don, his momentum pushed them back and they fell together against the shelves on the opposite side of the isle. Don's ribs hit one shelf and his head banged against a higher one leaving him momentarily winded and dazed. His attacker had a soft landing on Don, scrambled onto his feet and ran for the door. Shaking his head and ignoring the pain, Don jumped up and was after the fleeing man, close behind him. As the thief neared the passage to the door, he saw it was no longer ajar, spun around, brandishing a knife in his right hand that he had drawn while running towards the exit.

The man went into a crouch, slicing the knife in the air from side to side to stop Don coming too close while deciding whether to attack or back away towards the door and try to escape. Don saw a faint hardness come over his face, recognizing it from kumite or competitive karate fighting. He was familiar with the expression of resolve when his opponent was going to attack rather than wait defensively. The man suddenly lunged forward, but Don was ready and moved his back foot behind him to rotate and be side on presenting a smaller target. At the same time, he raised his right arm and brought a forearm block down hard onto his adversary's arm behind the knife in a painful blow, pushing the knife away from his body. Don then flicked his forearm back with his hand in a fist and hit the man on the bridge of his nose, hearing a crack as the blow crunched home. As the man tottered back, Don followed with a karate *mae geri* frontal kick to the base of his sternum, driving him further back and winding him. As he staggered backwards, he tripped on the cardboard boxes that Don had carefully positioned and fell flat onto his back.

Don was on him landing carefully with his knees on the man's rib cage to further wind him, but not break any of his ribs. He then slid his knees forward onto the man's upper arms to pin them and grabbed the knife hand which was still holding the weapon. Don twisted his hand painfully commanding him to drop it. The immobilized, would-be burglar with a look of pain, hate and defeat in his eyes, dropped the knife. Holding onto the empty hand with it still partially twisted in a disabling grip, Don stood up and rolled him over. Blood was pouring from the broken nose. Ignoring it for the moment, Don pulled the handcuffs out of his back pocket with his left hand and cuffed the right wrist then pulled the left arm back and cuffed it too. Don stood up then pulled the man up onto his feet. Holding the chain between the handcuffs he shuffled the man backwards towards the entrance so that he was not facing the door he was about to open and therefore unable to try and run even with his hands cuffed behind him.

Don stepped out the door while keeping the man just inside and with his free hand sent a worried looking Fran a thumbs up. He then beckoned her to drive down to him. She arrived with the window slightly open and he asked her to get his Police ID card out his wallet in the glove compartment. They could hear the siren of a police car rushing to the scene in response to her 911 call.

They spent about an hour at the police station as Don made out his report. Don had kept Fran with him so she could read the report that he compiled describing what happened inside the store. While he had been busy, she had plenty of time to ponder the event:

'In an emergency, this is obviously a man I can trust to protect me. Well as long as he is prudent and not some *gung ho* man seeking dangerous heroics and excitement. Between what I know of you Mr. Whitely, you are cautious and calculating – the engineer – and a responsible person. If not, I should not be moving in with you. Frankly it is a turn-on to know you are quite the macho guy. Don you passed my test to *get a man into my head* ... and this event does not change my decision to be with you. If anything, it has enhanced my impression of who and what you are. Looks like I may be in for some interesting experiences with you dear Don. And I am looking forward to finally getting into your bed.'

In the car Fran needed to discuss her thoughts. "Don, should I be worried about being in a relationship with you? I am interested in the engineer and philosopher, not a part-time police reservist that responds recklessly to any crime being committed without back-up?"

Smiling while gingerly touching the swelling on the back of his head, Don explained "I have never done anything solo as we are always in pairs when on duty. This was an unusual once-off. Assuming our relationship progresses, the novelty of part-time police work has already passed, and I will definitely be resigning."

Don's hand then moved to his ribs and Fran apologized. "Sorry, I should have first asked how much pain you are in. You seemed fine in the police station and said nothing, so I never expected you to have been hurt. You did write that you were shoved onto shelves with this guy on top of you and you are now touching the back of your head and ribs. How hurt are you?"

"I suppose that I may develop some bruises but not more than I ever received playing football at school or during kumite."

"Another foreign word" replied Fran. "What is kumite?"

"It is karate sparing so it is the contact part of the martial art. How were you doing in the car while waiting?"

"Worried! I had been with you for only a few minutes since we left my place when you were off on some dangerous crusade leaving me not quite stranded, but on my own full of concerns for you."

"My rationale for going in alone was based on a few facts. Petty thieves do not carry firearms. He was on his own. I have some unarmed combat training and experience so the situation did not feel like one that I could not manage. I was correct."

Her brow furrowed, Fran said "Well yes, but he had a knife, and you did get hurt albeit nothing serious. Lucky this time."

"There may be no next time so don't worry."

"Alright but I want specific details on where you are hurt."

"My head and ribs hit some of the display shelves when shoved back against them. Not too bad as I am fine, a bit sore and definitely not sufficient for an ER visit."

"It does give me a feeling of security that in an emergency you would be a good person to be with. While I hope that never happens, we have been discussing some anarchic scenarios. But I really pray we never go there."

Chapter 5   NEW BEGINNINGS

Sometimes our lives have
to be completely shaken up,
and rearranged to relocate us
to a place we are meant to be.
- Saul Speaking
The Funny Beaver.

"We have arrived" announced Don as he turned into a secure complex of condominium apartments. As a bachelor engineer, he could afford a more upmarket apartment as his first residence in a nice neighborhood. Don drove into the garage with his thoughts now lingering on Fran's gentle kiss on his lips when he arrived at her place followed by a hug as she whispered into his ear "I am pleased to be doing this."

Thinking about when he could try for the next kiss, Don jumped out and rushed around to open the door for Fran with his usual chivalry, extending a hand to help her out. "Welcome to your new abode that has waited many lonely moons for you to grace its halls."

Smiling she gracefully climbed out and said "Leave the luggage. I first would like a conducted tour of my new home – even if it is a temporary one." Then she thought `I should not have added that last bit.'

Ignoring her final comment Don gently took Fran by the elbow and led her out the garage to the front door. "This is a better entrance than through a service door into the scullery." He opened the front door and followed her into the passage.

She noted the pleasing pale grey passage walls with photographs of people and scenes hanging along it that Don had taken during his travels. There was a door slightly ajar on the left which was evidently a storeroom followed by a guest toilet. Opposite was a well laid out, open plan kitchen with ample cupboards and appliances. Fran paused and noticed the microwave, an air fryer, coffee machine, juicer, eye level oven, refrigerator with fridge and freezer doors, a double sink with mixer, gas hob and probably more kitchen equipment in drawers and cupboards. "Looks like I may be busy in here feeding my host. My man?"

Don smiled warmly with an equally fuzzy feeling inside. "I like the ring of that and am looking forward to mellow meals with good wine and extraordinarily special company. Let us continue with your conducted tour."

They walked into the dining room and lounge area that was tastefully decorated with a homeliness that surprised Fran who expected a more austere bachelor pad with cheap pine and melamine furniture. "I could be, no will be quite comfortable here" she said quietly, more to herself than to Don. She walked across to the sliding doors that led out onto a small patio with some garden furniture, a red Weber gas barbeque and a small lawn with a perimeter of flower beds, shrubs and small trees. "Weather permitting, I will be doing my yoga here" she mused quietly. "Now let's see your loft bedroom and bathroom."

"This way" said Don steering her back inside towards the stairs at the back of the lounge. Her skirt swirled as he followed her up hoping to see even more than her mini exposed causing his heart to pound even faster. With a sweep of his arm he said in a typical Canadian schoolboy's French accent "Voilà ta boudoir et la salle de bains est là" pointing to the bathroom door at the back.

Fran pushed him back onto the bed saying, "Your bedroom looks great and is where we are going to spend a lot of time." With that she clambered on top of Don and crawled forward to reach his face, Don pulled her down feeling the firm warmth of her body as she willingly pushing down onto him. With a smile she said, "I get the feeling, or can already feel, that you would like to start now." She softly touched his lips with her own then pressed harder with her tongue following. She fleetingly wondered whether Don had closed the garage and front door but quickly returned her focus to the matter at hand.

> On the science of global climate change, I'm an agnostic.
> I've seen Al Gore's movie, and I've read reports from
> the Intergovernment Panel on Climate change.
> I have also listened to the 'skeptics.'
> I don't know who's right.
> **- Robert Bryce,**
> **US author and journalist**

After settling into their lockdown routine, one day Fran said to Don "I would like to pick up on one of our messenger discussions about how to survive a possible, imminent ice age." They had been working on their respective computer notebooks on the dining room table with papers and folders strewn across the top. Needing a break Fran continued, "As an engineer who is quite technical, you would not have accepted such a scenario lightly and if you consider it having a reasonable possibility of happening, it merits a serious review."

"Dear sweet, delicious Fran …."

"Don't get sidetracked Mr. Insatiable. Focus on the subject, not me."

With a sigh and a deliberately look of helplessness, Don closed the lid of his notebook and continued. "Okay taskmaster, I shall meekly obey your every wish. Since there are so many variables, it is better to make some preliminary assumptions and decisions to simplify the decision-making process of this problem."

"What is the problem? Do you really think we will be in an ice age soon?"

"Yes, I do believe it, but I was thinking about where one should live if survival here becomes precarious. Not just the first, long Polar Vortex storm or the balance of that winter. But how much summer will there be afterwards, will we be able to grow enough food to survive the following winter and the ones after that? Will there even be enough survivors to farm the land?"

Pensively Fran answered, "Of course there are no answers now, but we should decide where to live based on food being the most paramount, apart from all the other important aspects of the 21st century modern living that may also collapse. I suppose this is working up the Maslow Hierarchy of Needs Pyramid."

"We?" asked Don.

"Don't you want me around during an ice age?"

"You know I do but you have not indicated in any way that after the lockdown, you want to remain locked down with me" replied a happily surprised Don.

"Well ask me" smiled back Fran.

"Are we now formally a team with expected serious longevity?"

Still smiling Fran said, "Ask me that again but not so formally like an engineer. Rather with more heart than head."

"I have absolutely loved having you here exclusively with me. Oh well, let me rather say it this way. I love you Fran. I want you forever. Where are you with that?"

"I am right in the middle of it, stuck with you. Stuck to you. It is where I want to be and where I should be as I love you too. Now get on with your explanation."

With the broadest grin on Don's face that Fran had ever seen, he grabbed her and said, "Sorry dearest, our discussion has to wait." He bent down and kissed her passionately, lifted her up and headed for the stairs up to their boudoir.

Lying contentedly in bed, Don did not want to pick up the thread of survival in an ice age, but Fran was concerned about what appeared to be a possible, impending reality. Considering how unprepared the world was for the Covid-19 virus, she felt that she had learnt a lesson even if the powers that be had not. Snuggling up to Don she asked "Where do you think we should live in view of this potential ice age? Continue here in Canada, which is close to the North Pole? Move down into the Southern United States? Or all the way to the tropics into a Third World country?"

With a reluctant sigh, Don looked at the love of life, and while stroking her still flushed cheek said, "Since you are now a fifty percent partner in this relationship, you have equal say in that decision. What do you feel?"

"Don't pass the ball back to me without any qualifications" replied Fran. "I first want to know what you think, and I suspect that I will accept your arguments between loving you and acknowledging your superior scientific and engineering knowledge on these matters. I have insufficient information and education on such matters to make such life changing decisions without professional guidance."

"This is crystal ball work, not rocket science" said Don worried that a choice would be affecting Fran as well now that she had become permanently entrenched in his life. "Remaining in North America keeps us in a familiar society with the advanced technologies we enjoy. Going south to a Third World country potentially gives us a better chance of survival at a most basic level to grow food and have more temperate weather. But we would be living in a completely different culture and type of life in say Africa. Depending on how the north fares after the first winter *hit* would indicate where the place to live should be. But we do not have that luxury of foretelling whether there will be this extreme climate shift and what the outcome of the first and subsequent winters' trend will be."

Fran interjected saying "If you are aware of this possibility, others must be too and more will become aware of it with time. I did an Internet search, which resulted in the usual contradictions but there were enough articles to suggest this scenario is possible. The Polar Vortices have been increasing in frequency, intensity and have been starting earlier in recent winters. My point is that in ten years or a bit more, enough people may also be preparing for this worst-case scenario. Then the country could be better prepared to survive such extreme storms."

"Then you think we should stay in Canada?" asked Don.

"If it is in a decade or more time, yes. This is my home, my roots, my family and friends, way of life and the culture I want to live in. If the ice age descends on us this coming winter, then we should flee before it arrives."

"That decision is a combination of emotion and rational sense considering that eventually enough people may prepare for an imminent ice age" replied Don. "I always become bogged down in too many details and alternatives to cut to the chase the way you have. Let us go with the decision to stay here for now and see where some planning takes us."

Fran asked, "Surely our priority is then to design and build a home that can survive weeks of exposure to frigid cold and a whole winter of repeated bouts of temperatures down to minus fifty?"

Smiling Don said "Of course but what about the cost? Such a home would be far more expensive to build per square meter than a typical house today and even jointly we could not afford it. Should it be in the city or outside where we could have some surrounding farmland to try and grow food in case supply becomes a problem? That then suggests we should have livestock as well, which would be a full-time job to look after. Add to that the stocking of animal food for a long winter as well as enough fuel to heat their quarters. That is why I have been saying there are too many variables to reach an easy decision."

Fran smiled back saying "I think that I can remove many of those options. If we cut our cloth according to our pockets, no farm. I also would be concerned about living isolated in a remote place during a time of what could become lawless with desperate people pillaging the land for food. If we had a commune with people sharing in the defense like an Israeli kibbutz, that could work. But with just the two of us, we may end up surviving winter but not the summer living on a remote farm being plundered for food."

Thoughtfully Don said "It is strange that over the years I read books and watched movies about these doomsday situations and saw what potentially could happen. One book that you mentioned was *Lucifer's Hammer* by Larry Niven and Jerry Pournelle. Not surprisingly considering all the other books we somehow have both read, I also read that one. As I recall, it was about a comet that broke up like the Shoemaker-Levy comet that hit Jupiter in 1994 and the 'calves,' or giant fragments, crashed into different parts of the earth. One landed in Baja California lifting tons of sea water and mud into the atmosphere. The other calves contributed to further atmospheric contamination resulting in the equivalent of a nuclear winter. The earth was covered in this cloud that reflected sunlight and heat back into space so the planet cooled dramatically. It rained salty mud, polluting rivers and farmland effectively collapsing civilization. The main part of the story took place between Los Angeles and Sacramento, and I happened to be reading the book while flying between the two cities for work. I remember reading about groups of desperate people who were stealing and killing just trying to survive, making it even more scary as I was where the story's horror was taking place."

"Don!" interjected a frantic Fran. "This is all quite terrifying. And the story is not that different to what an ice age could bring. I am not sure if I even want to continue this conversation. I can see insomnia and panic attacks coming down the track. Do we need to buy weapons, and must I learn how to use them proficiently to protect ourselves? Maybe it would be easier to simply freeze to death and not live in a post-apocalyptic world. Would we also become killers desperate to survive? This is all quite dreadful. What else did you read or watch? Do I even want to hear? What about children? Who would want to bring children into a world that could be like a Nostradamus or Apocalyptic prophesy?" Fran turned to Don and hugged him for reassurance, which he could not offer, only to return a warm, loving hug. After a minute Fran relaxed and continued "When I decided to move in with you, I had visions of being incarcerated during lockdown in a loving environment, to be followed by an equally happy life together. Now I feel I may still be looking forward to a different type of loving life with you, but one fraught with danger and extreme survival challenges. If that is what life holds in store for us, I still want it to be with you."

"Darling I cannot promise you anything as it may well become an uncertain future and many of the options are bleak. Stating anything milder would not help us address these potential life-threatening issues. Remember asking me whether I felt that I was I drawn to these books and movies because of some destiny that wants us to survive? Of course I don't know the answer regarding our destiny but my little DIY workshop is already stocked with things as simple as extra nuts and bolts since a collapse of industry could mean that no more would be produced, and for how long?

To what extent could civilization collapse? The history of humankind is fraught with hundreds if not thousands of catastrophes in which the indomitable spirit of people eventually bounce back after surviving unspeakable horrors. If an ice age comes, there will be survivors. As you asked, do we want to be part of such a different, difficult world?" With all these unanswered questions, they drifted into a heavy silence filed with thoughts fraught with the horrors that could soon be descending on the world, and onto them.

Chapter 7   MORE INTEL

North of the Arctic Circle there are only
two seasons – this winter and last winter.
Who would ever want to live there? …
The physics is straightforward,
but the engineering is not.
- Joseph Lstiburek,
Building in Extreme Cold

It was a balmy day and Fran had been on the lawn doing yoga. It ended sitting in a lotus position to meditate, which helped to center her for the conversation that she knew had to be continued. Finally, Fran rolled onto her back and stared up at the sky. On the periphery of her vision were some trees along Don and his neighbors' boundary walls. The leaves bobbed gently from a mild, warm breeze. A few clouds drifted so slowly that it was difficult to determine their direction.

`How peaceful this all is' she thought. `And how misleading. Around the corner is another winter that will be the same. But lurking below the surface are malevolent forces conspiring to turn our world into a deep freeze. How cunning to fool everyone first with global warming! Not with complacency as there is a serious concern where this heating trend is taking us. But is it a smoke screen, a red herring, a façade? I am really scared as there is little Don and I can do about it. We need a safe house, which we cannot afford. No, we need to find a way and between us, we must develop a strategy that will enable us to survival. This must be our top priority as we do not have the luxury of indefinite time or financial resources. Now is time for not a snow storm but a brain storm. The snowstorm can then follow. Mr. Whitely, ready yourself for BIG change.'

One day after one of Fran's yoga sessions, Don said "How about I show you some unarmed combat techniques? It is an opportunity for us to do something together, adds variety to our respective physical training, and may one day be invaluable in some post-apocalyptic world."

Grinning Fran said "If it teaches me how to throw you onto the ground, pin you down and make love to you, I am all for it. Let us start now." Enjoying all the maneuvers and techniques that Don showed her, Fran became an adept student and soon was challenging Don's initial dominance of the various dangerous situations he was teaching her to protect herself against. As her ability improved, so did her confidence.

Don supplemented some of these unarmed combat sessions by showing her the basics of using a handgun, rifle and shotgun. "Until lockdown is lifted when we can go to a shooting range, this is all theory, and you can learn all the basics leaving only the actual firing of these weapons to convert your theory into practice later." This new dimension of self-protection increased Fran's confidence even further although she did feel ambivalent about becoming proficient in what she considered on some level to be learning how to perform violent acts. This feeling fluctuated between considering it to be vital for the protection of her and her family, whereas at other times she would be quite uncomfortable learning these new skills.

Between work, domestic, and social commitments, Don had been drawing components on a computer CAD program of a house that would need to be adapted to a far colder environment than present Toronto experienced even in the harshest of winters. After one of her daily yoga sessions in the garden, Fran went inside to shower, then went to Don's desk casually dressed in a track suit and sneakers with wet hair still wrapped up in a towel. Putting her hands at the base of his neck she massaged his tense muscles. "Can you take a break so we can pick up our recent chat about how to live in a doomsday world?"

Don performed a few keystrokes to save his work, closed the lid so his notebook was in sleep mode, stood up, slowly turned and took Fran into his arms and said "I barely slept last few nights seeing how frantic you are with this conversation and wish I could say 'Just kidding!' so it would go away. But we need to confront this potential reality and at worst, we may spend money on a house that will withstand extreme winters that may never come. Or we may be one of the few survivors when the Horsemen of the Apocalypse ride through the country."

Fran took Don's hand and led him to the sofa where they sat down. "Let me summarize what I think I understood including what additional research I have done over the Internet. The current climate changes of global warming may tip the world into an ice age. Because of people's impact on the environment, primarily from fossil fuel combustion, the potential shift into an ice age has accelerated faster than any historical evidence scientists have found so their predictions based on past cycles can only be guesswork. For us living in Canada, relatively close to the North Pole, we would be exposed to extreme winters that have never been seen in our recorded history. If we wish to remain in Canada and in a big city, we need a different dwelling, provisions necessary to survive months and maybe things for years ahead if civilization as we know it, collapses or shrinks."

Don frowned and looking straight at Fran said "An accurate and scary summary. Since we seem to have converged on a few variables like wanting to remain in this city, a suitable house able to withstand incredibly cold temperatures and as you say, with stocks of important items that may no longer be available once the first terrible winter passes. The house design is what I was working on now. Considering design aspects of a home that can endure temperatures of -50°C for months."

Fran asked "Please tell me what some of the key attributes of such a house will be. But at the level of a layperson."

"This is a superficial overview, and I can give you additional details afterwards. I would increase the thickness of wall insulation and insulate all hot- and cold-water pipes against the cold ones freezing up and hot ones losing valuable heat. The double-glazed windows would need to be doubled as they are areas of greater heat loss than double-insulated walls. Also, not too many windows despite wanting more natural light and to see outside. The ratio should not exceed window area in a room to being more than 10% of the floor area. All lighting must be low energy LED's and easily accessible for globe replacement. Doors, ceiling lights and switches need to be caulked to either prevent heat loss going out or cold air leaking in. We would need an air vent heat exchanger that warms incoming freezing, fresh, replacement air rather than simply wasting stale, heated air being vented out the house. The roof will require substantial insulation and perhaps solar panels on the outside to contribute towards electricity generation and heat water in summer."

Fran asked "What about pitching a steep roof like homes in Nordic countries to minimize how much snow can collect on it? It also means summer melt would be less before exposing the roof underneath as the season warms. The solar and heating panels could then contribute sooner."

Nodding Don said "Great idea! That will definitely be added to any roof design. To continue, there are other places one can obtain electricity like water flowing in pipes through small turbines turning little generators. What also flows are the exhaust gases from one's heating as it goes into a ducting system. Using the same principle with water flowing, the smoke can turn a fan connected to a small generator. These small amounts of electricity can trickle charge a battery bank that has an inverter to provide electricity at 110 volts. If we have a basement and two floors, the ground and first floors would have ducting inside them that the burnt gas flows through on its way out, to recover as much of its heat as possible and generate some electricity before it is vented."

Fran commented, "Yes you mentioned heat from an exhaust smoke duct network during one of our messenger communications and reassured me that if people can have toxic gas in their refrigerators and air conditioning systems, we can have exhaust gas ducted through a house with equal safety."

Don said "Carbon monoxide and carbon dioxide detectors will be installed in the house as a precaution. For the heating, I would install a burner that can use either natural gas piped to homes or oil if this supply fails. We could have some 46-kilogram cylinders of LPG or Low Pressure Gas in reserve for say cooking and emergency heating. We would need a large oil storage tank of two to three thousand liters as back-up. I would also install a conventional wood and coal burning stove to the same heating system as a second back-up."

"When and how will the different heating systems be activated if you, no we have either the gas or oil system and solar heating in summer? If we use hot water for a shower and the heating is not currently running, the geyser thermostat should not immediately activate electric heating when the water temperature drops because of cold, replenishment water flowing into the geyser. For example, if we shower at night in summer when solar heating could be used in the day, surely the thermostat must not switch on the geyser's electric immersion heater and wait till the sun is up instead? Solar heating will then be able to start warming the geyser water the next morning."

Don answered while thinking aloud. "We need a small programmable controller that would override the thermostat switch in the geyser if an external temperature sensor indicates it is too cold outside for solar to heat water. A geyser will still have hot water after showering. If we need more hot or at least warm water, we can turn on the electricity manually. Otherwise heating would be delayed until there is solar heat the next morning. I wonder if standard solar heating systems come with something to not use other heating like electricity or gas at night when it could wait until morning? Developing an energy saving controller for solar heating systems seems like a nice little business opportunity on the side."

"What about standby electricity for the house?" asked Fran.

"There would be a bank of deep recycle batteries to collect electricity from the various generators, solar and a separate electrical circuit with inverter that only supplies essential services if the mains supply fails. I would not run refrigerators or freezers off the electricity as we can use ice from outside to keep them cold. We could also have a stand-by electrical generator that supplies at least five kilowatts as another back-up. Overall, there is enough technology and equipment available to build a house that will withstand such severe winters and all we need is the money."

Fran said "The Covid-19 lockdown is providing some experience of being confined for an extended period. Terrible winters could lock us down for much longer as one could not even escape to the shops and we need to consider many of the activities, resources and things necessary now that would be important then.

"We may need to ask our parents for loans and once the house is built, take out a mortgage bond to repay them" continued Fran. "I cannot think of anywhere else we could obtain funds and our joint salaries only cover our monthly expenses plus a bit. But your description sounds amazing and exciting. Given the gloomy future that may lie ahead, I seem to have hitched up with the right kind of guy to survive." She moved across the sofa, pushed Don back into a lying position and stretched out on top of him. "Life is all about balance and this topic requires rational thinking. But emotion is also part of life and I am feeling very, positively emotional towards you now. You need to change gear from being rational and make desperate love to me so I can shift my thoughts from a dire future to delicious feelings of pleasure right now."

PART 3

CONSTRUCTION

Chapter 8 THE PROJECT

While we would not want to attribute every
extreme weather event to climate change,
the pattern is building and the costs are rising
- the human costs and the financial costs.
- Sir Edward Jonathan Davey, British MP

After lockdown and a semblance of normalcy returned to everyday life, and Don and Fran planned to introduce each other to their respective parents. Fran's parents Robert and Sybil Brandt, and Don's parents Jake and Mary Whitely both lived in Toronto. Still there was some apprehension beforehand in case there were any surprising responses to the news about their relationship. Fran arranged a Saturday lunch for the parents at Don's house and wore a knee length, dark blue skirt with matching low heels and a lacey white blouse. Don had Chinos with a white and pale blue checked shirt, both being dressed smart casual without anything controversial to inadvertently raise any eyebrows.

Sybil, like Mary, were also dressed smart casual. Both had similar feelings of concern wanting their future son- or daughter-in-law to accept them knowing how animosity with their child-in-law could drive a wedge between them and their child. Gone are the days when the son- or daughter-in-law were the only ones concerned about the impression they made with their future parents-in-law.

Although Fran was a reasonable 168 centimeters tall, next to Don at 185 centimeters, she looked short. Similarly, Sybil who was almost Fran's height, looked short next to Robert who stood 180 centimeters tall. But Mary was taller than Sybil at 173 centimeters and closer in height to her husband Jake who stood 183 centimeters tall. Not surprising that Don was his height with tall parents. Don looked more like his mother with chiseled features and a straight jaw. Fran had the rounder facial features of her father with high cheek bones and his dark brown hair. Sybil was a blue-eyed blond with none of her genes apparent in Fran.

Both Sybil and Mary were overtly excited at all the prospects this marriage would bring, especially grandchildren. It was not surprising news as Fran and Don made regular telephone calls to their parents who had both been told about their respective beau and belle, and that they were living together. Soon after the introductions, the three couples had lunch accompanied with much conversation as the in-laws started getting to know each other. After desert, Don and Fran broached the sensitive topic of a house loan to both their parents. Fran and Don's parents could individually afford to loan their children the money to build a survival house rather than a dream one more typical of what newlyweds would be considering. While Don explained the concept of an impending ice age, Fran was quietly inspecting her future in-laws. Mary had arrived in casual pale beige slacks with a short sleeved matching blouse. Contrasting her simple attire, Fran's mother Sybil was more into fashion and wore a bright, floral dress with heeled shoes.

Fran thought, some of our mothers' husbands' personalities have rubbed off onto them. Dad is outgoing having to interact with many people whereas Jake is an engineer. Dad dresses to look smart for his many meetings where an external impression is important. Jake's clothing is more utilitarian for building sites and meeting with fellow technical employees, who judge him on his work rather than image. While everyone is well dressed as a reflection of what they can afford, my parents are definitely more flamboyant in their choice of garb. Does this extend to their personalities as well? Dad and Mom are quite extrovertish. Will Jake and Mary be similar or introverts? Mary is comfortable with her hair to have greyed whereas Mom dyes hers. An ego reflection of their respective personalities? Do I consider Don to be an extrovert or an introvert? No neither. Well balanced! In a short space of time, I will have my answer as I get to know the Whitelys.

The young couple had made good impressions on their prospective in-laws, which was a relief although neither felt it would be anything less. However, this did not reduce the skepticism both sets of parents had towards an imminent ice age. It made them quite reluctant to contribute towards the additional costs of building a more conventional home. Robert voiced his first concern. "One problem is that you are not yet married and if it does not materialize, who will own this expensive house?"

Jake had followed Robert's concern staying "The second problem is that definitely I consider such an investment to be one that would over capitalize a house with all the excessive features required to withstand the possible extreme storms that you have described Don if this ice age does not materialize. I expect Robert shares my sentiments on this point."

Don knew he would need to justify his plans for a dramatically changing climate that was predicted in about a decade. He gave them some frightening statistics to bolster his argument. "The coldest occupied village in the world is Oymyakon in Russia's Yakutia region. Temperatures can fall to below -70^0C or in the minus nineties Fahrenheit. But the world's coldest place ever recorded by NASA on August 10th, 2010 was in the East Antarctic Plateau at -135.8^0F or -93.2^0C. Therefore. minus fifty is quite possible. When storms generally contained in the polar regions by traditional cold winters around the poles break out of their vortices, this freezing air blasts towards the equator. You know the extreme storms we have been experiencing in the last few years. Well, it seems that this trend will tip the world into an ice age and it is relatively imminent. If people can live permanently in Oymyakon, it is possible for us to survive marginally warmer temperatures down to minus fifty with the appropriate housing."

Jake said "Climate continuously experiences cycles ranging from mini-ice ages to cataclysmic events. There are also shorter cycles and for many years the current global warming was considered to be another short-term warming cycle rather than a serious trend. Are these Polar Vortex storms you are describing not merely another temporary trend?"

Don said "I did not want to overload you with all the various information published on the Internet. But one in particular called `Severe Weather Europe' focuses on trying to predict whether the `Arctic hounds' or `Beast from the East' would release extreme weather into Europe and other parts of the globe due to a collapse of the containment conditions of the Polar Vortex. Their January 2021 forecast said these containment conditions are collapsing and you know what horrendous weather spilled out of the arctic region last winter."

To address the problem of the couple not being married, Don and Fran's response was to rush through a civil marriage in Court with a statement to their parents that a more formal ceremony in church could follow within a reasonable period if everyone wanted something more traditional.

Eventually the parents capitulated on a building loan after not much more persuasion saying that it was their children's decision and they needed to take responsibility for what they proposed building.

Around a fortnight later, Don was chatting to his father Jake on the phone. "Dad, you know I always planned to go into my own business. This is an opportunity to build a show house and offer similar ones to other people who would also like to insure against the possibility of an ice age. Initially I suspect there would be limited interest, but as the severity of our winters continues to increase as has happened over the last few years, media reports will increase their coverage of this phenomenon. A show house will help to sell the concept to buyers, augmented by our own independent marketing initiatives. This could then make the asset work in another way too. Being a physical object for potential buyers to see, it will promote the idea better by being a tangible reality. An existing home enhances the credibility of a mere concept into something palpable and our house would then become an investment that gives a monetary return."

"Don, you had already persuaded us to give you a loan, but this dimension represents a new level of interest for me. Perhaps the loan should be considered an investment in a new company with which I buy shares? If you would have your father as a partner?"

"Of course, Dad. I did civil engineering to follow in your footsteps and you have decades of experience that would undoubtedly have many invaluable contributions towards aspects of the designs of the various system."

"Once I moved beyond my reluctance to believe than an ice age could be around the corner, I have been doing research on the Internet on these Polar Vortex occurrences and giving the construction much thought, which I would love to discuss with you. We should have a barbeque soon to chat about some of the design features with Robert and Sybil to ensure they do not feel excluded?"

Fran's economic and MBA background automatically assigned her the task of administrator for the project including control of finances. After some thought about the scope of her responsibilities, she said to Don, "As the woman on this project, my role with your blessing must include the decorating of the house from paint color to furniture, choice of books and even the choice of offline movies to pass the time, what first aid and medicine to stock, linen, cutlery, crockery, kitchen equipment and what would be needed for our children."

"Our children" replied Don in a quizzical tone. "I don't remember this as part of our roadmap."

"Does that mean you don't want children" said a disappointed Fran pulling a most dejected expression. "We were so busy discussing and planning the house project that other aspects of our lives such as children seem to have been relegated to an indefinitely pending inbox. Now is an appropriate time to afford it the airtime such an important decision warrants."

"Yes, we never raised the subject of children and my first thoughts are whether we want to bring them into a potentially bleak world," said Don. "But if we do want children, I would not want to delay and be an older father, nor want you to have pregnancies when the country's medical services may have collapsed. If we have around a decade to go, having children soon would mean they would be reasonably independent and therefore easier to manage when the ice age descends on us. Okay you win. Let's go upstairs to bed and start now."

"This will have to be a practice run since I have to come off the pill and let my normal cycle resume. But I intend to practice as much as possible between now and then, so yes we are going upstairs immediately."

After long days at work on their regular jobs, the couple would still spend hours at night and on weekends designing, setting up accounting programs, project management spreadsheets, Bill of Materials and Material Requirements Planning programs, project planning and control bar charts with critical path analysis, and requesting quotes. Fran said "We covered many of these subjects during the Operations Research module in my MBA course that I felt had no relevance for anything I would ever do or need in my life. Now some of these techniques and methodologies are cornerstones of the project. Who would have thought? We never know what life has in store for us."

One of Don's father's work associates and personal friend who was an architect started on the house design, guided by Don and Jake. One evening Fran asked Don "What are you doing to recycle heat from appliances like a tumble dryer, heat off the oven and hob, and anything else that may generate a reasonable amount of heat? And assuming city electricity and gas do fail, how do we run a washing machine and then dry its contents, especially towels and sheets, and similar, large items? What about ironing clothes if there is too little electricity? Can you produce steam from the gas burner for a steam iron? We should have kids' clothes then as well that need to be washed, dried and maybe pressed."

Surprised at these important points, Don said "I am supposed to be the engineer and I never thought about those things. They are really valuable heat recovery sources. Would we be able to produce sufficient electricity? A generator would have the power, but I am not sure we would have sufficient fuel to last a long winter with all these extra requirements. Apparently, diesel engines will run off heating oil to avoid storing two types of oil. But there are additives in diesel for better performance and keeping an engine clean that are not added to heating oil. This topic requires more investigation, especially because of limited space and not compromising the long-term condition of a diesel engine with poor quality fuel."

"Maybe the heat from some of these appliances can be ducted into a clothes and linen drying cabinet. But I will leave it in your capable hands babe," said Fran. "I also thought that perhaps at the end of year when we were considering a winter break, what about Kenya? As this project progresses and we treat an ice age as an inevitable reality, my thoughts about extended periods of freezing cold are drifting towards the longer term, especially once we have children. If Canada becomes relatively uninhabitable, we may have to move if it is not too late. Then I would like to have a feel for some warmer country but only know a trivial amount about Africa from books and movies."

"I have always wanted to do a safari and we could combine the two. Say a week in the bush and a week travelling around looking at the land. Ideally, I would love a farm near a town on a river by the sea. That would give us many resources like fresh water, sea fish and shellfish, and provisions in a nearby town. But I imagine such prime land is already owned and would be expensive to buy. And we do not have money to buy anything abroad."

Fran said "When we were studying finance, there was an old book called The Crash of '79 by Paul Erdman. It is a fictional collapse of the world's monetary systems in 1979 and the protagonist gets wind of it probably going to happen."

"Sounds not unlike the situation we may be confronted with soon."

"Yes," continued Fran, "and I suppose I have also read other doomsday material without realizing it. Anyway, in the Crash of '79 he sells all his assets, buys a farm on the Californian coast that is stocked with everything to be self-sufficient, and converts the balance of his cash into Kruger Rands. He felt that over the centuries the one commodity that was the most highly valued for trading was gold and hedged his remaining liquid assets into that form. As you said, not that we have cash to convert to Kruger Rands and this strategy should be implemented before any ice age. But into a tradable commodity if currencies fail as it would need to be something reasonably portable and negotiable to buy land and other necessities in Kenya."

Don asked, "Have you read anything about the politics, the country's infrastructure and other important aspects of potentially making it the optimal country of choice on the equator?"

"Not really. South Africa would probably be the best African country to move to as it probably has the best infrastructure in Africa. But it stretches as far as 34^0 South and therefore may be too far from the equator."

"How on earth do you know its latitude?" asked Don.

"Cape Town is the same distance south from the equator as Los Angeles is north. A bit of Trivial Pursuit's knowledge I picked up somewhere."

"Why did you select Kenya of the many countries around the world on or close to the equator? Because English is their second language?"

Fran answered "As an ex British colony and like Canada, it is part of the British Commonwealth. Therefore, there is some culture and affinity for the English ways that is still entrenched in Kenya. Remember the only other English-speaking countries on the equator are the adjacent Uganda and Tanzania. However, Uganda is inland with no sea access, which I think is important. And I think Kenya is more developed than Tanzania, but I would need to do more research. South Africa is even more developed, includes English amongst its eleven official languages, but I am sure too far from the equator."

Don pulled out his smartphone and asked Google "What is the latitude of South Africa's northern border." A list of over 200 hundred countries' border coordinates came up and after scrolling through it for South Africa he announced "It says the most northern part of South Africa is Beit Bridge at 22.2° South. I need to look at a map but yes, it is still too far from the equator if we are going into an ice age. You know the eastern side of parts of America and Africa appear to be wetter and the western side can have deserts. Look at California versus the US East Coast. Chile on the west and Argentina on the east. Similarly, in Southern Africa with the Namibian deserts on the west and tropical Zululand in South Africa on the east. But as I recall, they have this resistant malaria in Zululand, and I need to check what the malaria status is in East Africa. Not merely for our proposed vacation there but long-term living. A collapse of civilization could mean no sophisticated drugs manufactured anymore. This is all quite depressing!"

It was summer and that Sunday their parents came around for a barbeque. Fran's parents Sybil and Robert arrived early as he wanted to tell them something important. "Sybil wants to be close to Fran to help with any grandchildren. We have decided that we finally want to build an ice age resistant home next door to you, and I have the ideal location for us. We would sell our present house once the new one is complete, which ideally will be ready by winter."

Fran jumped up and grabbed her mother in a hug saying "I am so excited! Thank you, thank you." She turned to Don grinning broadly asking "Isn't that fantastic news? I am so excited and happy?"

Don stood up and went to hug his father-in-law saying "This is great news. Now this may swing my parents as well who have been vacillating about taking a similar plunge."

At that moment, his parents Jake and Mary came in. "What are we celebrating?" she asked.

Sybil went up to Mary, took her hands and said smiling "We have decided to move next door and build an ice age house too. Now it is time for you two to move next door on the other side."

Mary looked at Jake with a twinkle in her eyes and said "Well Jake, we have been speaking about doing this but never quite saying yes. I think we need to also build next door."

Jake looked a bit uncomfortable replying "Yes we have been considering it. By the way hello everybody. I was not sure what would finalize a yea or nay decision and maybe this is the catalyst to finally do it. I am feeling quite good about the thought, especially as doing three houses together will give the project various efficiencies and economies of scale."

Mary shrugged her shoulders and smiling said "That's my engineer. Always being pragmatic. But I think we won the day. I am in and Jake, you better follow." After a few beers, before the afternoon ended, Jake formally agreed to build a house for them on the other side of Fran and Don's house from where Robert and Mary would build.

Don needed to discuss the housing business as well. "Guys, you have expressed some interest in a joint business venture building these houses. I would like to finally register a new company and test the water. Unless we make a firm commitment, it will merely be a nice idea but not have any drive towards making it a reality. Now that you are in with a specialized house each, can we go the next step together?"

Sybil shouted excitedly before the men indicated a yes or no "I would love to call the company Iceberg or Glacier."

"For now dear, maybe just Newco for New Company until we confirm if we even want to enter into this type of business" said Robert. "I have not spoken to Jake enough to know what his sentiments are. Jake, what do you feel?"

"I have enjoyed helping Don with an excitement that I have not really felt since I was young and just embarking on a career as an engineer, creating things for the first time. I have also seen your equally enthusiastic interest and am keen to embark on this new business phase of life at a time when I was only thinking of retirement."

Smiling, Fran said "Mom, let us consider your one suggestion. I want to propose a name I have been thinking of for a Newco that is close to what you suggested. How about Nice Age Construction instead of Ice Age. The N in Nice could be a different color so one can still see 'Ice Age' embedded in the name. Or a small n and capital I?"

"Well, it will be your company even if we become shareholders, so you have the final say" replied Sybil. "What do you think Don?"

"I think my astute wife that is a financial specialist also understands marketing and if she feels that is what Newco should be called, Fran has my vote. I do think it has a *nice* ring to it."

Mary added "Specialists in home construction for extreme subzero temperatures."

Robert then opened the subject of location. "When Fran was young, I bought a small farm holding on what then then just out of the city as an investment intended for her. But over time the city expanded and eventually enveloped the smallholding, which is in the northeast of Scugog in the Durham municipality. It is now designated as peri urban as it has rural qualities in an urban area. Once its status was changed, I decided to apply for it to be re-zoned as a township for development and the application was successful. It requires services such as roads, water, electricity, gas, a sewerage system, and communications that are straightforward tasks to implement. I feel it would be ideal to build a like-minded community in this area and has many benefits, which we can discuss."

Everyone stared in surprise at Robert's announcement and the shocked silence was eventually broken by Don who said "Robert, that is unbelievable. Fran did you know about this land?" Continuing without pause for an answer he shifted into engineer mode. "Since we are planning for extreme conditions, these services will not be so easy to implement as they need to withstand extremes of cold that current services will not. Therefore, it will not be straightforward and will be more costly."

"Dad," said Fran, "in case you are thinking of merely giving the land to the project, I need to say upfront that it is an extremely valuable asset. We either need to buy from you with funds we must raise or alternatively it can be accepted by Newco as an asset with a loan account to you at its fair value. Or maybe used to acquire shares in the company. You need to decide which option you feel comfortable with and I am sure everyone will agree with your choice."

"You are already the financial controller" replied Robert. "I said this was bought to be an inheritance for you, and Mom and I would like to give it to you now. It will help you or us get the new company started and benefits us as we will all be together. Also, the expense of land will not be one of the funding requirements of the new company."

Don said "We need to see the land and its location as soon as possible so we can start planning. And as Fran said, this is your land for which you will be compensated. At least in the form of shares and I am sure you and Fran will decide on something fair and appropriate. I will accept whatever you two decide and Dad, Mom, do you agree?"

"Of course, we do." answered Jake and Mary simultaneously. "This is a really big kickstart to the project. Thank you, Robert," added Jake.

An unexpected bonus materialized. The grandparents had been talking about their children's project to friends and once they had both decided to follow suit with their own houses, two of their friends, Evan and Lily Thomson, and James and Amelia Jones, said they would also like to buy one of these specialized survival houses. They had become equally concerned about an imminent ice age, having researched the possibility on the Internet. They concluded it to be sufficiently probable to prepare for it, especially as they could afford these specialized houses.

Don decided to resign from work to be involved fulltime with the project. Jake and Robert insisted on paying retail prices for their homes to help Don and Fran's income as they needed to have a nest egg for winter. Before the end of summer, they had another firm buyer plus two possibles enabling Fran and Don to feel reasonably secure that they could survive financially doing these housing projects. Don offered a lesser designed house to the one ambivalent couple that was adequate for the present winters. The house would be enhanced with the extra systems needed to make the inhabitants self-sufficient down to minus fifty at a rate that their personal cash flow could afford. But the house would have additional insulation in walls, windows and doors that could not be added later. The nIce Age partners were upbeat with the increasing positive interest, so additional stands were prepared in anticipation of even more sales.

Chapter 9   NOAH'S ARK

13. And God said to Noah,
"The end of all flesh is come before me;
for the earth is filled with violence through them;
And behold, I will destroy them with the earth.
14. Make thee an ark …
- Noah, Genesis VI

The excavation of the first basement marked the start of their project. Fran, Don and their parents were there at 9 o'clock on a Monday morning on Scugog land lying on the outskirts of Toronto. Although it was spring, the air was still cold. The sky was overcast with sporadic gaps of blue and a light breeze blew from the northwest. They stood at the spot where Don had pegged out the site that the couple had chosen for the first house. The terrain was dry, sandy and with sparse grass tufts here and there. The land had never been developed and its surface was sufficiently flat and barren not to need much preparation. The digger's engine roared into life with a deep throb declaring its power, ready to rend the earth asunder. They watched mesmerized as the excavator started scrapping into the hard earth, digging into the ground, lifting out the first scoop of soil. There was a collective sense of jubilation as fantasy started to become a reality. Jake popped the cork from a bottle of bubbly as the first sand was tipped into a truck. Glasses were filled to celebrate the start of the building, a short dedication was made by Robert and everyone sipped the champagne as they drank in the general excitement which they all had, watching the project commence. Fran suddenly giggled and said, "We must look quite incongruous wearing helmets, standing in the dust, drinking champagne."

Fran had found articles on geothermal heating where underground temperatures from about 5 meters down remain fairly constant all year round and were slowly being phased in around Ontario for free winter heating and summer cooling. Don was excited at this relatively unlimited supply of energy, which is partly why a basement became an even more essential part of the design. Once the original basement floor level had been reached, additional depth was excavated to lay a liquid filled pipe in a series of loops, which would absorb heat from the warmer ground in winter. Don discussed with his father how best to use this heat source. There were various designs and they finalized on the heat to be used to keep the basement and its ceiling warm. These were not living areas and therefore had a lower temperature requirement. As the warm air rose to the ceiling, it could be ducted with a small fan back to floor level. A computer cooling fan would be fitted to the base of a plastic rainwater downpipe that was the height of the basement and warm air would be sucked in at the top and expelled at the bottom to recirculate the heat.

One day Don asked his father "I am concerned at the amount of electricity all these systems require. For example, there is the geothermal circulation pump, the air vent heat exchanger fan, a microwave oven, all the lighting, computers, TV's and various electrical appliances, which may be small individually, but accumulate into additional kilowatts. We either need to convert more energy or find a cheaper way to generate electricity. What else can you think of?"

His father immediately suggested "You could use a windmill generator but with small blades considering the expected force of vortex storm winds. Or a few smaller windmill generators since a large one is too big to install on our stands and would be far too expensive. If you think of the various free and sustainable energy sources, other than wind, I think we have covered all of what is currently available. You have solar heating and solar electricity, which is very weather and light dependent. There is geothermal heating under the basement floor. There is heat recovery from your burners and other heat-producing appliances. Flowing gases and liquids are being used to turn micro turbine electricity generators. The large battery bank should be able to store all generated electricity, so none is wasted. Fran suggested motion detecting lights in passages and other non-living areas to save energy, which is a great idea."

Don added "And all lights are low energy LED's. Where there are options, appliances being bought are the smaller ones with lower power consumption. Our first winter will give a good indication as to whether the combined contribution of these systems provide adequate energy. We will need to turn off city gas and electricity in our houses during a peak cold period to see what the usage averages over a week or longer to obtain a reasonable indication of what the demand will be."

Jake said "This will only give an indication as we are planning for future temperatures that are expected to drop well below what we currently experience in winter. It is important to confirm that we have surplus heat and electrical energy now to survive these more extreme temperatures in a few years' time."

The decision was to first build Fran and Don's house, to see how it worked out before committing to the other four houses on order. Any conspicuous problems or modifications could then be part of the other houses' specifications. Contractors were chosen who were specialists in their respective fields with instructions where applicable, to exceed the normal building specifications. Increasing the thickness of polyurethane foam made no sense to the one contractor Jim. When he saw the specification from Don he asked, "Why do you want to waste all this additional foam that is far more than necessary for even our harshest winters?"

Don replied, "I think winters will be getting worse because of these Polar Vortex storms and I want to see how much more energy efficient a house can be built in case the trend continues. Other design features in the house will reduce heat loses even more and we want to build a show house that others may want us to build for them during the next few years."

"Well, your new name will be Noah, building your Ark when everyone around you is anticipating a global warming rather than some Big Freeze" commented Jim. "I suppose the added insulation will also keep heat out if summers get much hotter and that would reduce the energy consumption of air conditioning. But the additional cost may be a serious disincentive for other buyers."

"If I am to be Noah, who are you? Doubting Thomas?" said a smiling Don, unfazed by his contractor's comment, ensuring it was trivialized rather than become an issue that could quickly spread this nickname to the other contractors. He did not feel like justifying his design decisions to Jim or anyone else who came on site but knew there would be others who also queried their respective specs. "Anyway, we already have orders for four more houses. Do a great job with the first one and you will remain our preferred contracted for the future ones."

"Deal!" said Jim. "I always do my best so the quality of my work will not improve with this incentive. As I am hands-on and work with my team, I am always present to ensure you receive the best we can do."

One Saturday some friends, Ellen and Frank had invited Fran and Don to join them for an evening in a new British pub called the Horse and Hound. It even had imported kegs of English beer and was original in every way including the menu with bangers and mash, and ploughman's lunch. After they were seated, Don gazed around inspecting the authenticity of the décor and recognized one of their insulation contractor Jim's employees who was quite drunk, rowdy, and shooting pool with some friends at the back of the pub. At one point he looked across towards them and waved at Ellen. She commented "His name is Carl. What an ass. His son is in our daughter Candy's class and at PTA and sports meetings, has too much to say, always complains and is not at all popular. I hope he does not come across to chat as he looks quite drunk."

Don replied, "He has been working on our houses, so I have seen him, but my interaction has been only with his employer. I have no idea what kind of a person he is."

"Trust me," said Ellen, "you do not want to know him."

Of course, Carl staggered over from his game and stood at their table looking at them. "Hello Ellen. Hello Mr. Whitely. What brings you to this end of town? Pub crawling? How about a game of pool Mr. W? Small stakes. Only five Dollars a game. I am quite good but having had so much delicious Watney's English Ale, you would have a decided advantage."

Don answered shaking his head with a "No thanks. Tonight is a social night with the ladies, not a boys' night out."

Talking loudly so people around could hear him, Carl virtually shouted saying "Chicken Mr. W. You too afraid to play drunk in case I beat you? Show some courage. Only one game. The ladies wont' mind."

People were looking around making them feel uncomfortable. Fran said quietly to Don "You said you can play a reasonable game. Just do the one game to placate him and stop having our evening spoiled by his uncouth manner."

Reluctantly, Don stood up muttering "I am sure he will want more than one game." He walked across to the pool table with Carl trailing behind where his friends had been watching and were grinning at is escapade. "Going to take a few bucks off Carl are you?" joked one of his friends. The balls are set up and I am sure Carl will let you do the opening break."

Don took a cue, chalked it and did the break. "Nothing sunk Noah?" slurred Carl. "Like your house we are building to float on ice." He roared with laughter while his friends looked at him quizzically. Turning to them, Carl said "The polar ice caps are melting with global warming and Mr. Noah here is building an ark for an ice age. I want some of whatever he has been smoking" and roared with laughter again."

Don turned at looked angrily at him. "Stick to the game and shut up."

"Or else what?" said a now aggressive Carl who evidently wanted to have a fight.

"Or else I am going back to my table and you can play with your friends."

"If you want to do something stupid like build an icehouse, be prepared to be mocked" snorted Carl, showing off in front of his cronies who were enjoying his insulting banter." He hit a ball, which did not go into any pocket. Don took his turn and sunk a striped ball. "Earned your stripes Noah. But you failed to understand elementary climatology."

Don looked at him and simply said "Cheers!", placed his cue on the side of the pool table and started walking back. Fran was staring across the room with a worried look, which he saw. He then saw Fran gasp and spun around to see Carl swinging his cue at his head. Instinctively his arm went into a karate block, deflecting the cue away from him. In his other hand, Carl had a pool ball, which he swung at Don's head. Being so drunk and untrained, his blow was slow giving Don plenty of time to parry the arm,

70

striking it hard. The ball flew of out Carl's hand and landed on a table where it shattered a plate and continued knocking over a wine glass before rolling onto the floor. Carl lunged forward, knocking Don back against a table sending its contents everywhere and spilling beer and water onto some of the people seated there. Don was pressed back against the table with Carl's head down and arms around his waist. Don did a chop down onto Carl's neck causing him to collapse onto the floor, falling more from his drunken stupor than the blow.

As Don stood up away from the table, Carl's friends and some of the staff rushed up. The manager said to Don "I was worried about this guy as I saw how progressively drunk and loud he was becoming. I saw you walk away and how he attacked you. I apologize and tonight's food and drink are on the house. We have called the police and charges will be laid against him."

By now Fran was also standing there, everyone in the pub was staring at the altercation, and she gently led Don away back to their table."

"Oh, Don I am so sorry," said a nervous Ellen who could not stop talking from nerves. "I knew he was a pain but did not expect him to become violent. That was quite a bit of martial arts you did there. I did not know you were so adept. Are you going to lay assault charges against him? I think you should. He needs to learn a lesson."

Don was fuming and Fran was concerned about what he may say so she quickly replied to Ellen's question. "It seems the right thing to do and Don probably will. The manager said they will be laying charges and Don will be drawn in anyway. But he said tonight's food and drink are on the house and we should try to make the most of the rest of the evening."

Don continued to remain quiet trying to subside as Fran and Ellen tried to restore the evening's original mood. Frank had been quiet and

71

finally said to Don "I am really pleased that you thrashed that pig. As Ellen said, no one likes him and now he may realize that he cannot behave in this unacceptable manner."

Don finally spoke. "I do not care about his puny attack or snide comments. But he was directly insulting, which I will take up with his boss Jim who must have said something slighting to Carl about us. He was deliberately insulting, trying to goad me and I am pleased that I merely walked away. You are right, Ellen. He needs to learn a lesson and he will be confronted with a list of charges including assault, drunk and disorderly conduct in a public place, damage to property and maybe other charges as well. That will sober him up and maybe stop him from becoming drunk when not at home. I wonder how he treats his wife and children if he can become violent like this quite easily in public."

They made the most of the rest of the evening. The waiters quickly cleaned up and soon the pub was noisy with people enjoying themselves as though nothing had happened. As soon as they were back in the car returning home, Fran said "Don I am sorry that I suggested you appease Carl with a quick game."

"That's okay Fran. It made sense at the time, we did not know the guy and it happened. I was not hurt, and we even had a free meal. But what I have not been able to tell you is that Carl was calling me a stupid Noah, building an icehouse as I was too stupid to understand the concept of global warming."

Fran was stunned. "Where did that come from?"

"His boss Jim who has been doing our polyurethane insulation called me a Noah building an ark when the world is experiencing global warming. He must have joked about me and what we are doing to his staff

72

afterwards. Not okay and I am going to pull him off the job. When he takes it up with Carl, he may learn another lesson if Jim lets him go. There are plenty other contractors that can do this type of insulation who will appreciate the work and not deride their clients to their staff."

"He definitely has to go. Maligning his principles who are paying his salary! Absolutely must go!"

Jim and his crew arrived on the Monday and started setting up their equipment as though nothing had happened. It was impossible that Jim was unaware of what happened between Carl and Don, and Jim was trying to discretely ignore the event. Don gave him ten minutes to broach the subject and perhaps show some contrition. When nothing transpired, Don simply walked up to him and said "After the insults and attack that I endured from your Carl about me being a stupid Noah, your work here has ended. Talking disparagingly behind my back about me to your staff and not even bothering to apologize! Just pack up and leave. This is not the type of contractor I am prepared to work with." Don turned around and left, not interested in entering into any debate or listening to a 'woe is me' plea from Jim.

As the houses progressed into three dimensions off the plans, various changes and additions became evident, challenging particularly Don's attempts at remaining within budget. Fran too who was tracking their expenditure was concerned. They had 10% contingency built into the budget and it looked that they would need at least twice that amount to complete the house. Their parents could afford more and were less concerned about overruns. Jake said to Don, "You were right to delay building all the units at once, despite the possible benefits of scale we may have had. These changes would have cost more than any savings if repeated in five homes rather than one."

Fran had researched some of the design criteria of arctic circle homes built in other countries such as Alaskan, Scandinavian and Russian houses, that added even more features to the original design. But one day she surprised Don by asking "What happens if a fire starts in the house? We can install fire extinguishers and have strategically placed hoses fed from the cold and hot water tanks and geyser. But what if we must flee the house? Maybe we need a shed or granny cottage as a backstop. And how would we get to it in a vortex storm? This is an unplanned expense, but can we ignore such an event even if highly unlikely?"

The next budget set back followed a statement by Fran who told Don "I was looking at some off-the-grid container houses and one of the advertisers said they include grey waste recycling and rainwater collection. I looked it up and it seems rather important. Do you know anything about *grey waste?*"

"Yes, rainwater collection is a good idea in summer."

"Very funny. You are going to only shower in grey wastewater as punishment for poor humor and not making provision for it."

Don took Fran in his arms and said "I need to confiscate your computer until after the project before you cripple us with all these important additions. If we collect water from the bath, shower and basins, it is reasonably clean to recycle into toilets and in summer, for plants growing in the garden."

"What about kitchen wastewater?" asked Fran. "It is not classified as toilet blackwater and is easier to clean than black waste."

"Yes, but it has more fats and oils, and other organic matter than shower and basin water so it needs more treatment. The cheapest is a sand filter but the sand needs to be regenerated or replaced periodically as there is no place on the property for some biological digester to process the organic matter even if greywater has a lower level of contamination than blackwater waste."

"What is the bottom line? Is it viable and appropriate for us?"

Don continued explaining "In winter we have ice and snow as a water source although it does need to be melted, which does consume heat."

"That is what we are using the warm air for that is being vented, which would otherwise be wasted, lost heat."

Don continued "Since we have winter snow and ice to melt into water, greywater is more of a summer requirement, especially if the city water supply has been compromised. That also means we should be storing thawed, frozen water in a large tank, which is something else we have not made provision for. I had thought about it in passing and even wondered about a borehole as a water source in case of a mains water failure continuing into summer."

Fran said "We could put a large tank in the basement considering the weight and fill it in winter. As long as we have the city's water supply flowing, I think mains water should run into the ice melt tank, so it is always filled with fresh water. We then would have one pumping system feeding the house with water."

Don said "We would then be running a pressure pump all the time for the house's plumbing. If the municipal mains supply is still working, using its pressure would save on the electricity to run a pressure pump. A simple valve can swap the feed from mains to auxiliary pump if the municipal feed fails."

Fran nodded and asked, "That would be separate to any greywater system, which is another exercise that needs more investigation."

"For additional water sources apart from greywater, we can run rainwater off the roof into the tank as well, probably first through a small filter." answered the engineer. "With greywater perhaps the simplest start would be to run it into a separate tank, pump it through a swimming pool filter as a cheap, off-the-shelf filtration, and then into a small tank in the roof where it would gravity feed the toilets". The filter would be backwashed periodically, which would minimize sand contamination. But it may require a separate loop for caustic soda cleaning to dissolve the fats and soaps which I need to consider."

Fran asked "So are we doing this then? That was a quick decision. All of it including the large storage tank or just the filter and smaller tanks? I need to get quotes and put them in the project spread sheet."

"I think in principle yes but subject to what it is going to cost. You realize this also requires some new plumbing and changes to the existing pipework" commented Don. "Maybe we do the plumbing now and add the tanks next year so we do not cripple our cashflow."

A week later Don came to Fran looking serious. "Remember when I said there are so many variables including unforeseen ones in planning to survive an ice age? After your grey waste bombshell and fire query, I feel both are essential."

"Okay. And ..?"

"The we must plan how to manage a fire and install suitable firefighting systems. This is like a bottomless pit with all the extras and necessary options."

"Don I am also concerned that we will not have enough electricity to power all these systems designed to give us self-sufficiency plus our normal requirements like lighting, computers, TV, kitchen appliances and other things."

"That is exactly what my dad raised recently when he suggested some windmill generators to boost the supply. Some of these extras will have to be added over the next few years as we can afford them. We still have a few more years' grace and can introduce these additional investments over time."

"Maybe this winter we should see how we fare for say a month off the grid when temperatures plummet during a Polar Vortex storm" said Fran. "It will increase our consumption costs if we use more expensive stored gas and oil. But the value of testing everything running together rather than individual components will give us the data we need to help confirm everything works and we have adequate capacity to last one of these terrible winters."

Don added "Remember our parents must do similar trials in their homes. Our home is not only a show house but a test prototype, which we could sell, build another for ourselves with the accumulated experience and have a superior one to this initial attempt to create a sound survival home. Therefore, we should not panic about any omissions or mistakes in the first house."

"Refining it with a new house is reassuring that we will have the luxury of learning from any mistakes" said Fran. But we would need to rectify any problems in this house before we could ethically sell it."

"Remember word of mouth sales by satisfied customers is worth more than any expensive marketing. Therefore, we only want happy buyers so the house must be equal to all the others we sell. There is a lot depending on our success with the initial ones and I agree, any existing units we sell must have been modified with any changes that are built into new homes."

"Agreed!" said Fran. "And we need to tell our parents about the new features we have decided to add. I am going to invite them over for a barbeque on Sunday to discuss it with them."

Part 4

Kenya

Chapter 10   THE EQUATOR

> One spoon of soup in need
> has more value than a pot of soup
> when we have an abundance of food.
> **- Angolan Proverb**

The Kenyan holiday trip finally arrived. With mixed feelings having to leave their construction project before it was completed, they boarded a plane to London and after a three hour wait, caught their connection on Kenyan Air to Nairobi. Even their Canadian summer clothes were too hot for the tropical heat that hit them and after checking into their hotel, went straight out to shop for more suitable apparel. "This heat is unbelievably oppressive" complained Fran. "It feels like another planet as we are planning for -50°C below whereas it feels like 50°C here. This heat challenges any thoughts of an ice age if it can be so hot here."

"This is really a shock. I have been to the Caribbean and experienced heat, but one tends to forget the clammy humidity of the tropics. I cannot imagine anyone here considering our project to be even vaguely plausible. Do you feel this is a challenge to our vision?"

"Superficially yes, but after all the research we have done, I still feel it is highly probability. I am keen to see what farming infrastructure there is as an indication of how well they could gear up to meet an enormous export demand for food. We once discussed how First World countries may want to colonize Third World countries if they are unable to rise to the occasion and ramp up their farming efficiencies and output to feed a freezing world. Now we can see whether this may or may not be necessary."

80

"Another problem," continued Don, "is that if temperatures here also fall, which they must, will the current crops grown still be viable? To change to more suitable crops for cooler weather, they will not have stores of seed and experience to grow other more cold hardy crops."

"Not only that but if most of the land suitable for farming is currently used, to increase it for additional output takes time to prepare new areas to be arable. With the potential of millions if not billions of people in colder regions desperate for food, there will not be the luxury of any long preparation time. And as you said, what about seeds, fertilizers, insecticides, equipment, food processing manufacturers, refrigerated storage and transport, and the whole logistics chain from field to an overseas supermarket. Starting up here would require a lot of capital. That farm in Kwale of 8 hectares which is about 20 acres cost $430,000 Canadian Dollars."

Don asked "What were the details again? Now that we are here, I can concentrate on the specifics"

"This is what I copied down from the ad:

20 Acres agricultural land in Msambweni, Kwale county. Very good for agriculture with a 3 bedrooms residential bungalow, chicken houses, staff houses, vegetable plants, mango trees, maize, fully connected irrigation system. Price negotiable with a 10% down payment and a two-year loan at 13%.

Fran added "From Google Earth, Msambweni is a village with a river close by and the coast only a kilometer or two away. Without farm coordinates, I could not tell whether it was in a prime position or merely close to resources we would ideally like to have. We need to check with the

81

estate agent whether it is still for sale and whether there is anything else in the area. Although there is a loan available, if it is not taken now but after the first horrendous winter, prices may soar around the equator. And loans may not be available, especially for non-residents."

"Well, we are here on a look-and-see to get a feel for Kenya rather than a buying trip. The farm sounds like it has some infrastructure even if it is basic. But we are following your suggestion to rather go to the Kenyan Highlands to see what is grown there since it is cooler at the higher altitude and their crops may be the ones to grow at sea level if the earth cools down."

"Yes, that way existing country resources and experience would be shifted to a more appropriate region if the climate changes."

Don said "What is our arrangement with the estate agent in the Highlands? I doubt they would collect us so we may need to rent an automobile, which I never thought about."

"We are due in Kericho in three days' time."

"How far is it?"

"About three hundred kilometers or five hours travelling because of the quality of the roads" answered Fran.

"That is not a quick drive and means we are going to lose a day travelling each way. Maybe we should fly."

"No!" said Fran. "We need to see the countryside to get a feel for the country."

"Then we need to rent a car. I wonder if some of the major rental companies are in this country. We really should have checked this out before leaving and would probably have secured a better rate if we booked from home."

"Yes, ideally we would have but between life in general, building the houses and preparing to leave, it was too hectic to attend to such details."

Don's Internet search included a car rental offer for vintage Land Rovers. "I would really like to rent one of these old Series 3 vehicles. It is probably over 40 years old and I am sure we will feel like old, intrepid explorers." The fantasy hardly materialized as the reality was a grossly difference experience. While the 4x4 off-road vehicle was rugged for the sand roads they were driving on, it was slow and had no basics that one expects in a more modern car. These included no air conditioning, no power steering, no boosted brakes and a maximum speed of around 80 kph by which time the hard suspension had the occupants bouncing around badly and the engine so noisy that the only communication was by shouting, especially as the windows were open for some ventilation. During a stop a miserable Don said "With our slow progress I am afraid we will only reach Kericho after dark. I hope this veteran car's lights work. This was such a bad idea."

After a quick pee stop down a quiet, dusty sidetrack Fran said "I don't want to complain. But I really do want to complain. As I won't feel better and you will feel worse, let's endure as best we can and hope there is a rental branch in Kericho where we can swap the car for anything else, even a modern pick-up to get back to Nairobi." She gave Don a hug and climbed back into the Land Rover.

It was close to sunset when the engine sputtered and died. Don pulled over to the side of the road with the car's last bit of momentum, pulled up the handbrake and turned the ignition key. The starter cranked the engine, but it was dead. With a sigh he climbed out, lifted the hood and started prodding around. After about five minutes Don shouted "Here is the

83

problem. The fuel line has slipped off the carburetor. The clip is old and was not tight enough considering the bumpy road we are on.

Moments later Fran called out "Don, there are some young armed men with spears coming down the road. They have seen us and are now running towards the car."

Don looked around and shouted "Slide across to behind the wheel while I try to be quick. Lock all the doors and close the windows. They look like young Masai probably in their regalia for a transition into manhood ceremony. I hope it does not involve showing how brave one is like the old days when groups of youngsters would fight a lion to prove their manhood." Fran quickly took her phone and took some photographs of the warriors as they ran towards them. She thought they may need some evidence and a way of identifying the men if things turned ugly. Don pushed the hose onto the carburetor's intake pipe and forced the clip on. He dropped the hood and shouted to Fran "Try and start the engine." After a few turns, gas was sucked through the pipe by the petrol pump into the carb and the engine fired into life. But by then the young men had arrived preventing Don from moving. "Hello" he said raising his hand hoping they were merely curious and wanted to help.

The young men held up their shields, were peering over the top, holding their spears with the traditional long blades pointed towards him. The man in the center said "We want your money, cell phones, passports, cameras and any other valuables. We will take them whether you are dead or alive."

Knowing that these testosterone-high young men may injure or kill them anyway to justify their transition into manhood, he knew that he must not show he is intimidated. Don said loudly to Fran "If they attack together, drive through them and go for help." He then addressed them saying "You know that there will be trouble from your elders and the police if you attack tourists and do anything stupid. Just go on your way ..." Before he could finish his sentence, one of the young men, eager to prove himself, dropped his shield and charged at Don. He held the spear horizontal to stab Don who turned to face him head on.

Don thought 'When we did bayonet charges during unarmed combat training, I thought what a useless exercise since warfare had changed so much. If I had only known. I must first deflect the spear ...'

Don side stepped away from the point and started falling backwards to use his assailant's momentum against him. With his arms outstretched, he grabbed the man's arms as he rolled back onto the ground and with his one foot in the moving man's abdomen, lifted him over his head. Don hung onto the man's arms as he sailed in a circle over him, holding his assailant's arms up so that the man landed hard on his back. He fell with a thud, winding himself. Don was up and on him in a flash, rolled him over, pulled his arms back to pin them, then pulled him up onto his feet. Don saw a group of adults running down the road towards them and said to the surprised group "It seems your parents are running towards us. Who else wants to do something stupid and try again?" The group became agitated knowing they were now in serious trouble and waited for the inevitable.

One of the men arrived first and panting said "I am so sorry sir. These young men will be severely disciplined. They have been involved in the traditional initiation into manhood and wanted to prove it with some stupid bravery that is obviously illegal. Please forgive us for such appalling treatment."

Don replied "Yes, I realized that is what was happening since the boys were dressed up as warriors. But they demanded all our possessions and then this youngster tried to stab me with his spear."

"We saw what he was doing in the distance and he will be even more severely punished than the rest of them for his foolishness. Although this was attempted theft, we would like to discipline them according to our custom. I hope you do not lay charges of assault and attempted theft with the police so we can administer tribal justice. We live nearby and as it is late, please let us make amends by offering you a place to sleep, some food and the congenial hospitality for which Kenyans are better known."

Don said "I will ask my wife first as we are on our way to Kericho where we have accommodation booked. May I add that you speak excellent English."

"My name is Abraham; I am the village teacher and I have had tertiary education."

Don walked around to the driver's window where a worried Fran was impatiently waiting for his report. He said "You can turn off the engine. These are the youngsters' parents who are furious at what they tried to do." She turned off the engine with a trembling hand as Don continued. "We have been invited back to their village to try and make amends for the incident with the offer of food and a place to sleep. I said that we need to first discuss it and wonder what you feel."

Two tears ran down Fran's cheeks as she tried not to start crying. "I was not scared but terrified. You keep surprising me with your unusual skills. I hardly saw what you did as you fell back below the side of the car where I could not see what you did to disarm him. I thought you had been stabbed and moments later were up with the man's arms pinned behind him. I am too emotional. You decide."

86

"We wanted to see the country and whether it was a place we could live in if things back home deteriorated so badly that we must leave. This is an opportunity to experience the locals firsthand and it offers them an opportunity to make good the wrong their youngsters did. It is getting dark and still quite a way from Kericho so I am keen to stay, but only if you are."

Fran began to feel more composed and said "I am sure it is a small village with limited place where we could sleep. Do you think their traditional food is something we could stomach? Masai are known for drinking cow and goat blood mixed with urine so it does not curdle and other weird foods. In principle yes, but in practice it may backfire."

"I will ask Abraham who said he is the school's teacher with a tertiary education. I am sure he can be asked directly." Don went towards the group of adults noticing that the youngsters had been herded away. Abraham saw him approaching and stepped forward to meet him. "We think that we would like to accept your offer but have some concerns. We are Canadians and are accustomed to food that is probably quite different to your local staples and we are worried about possibly offending some of you if we find it unpalatable. Also, if you are in a small village, what accommodation are you offering? If it displaces anyone or is of a nature that we find uncomfortable or unpleasant, do we insult the owner and say we wish to leave and continue to Kericho?"

"Regarding the first, our supper would be fresh meat or chicken stew with a maize porridge, which I think you call polenta or cornmeal, plus some vegetables. Masai are traditional herders in arid regions and do have a completely different way of life. But some of us live here in the highlands with a more urbanized lifestyle. Here we are not nomadic and have permanent homes rather than grass and wood huts with walls of cattle dung." Don looked shocked and Abraham smiled, continuing. You would

87

sleep in my spare room; the place is spotless and the bed is comfortable. If you wish to leave prematurely for any reason, we will thank you for trying."

Don nodded and said "It is late, we are keen to experience rural life and thank you for your offer. You can all pile into the back of the Land Rover and we will go together to your village."

Abraham announced to the villagers that they had visitors, who offered them a lift at the back of the car. They all climbed in quite squashed but managed with the ladies along the bench seats and the men on the floor in the middle of the Land Rover. Don made Fran drive to help settle her further, forcing her to concentrate by not making the ride too bumpy for the passengers along a sand road full of corrugations and potholes. After a kilometer, Abraham instructed Fran to turn off the road onto what was more of a track and even more bumpy but the villagers seemed quite accustomed to it. The village lay just over the crest of a nearby hill. Although it was almost dark, they saw perhaps thirty small houses made of bare brick walls and corrugated iron sheet roofs spread out in a haphazard fashion looking like temporary DIY homes. It was typical of the villages they had passed and Fran was quite excited as it was not an experience they would normally have had."

Abraham's wife was surprised to receive two white people for supper and to sleep the night. She asked Abraham for a quick explanation with furtive glances over his shoulder at the couple standing just inside the doorway who were beginning to feel quite uncomfortable. But she then moved towards them smiling, shook their hands which moved from a normal hold to gripping the thumb, then back to an ordinary handshake. His wife was a typical lanky Masai with a shaven head, dark piercing eyes and gaps between her teeth when she smiled. She spoke in Masai which

Abraham translated. "My name is Lankenua, which means I am lucky. I only know a few English words so my husband will repeat in English. His Masai name is Sironka or Pure One. I am sorry you were attacked by our young warriors and hope our hospitality will help you feel less angry about the unpleasant experience." She led them through their penurious abode that was spotlessly clean to a second bedroom that served as Abraham's office where a table next to the window was strewn with piles of student papers and exercise books.

Planning to be away for a few days, the couple had only brought a small roll-on case having left their suitcases at the Nairobi hotel. Don swung it up onto the bed, unzipped the top and opened it. He then turned, leaned back against the bed to face Fran who had sat down wearily in the only chair. "What do you think?" he asked Fran.

"Too soon to tell. It is clean and comfortable, but I am sure we must share the bathroom with our hosts. I hope it has a toilet and not some privy outside. Frankly I am too tired to care and pleased we are not still on a night long drive with an unreliable car, cows and who knows what else on the road."

"Agreed! I think we need to join them and not have a quick rest." Fran nodded and rose up from the chair and Don opened the door for her, following her into the open plan kitchen – living area where Lankenua was cooking and Abraham was setting the table."

Abraham said let me show you the bathroom, which I am afraid we must share. I think you may want to wash Don's shirt and perhaps trousers as he rolled back onto the ground when disarming his would-be attacker."

Fran replied "Thank you I will and am sure it will dry quickly. Meanwhile how can we help with supper's preparation?"

"You are our guests" answered a smiling Abraham, evidently pleased to have them. "Please relax and come sit on the couch. What can I give you something to drink? I have Coldrinks or sodas as I think you call them. And I would like to hear why you are visiting Kenya. To go to the bush? But Kericho is in the wrong direction."

"Walking across to the couch, Fran answered for both saying "Anything that is open will be fine. And with some ice please as it is still so hot."

Don said "To answer your question, we have already been into the bush but also want to see other parts of the country. We are curious as to how Kenyans live, and how developed the economy is, especially with farming and food processing. I believe there are opportunities to enhance efficiencies in these sectors to improve yields and exploit foreign markets. Your coffee production is an excellent example of where this has happened as Kenyan responded well to international demand. Perhaps because the price per ton price is better with coffee than other crops you also grow, or simply that there is such a great international demand, it ensures all coffee beans get sold. I believe that Kenyan coffee farmers are only allowed to sell their beans to the government, who therefore make a profit on the international sales. Is there control on other food products?"

"Are you interested in investing in Kenyan as you did not say you wanted to live here? Regarding food production, the high rainfall region of the country only produces about 10% of our food. We are a food deficit growing country needing to supplement our basics such as maize, wheat, rice and sugar with imports. We are the world's major producer of black tea. Why are you so interested in Kenyan agriculture and food production?"

Don said "No we are not interested in emigrating to Kenyan and are merely interested in aspects of the African country we chose to visit.

"I am the economist of the family," said Fran, "and the efficiencies of your core GDP contributors interest me. You have many rural famers and a few large estates. One expects a significant disparity between the efficiency of the two extremes and I am disappointed to hear you are a net importer of staples. In 1965 India embarked on a project called The Green Revolution, introducing higher yielding varieties of seeds and turned the country from a net importer to a net exporter of food products. It is therefore possible to do this in other Third World countries, but I suspect politicians and grass roots competence are barriers to the success of such initiatives. What about Kenyan coffee production, which may be an example of this type of initiative?"

"Luckily, we did a project at school last year where we investigated farming and it did include coffee" replied Abraham. "I therefore do have some interesting facts. For example, coffee is the second largest traded commodity worldwide after oil. The Coffee Board of Kenyan did all the marketing and sales of locally grown coffee, but the relaxation of various regulations some years ago did lift that constraint. There are only a few large estates and many small farmers growing coffee. It is therefore difficult to implement increased efficiencies on these smaller, more basic farms. Because coffee comes from beans which is a tree crop, one cannot enhance yields like annual crops where improved seeds and fertilizers can be used with each subsequent year's crop."

"I could chat about farming efficiencies all night, but we also would like to know about the people and what it is like living in Kenyan," said Don.

After three quarters of an hour of talking, Lankenua announced that supper was ready. The Canadians were keen to see what they were going to eat and were marginally apprehensive that it would be something offensive to their Western palate. Abraham ushered them to the dining room table and announced "Tonight's supper is a stew of goat meat with maize and black beans with local herbs and seasoning. It is tasty and overlaps with Western tastes."

Fran's smile was both warm and beaming with relief as she sat down. "I am sure it will be delicious and look forward to tasting your cooking Lankenua."

The food was delicious, partly because of how hungry they were. Don sealed the relief of their hosts by asking for a second helping. Shortly after supper while all four were in the lounge area there was a knock at the door and Abraham went to see who was there. He returned with an entourage of people following him. Don recognized the youngsters who had accosted him with their grim parents behind them. The young men were now dressed in T-shirts, short pants and sandals made from old car tires. The man who had charged Don with his spear stepped slightly forward, his head hanging down dejectedly and hands clasped in front of him. "My name is Leboo and I am sorry sir for what I did" he said a subdued voice. "I do not think that I can be forgiven for what I tried to do to you and am pleased you were not hurt. My parents and other elders explained what could have happened and how we could be in jail right now."

Don had an angry gleam in his eyes and Fran felt her reply may be more appropriate although in a male dominated culture, it may be inappropriate for a woman to speak on behalf of an aggrieved man. But what the heck. She was a foreigner from a country which they knew was more liberal and would therefore have to tolerate it. "I was terrified by your attack and as you speak well, I assume you have had reasonable education. You therefore must have known that any attack on another person is against the law. We could have chosen to file an assault charge with the

92

police and all of you could be locked up right now in jail. No, you cannot ask for forgiveness. They would be empty words from us, and we would never know if you learnt from what you did. Instead, we would like to hear what your parents and the other elders propose you must do for your punishment. If you do not learn from what happened, this type of reckless attack on innocent people will be repeated, possibly more than once until something terrible happens."

Fran suddenly felt quite emotional and sensing this, Don stepped in. "We did not lay charges as we think that we understood your motivation in trying to prove your manhood and think that you are essentially good people. We do not want to be the ones who could ruin your lives with criminal records and assume your families and village elders know best how you should be reprimanded." Looking past the group at the older adults behind them he asked, "What punishment have you decided on?"

Abraham and some of the others were quietly translating to Lankenua and those who did not speak English One of the men shuffled forward in the confined space to answer Don's question. "I am the head man Lemuani and it is our custom to have a kutana or meeting of all the men. Because of the seriousness of what happened and how many were involved, this cannot be a quick decision by me alone. In the old days, their punishment would have been a flogging, but it is now forbidden by law. The law has also banned young men from attacking a lion to prove their manhood. If they had, there would have been no interest in you. But times have changed, old traditions have died, and these men do not have the time-honored way of showing bravery for them to prove they are men. I can only try to reassure you that these men will not get off lightly and will definitely learn from their folly. I beg you to trust us that we will do what is considered appropriate and necessary in our culture."

Fran had recovered and was about to reply but Don had suspected she may plead some leniency for them. He was the one who faced the deadly spear attack and as a police reservist, needed to know there would be adequate punishment. "I am a police reservist and therefore have strong feelings about justice. As I will not be here to see what that decision is, I must rely on their punishment being fitting. I feel that this community was horrified and angry at what these young men did. I therefore feel confident that you will do what you consider necessary according to your traditions and wish to leave it at that. I will ask Abraham to write to me with a summary of what finally happens to them and hope they learn from this foolish deed without it ruining any of their lives."

Lemuani gave a small nod saying "Thank you for leaving the matter to us. Your trust in our justice being suitable is appreciated."

Turning to the young men, most of whom did not speak English well enough to follow the discussion, the chief simply said "Come." Everyone filed out the house leaving a silent vacuum.

Lost in their respective thoughts about the incident, Fran eventually said "While their action was unfortunate, it has given us the opportunity to see and even experience village life up close and meet you. I feel comfortable that justice will be upheld and as we wish to make the most of the situation, let us move on and talk more about Kenya and the way of life here."

The rest of the trip was uneventful, informative, and left them with concern about how primitive much of the country still was. There was neither the infrastructure nor much knowledge to ramp up food production by many orders of magnitude if the opportunity or need arose. Tribal politics and the power of local headmen created barriers to outsiders moving in and trying to set up anything on a major scale. They returned from Kenyan without much enthusiasm about it being a potential haven with many farming opportunities. Subsistence farming yes, but not with major export potential. For a vacation, it was a beautiful country, and the wildlife was amazing. But as a new home, it felt more like a last resort destination.

Part 5

The Project Progresses

Chapter 11 NEWCO

The way to get started is to
quit talking and begin doing.
- **Walt Disney**

A pregnant Fran put her mind to a stock of winter provisions that had to include those required for a baby due in January. Although they neither anticipated some lockdown event nor a horrendous winter preventing them from necessary excursions to shops and service providers, their objective was to try and weather the coming winter weather as though they were already enduring fifty degrees below zero. Included were baby clothes, diapers, formula, special washing powder, bottles, medication, and a host of other provisions, all on her long list. Fran asked friends experienced with their own young children for additional suggestions. "Don, what do we do with all our waste? Adding diapers to our normal garbage is going to exacerbate the problem of it when the ice age hits. "

"Hopefully, our kids will be out of diapers by then. But we will still have a disposal or storage challenge if we become snow bound. I had an area excavated in the basement outside the outer wall and built a holding room that is not insulated although it is deep enough to benefit from some geothermal heat. Whatever we put in there will probably freeze and preserve the contents. Anything that could rot at room temperature will therefore either be frozen or close to zero. I will monitor how low the temperature drops this winter in the room."

Fran asked "What about toilet waste? It is something I left to you, but I ought to know what provision you made."

"We have a septic tank quite deep under the house, well below the permafrost at this latitude. City by laws do not allow for this type of sewage treatment in the suburbs so it will remain inactive until we need it. There are two large valves that need to be shut and opened to re-direct the waste from the municipal sewage system to the tank."

Fran shook her head saying "There is just so much we have had to consider and incorporate into a self-sufficient home when frozen in. This winter will be another interesting test of what works, what does not, what we have not thought of, what fails, and what works reliably. It is important we only go shopping for goods like fresh foods such as salad and vegetables products. The rest needs to come from the stocks we have put in." Smiling she added "And what if we do end up with an overheated planet instead?"

"We will have a well-insulated house and be cool and comfortable inside" replied Don grinning. "Are you being a cynic or a realist?"

"I don't know. Both! Neither! We have been so occupied with the ice age scenario that continued global warming has not been considered at all. You know I share your convictions, have listened to your esoteric sources predicting an imminent ice age, and do believe that is where the world is heading."

With a wry smile Don said "Our friends continue to think we have lost the plot and the title Noah has been popping up with increasing frequency. I almost want to be vindicated, but that would mean praying for a scenario that brings with it, incredible suffering, death and survival challenges for those who are not wiped out in the first extreme winter. I feel more like Jonah who tried to run away knowing what the future held in store for the Children of Israel who were too intransigent to mend their evil and irreligious ways."

"Well Mr. Prophet Jonah, which of our friends are the sinners who are attracting the wrath of God?" Fortunately, Fran then winked, indicating that she was joking and not serious. Don shrugged, meekly smiled back, but did not respond, feeling how serious a sudden ice age will be for the city, the country, and the rest of the world.

Towards the end of summer, the street took shape. The house shells were complete, interiors were being fitted with the various systems that Don and Jake had designed, and it was time to paint the outsides. Fran convened the family in their role as project partners, to discuss the aesthetics of the house exteriors. "At first, I considered uniformity, but the street would look like a row of terraced housing in England. I feel they should be individualized to enhance the street's appearance and to reflect the characters of people living in each one. What do others think? "

Sybil said "I agree but we should still set a standard, so no one does anything too garish. We would then need an aesthetics committee with guidelines and recommendations. "

"Makes sense and I agree," said Robert. "You have both my vote and nomination to form and lead the committee. "

Mary asked "Is this just for the color of the outside walls or are we extending this to gardens as well? I would not like to see sterile yards of artificial grass or cement."

"Lots of hard work for the guys, mowing lawns and other laborious chores" muttered Jake.

Don said "Or we can employ a garden service that is paid for from the monthly levy. "

"Okay after we have our aesthetics committee formed and drawn up guidelines, we can hold a general meeting to see what the majority's sentiment is." said Fran feeling new variables she had not considered would start complicated her simple question about the color of the houses.

With a project to occupy her, an excited Sybil had her committee formed within a few days and soon had the permitted house colors and garden guidelines complete. The future residents met in Sybil's home for the discussion and decision of how the street would soon look. Sybil enjoyed being in charge for once and addressed the gathering. "We need to know what color paint each owner wants for their house. As I wanted nursery pink and Robert wanted fire engine red …" pausing as everyone tittered, "…we decided to form an aesthetics committee to set guidelines. This will ensure we conform to standards and have a great looking neighborhood. It extends to gardens as well, but first the color. We feel the choice should be a pale earthy or a grey color. Within those parameters, I am sure there are more than enough colors to satisfy everyone. I have a color chart from our proposed supplier for you to look at. There is a form with everyone's name listed and would like you to write down the code next to the color you choose. I will pass around a clip board and the charts for everyone to look at. And while it is being circulated, I want to tell you what we have considered for gardens. The objective is to have typical urban gardens that are pretty and practical for both children and maintenance work. Nothing is cast in stone so ideas and suggestions will be considered."

Soon the street took on the garb of Joseph's coat of many colors, but with a pleasing effect. Some owners had started laying out their gardens but with fall approaching, there was a limit to what could be accomplished. Don took his pregnant wife for a walk down the street of new houses one late afternoon as the sun started setting, blazing colors across the scattered clouds. A gentle breeze was blowing creating a mild nip in the air, which heralded the end of summer. This was confirmed by leaves that were starting to change color. "Look at what we have created" he declared proudly with a sweep of his arm up and down the street. "Who would have thought? Doesn't it make you feel proud?"

Fran pulled Don to a stop, turned to him, stood on her toes and gave him a gentle kiss on the lips. "Who would have thought during our Covid lockdown messages that this is where it would lead? I am so pleased to have followed my heart rather than be discouraged by some weirdo talking of an ice age during global warming." They smiled at each other and Fran continued. "We have homes for us and our family to weather the impending storms, we are self-employed in our own business, and we have a group of like-minded people in the development, many of whom already feel like extended family. Not to forget mentioning being married to a man who I am deeply in love with and will soon be giving a child. How much more blessed can we be?"

During the winter, they were relieved to find most things worked as designed and the handy engineers were able to modify or repair anything that went wrong. His well-stocked workshop ensured that Don could do minor maintenance unless it required some specialized component. At times Jake and Don assisted each other in any of the homes if a repair or maintenance problem needed two people. Their stocks lasted, supplemented only with perishable produce that they agreed they should have for health reasons, especially with Fran's pregnancy.

Baby Sean was born in mid-January, in a hospital with no complications and overnight, their lives changed. Their son was tiny yet demanded continuous attention on a 24-hour basis. Rising to the occasion, the novice parents soon developed a competent rhythm with the balance of winter having this additional dimension to their lives.

Don kept a diary and notes of his observations, people's suggestions, problems, and anything requiring modification, tweaking or serious re-evaluation. When the grannies came to visit, the grandfathers would discuss aspects of the ice arks with Don. Orders for more houses came in after some extreme storms during the winter. When the weather had become sufficiently clement, in their spare time outside of construction work, Don and Jake worked on their changes, adjustments and alterations to all the houses. Meanwhile Fran continued to be locked down tending to baby Sean.

Chapter 12   THE DEVELOPMENT

While we would not want to attribute every
extreme weather event to climate change,
the pattern is building and the costs are rising
- the human costs and the financial costs.
- **Sir Edward Jonathan Davey, British MP**

Now that *nIce Age* had orders and plans for another round of building during the coming summer, Don, Fran and their parents walked around the site to assess how best to situate the next row of houses. Afterwards they went for lunch to a nearby restaurant to continue discussing thoughts, suggestions, and concerns. The men put two four-seater tables together to accommodate six people, some drinks were ordered, and everyone scanned the menus. Being late morning, it would be brunch. The men ordered egg dishes whereas the women gravitated to the healthier muesli options. Don then asked Fran to take notes but before he could start, Mary said "Tunnels!" Everyone turned to look at her in surprise and she said, "From what you describe about the severity of the storms where no one can go out of a house, let us build a tunnel system that links the homes using precast box concrete culvert sections."

"I beg your pardon," said Fran. "What is that and where do you know about such things?"

"Well, I have been married to an engineer for decades and helped Jake with his blueprints, documents and admin for something useful to have rubbed off. Some of the services can also be moved into the tunnels to protect them from the elements" added Mary.

"Right!" said Don. "You are appointed the task of designing the tunnel concept and I suspect you will be most adept in your design."

Sybil then surprised everyone by making another suggestion as she never ventured into the business field. "We must increase the number buyers of our survival houses to help us be more financially sustainable and earn an adequate income from this venture. What I suggest is that we formally offer an entry level of well-insulated homes that are energy efficient for either severe global warming or cooling as you did for the Robertsons, Don. We advertise that many of the additional features we have for the extreme cold will be added afterwards if buyers wish to commit and as houses will cost less, we should sell more on this basis. Even Fran and Don deferred some features they cannot afford now for later as well, and this policy can be formalized as a selling point. The houses will be flexible for hot or cold climate conditions and we should be exploiting this selling concept. The more people we have on board, the wider the diversity of members of our group will be, many with specialized skills that may prove to be invaluable." Quite surprised by Sybil's unusual contribution and excellent suggestion, there was a stunned silence. "Oh dear. Seems to be a damp squid with no one agreeing" she said despondently.

'No' everyone effused. 'Great idea – well done – we were simply quite surprised at such useful insight – wonderful suggestion – we should have capitalized on the idea when it secured the Robertson's commitment - we will start on it tomorrow.'

A few days later an excited Mary called the partners together to present her seriously considered tunnel design. Standing up next to her dining room table around which everyone was seated, Mary opened a lever arch file to work through a list she had prepared with some drawings, starting with the tunnel. "The box culverts come in finite dimensions and I chose a size that people can walk in. It means excavating a two-meter-deep trench with a concrete floor. Since the culverts have straight sides, the rows of houses will have to continue to be in straight lines the way the existing ones have been laid out with no curves. The engineers will decide on how to run pipes and cables along the vertical sides, how to create openings into house basements and whatever other design considerations a mere lay person like me cannot do.

"Although some of the services have already been installed, Jake and Don can decide whether they should be moved into the tunnel or only future services need to be installed in the tunnel. If Don's prediction about the collapse of utility services is serious," continued Mary, "we will have home generators but eventually we should have a large generator to share with adequate oil storage to last through an extended winter. It will be more efficient than many little ones in each home and probably be more reliable. This generator would need to be in its own building. We can store extra gas cylinders inside it as well, run a communication infrastructure between houses and maybe a way of disposing of bulk sewage as the municipal sewerage system will probably freeze up. The engineers have done most of the resource sizing of these services based on estimates of how much we may use at those low temperatures lasting for an extended winter in case they cannot be replenished until summer.

"The tunnels will need some heating as they must shelter people from the elements. If the tunnel is extremely cold, it will be difficult to move around inside for visits or working to perform any repairs and service. I have heard discussions about what to do in the event of an uncontrolled house fire. People can evacuate through the tunnel rather than forced out the front door during a Polar Vortex storm." Mary handed out a rough sketch showing the street's straight row of houses with a tunnel next to them. A few sections in the first street representing the houses built the previous summer had been called Delaney Street with areas marked 'Generator House,' oil tanks' and 'gas tanks.' They were positioned centrally to minimize the maximum distance to the furthest houses. She then made a little bow, and everyone applauded her thoughtful efforts.

Fran asked "Mary, why have you named the first street Delaney?"

"I like the possible French origin which would be *De-la-née*. This means 'Of the birth' and we are giving birth to a new concept, a new type of housing development and a new lifestyle as this is how we will survive with a new lease on life."

Sybil suggested "Mary, how about a site visit tomorrow after our Sunday lunch date to inspect the land where your proposed tunnel and the next street would run? The land contours and other possible obstructions may create problems, which would be better to identify now rather than later."

Mary said, "Sure and Fran, please join us as well."

In turn Fran turned to Don and asked, "Can you join us on site too, say at two thirty as any problems will probably require your input to resolve."

Don said, "I was planning to go to site at some stage tomorrow, in particular to check the work of a fence repair on the northeast side of the land."

As Don drove towards the housing development gate, he saw Fran's car ahead turning in. He honked his horn as he drove passed to inspect the fence before joining them. He briefly noticed two vagrants walking along their boundary fence and wondered whether they were sleeping somewhere on the property as there were not many alternative places in the area. He drove on hoping he would remember to check.

Meanwhile the two vagrants had seen Fran's car drive onto the site, which was vacant being a Sunday with no one working there. When two ladies stepped out of the car they slipped through the gate and moved quickly towards Fran and Mary. Sybil was completing a telephone call and with the car's tinted windows, the two men did not notice her still sitting in the car at the back. The one ran up to Mary from behind, grabbed her handbag while pushing her over. She stumbled and fell, which is what her assailant had intended.

Sybil saw this from inside the car, cut her call short and phoned Don. As he answered she shrieked "Help, two men are attacking us. Come quickly." Don ran back to the car and drove like a Formula One driver towards the entrance gate.

Meanwhile the second assailant was more interested in sexy Fran than her handbag and grabbed her from behind before she realized what was happening. He put his arms around her and with one hand on her breast and the other between her legs, pulled her backwards so she was off balance and dropped her onto the ground. The fall winded her and before she could do anything, the man had dropped down on top her. Fran tried to bring her knee up in between his legs but between his weight and position, she was pinned down and unable to move.

As Don drove through the gate, he saw Mary on the ground with the one man's foot on her to keep her down. He was rifling her handbag, obviously looking for her purse, cell phone and any other valuables. The man heard the car approaching and bolted. Don drove after him across the open ground, pleased to be driving his Rav4 SUV. He drove passed the man, deliberately just missing him and as he went passed, Don opened the door using it to hit the man. The impact knocked him off his feet and in his rearview mirror Don saw him lying motionless on the ground. He spun the car around and rushed back to where Mary was now sitting, desperately looking around for Fran.

As he neared Mary, he saw the man on top of a wriggling Fran, trying to subdue her. Don braked hard, bolted out and was on top of the man who was so focused on raping Fran that he was oblivious to anything else around him. Don had his left arm around the man's neck as he rolled both of them off Fran and continued to roll so he landed on top of the man. Don locked this arm around the neck by placing his right arm behind his head, his left arm in the crook of his right elbow, and the right hand on the back of the man's head. The man could not pull Don's arm off his neck while Don's arms were locked in this position. Don straddled him, then pulled him up onto his feet. He jerked the man backwards and pushed him hard onto the ground to wind him. Don rolled him onto his stomach, pulled an arm behind him to be able to bend it further with pain to immobilize the man if he resisted. Fran had jumped up and with eyes blazing, kicked the man in his side screaming "You bastard!"

Before she got carried away, Don said "There is some nylon rope in my trunk. Fetch it so I can tie him and the other man up. There is a pen knife in the car door to cut the rope."

Trying to control her anger, Fran spun around and ran off towards the car. Mary was still sitting on the ground with Sybil consoling her, both looking terrified. Fran first went to help her up and with her arm and mother's arms around Mary, walked her a few steps back to Don's car. "Wait here and I will be back in a moment. Don asked me for some rope to tie up these bastards, which we need to do quickly. No go to my car and call 911 now." Fran grabbed the nylon rope and penknife and ran back to Don. "I think he should be tied around the neck and pulled behind the Rav!" she shouted, glaring at her attacker.

The retired police reservist knew that Fran must not make statements that the man could use against her and while taking the rope, said "Yes, he deserves serious punishment, and the law will do so in due course. Has either of our mothers called 911?"

Fran picked up Don's indirect message and replied "Yes, I asked our mothers to make the call. And I am looking forward to hearing what the Court mete's out to these criminals." Wanting to say much more, Fran prudently maintained silence while watching Don tie the man up and cut the rope. He yanked the man to his feet and marched him towards his friend who was still lying motionless on the ground. Worried that the car door impact may have injured him seriously, Don forced the tied assailant into a lying position. He knelt beside the other man and rolled him over. The man looked at him with glazed eyes then tried to get up. Don pushed him back down onto the ground, rolled him over, pulled his arms behind him and tied his wrists. In the distance they could hear a siren and decided to wait where he was with the two men. The police could come to him rather than Don trying to herd the two felons towards the gate.

After the police took custody of the men and obtained a preliminary statement, they were instructed to go to the nearby police station and file a formal assault report. As the police drove off with the men, the four stood there silently with everyone's thoughts running wild. Finally, Sybil spoke up. "Okay everyone. Thank God Don was nearby, and this ended without anyone injured or … assaulted. I am sure no one is in the mood to do a site inspection, which we can reschedule for tomorrow or soon after. I am going to drive Fran's car to the police station with Mary and Fran will ride with Don. Let us not hang around here any longer and get this over with."

In his car while driving, Don took Fran's hand and said "I was frantic when your mom phoned me. And this continued until I saw you struggling with that man on top of you. I flew at him with such rage and luckily as I rolled him off you, recovered my senses. Until then I was determined to kill him."

Fran looked at Don with so much love, whose vision of him soon blurred as her tears started to flow. "My hero and savior. I was terrified. He smelled of B.O., had halitosis and the thought of being raped …" Unable to speak for a few moments, Don waited patiently for her to regain some composure while gently squeezing her hand. "I knew you were nearby but did not know how long you would be. I tried to jerk my knee into his groin once I had been thrown onto the ground, which had winded me. It was the only thing I could try in that position but he landed on top of me off-center so I could not get my knee between his legs. My mother saved the day by chatting on her cell phone and not getting out of the car with us. Luckily, they never noticed her."

Fran fell silent again so Don, wanting to maintain conversation flow said "Remember when we spoke about the potential collapse of civilization, how anarchy could reign? This is the kind of predation we could be exposed to. How do we become extra vigilant? What do you think we should do once we are living in Delancey Street?"

After a short pause Fran responded. "You are the ex-policeman and know better than me. But there are fundamentals like CCTV cameras, locked doors and barred windows, and weapons that we know how to use that must be readily accessible."

"Yes, all of those. But intruders can be wily, and the challenge is how to respond when they sneak passed our various security systems. Today's incident is an example of villains taking us by surprise. Apart from basic security protocols like CCTV, remember we are soft targets. We need to plan how handle trespassers who have managed to circumvent our front-line defenses."

"Oh, Don, I have said this before. What kind of a world have we brought our children into?"

"This horrible incident has nothing to do with any post-apocalyptic event, but I suppose it heralds what could become commonplace."

Chapter 13   TASTE OF THE FUTURE

The last buyer in Delaney Street was Simon O'Connell who asked Fran to assemble a meeting of the street's homeowners. He felt there was merit in everyone meeting regularly to get to know each other. He explained, "In extreme winters, there would probably be times when we will need to help one another as friends and not strangers."

Fran opened the meeting saying "Hello family, friends and friends to be. Welcome to our not yet icy gathering and what I hope will be the first of many. We are here because there may be an ice age soon. Or maybe there will not. Maybe global warming will continue. Or maybe things will continue as they are. I am here because I believe the world is about to give me the cold shoulder. And even Jack Frost will get frost bite because of the extreme cold that is predicted. If that happens, our lives will become extremely difficult. Only those of us able to remember our previous incarnations as cave men and women fighting woolly mammoths on glaciers, will be able to draw on past experiences to survive in extreme cold. For the rest of us, our preparations are based mainly on trying to anticipate what is coming and what we need to survive the impending extremes. All suggestions welcome. Which is one of the reasons why our latest members, Simon O'Connell with his partner Emma Taylor, requested we gather on this balmy summer day to contemplate our inevitable chilblains. So over to Simon."

"Thank you, Fran, and everyone for coming. Apart from all of us possibly having to pool and share limited resources in this apocalyptic future, I have had some thoughts about enhancing our survival with two things in particular.

As Simon spoke Fran tried to assess the man. `You look in your late fifties, immaculately dressed in your flannel pants with a pastel green shirt, smart shoes, presenting yourself as a leader and speaking with confidence. I wonder what your vocation had been. Business, your own company, the CEO, self-made? Time will tell but should we be watching you? Simon, will you try to usurp us? Will you be a bonus or bone of contention to our group?'

Simon continued. "My first important thought is that although there is a central, large generator contemplated for the future, we should all contribute to one now as I feel electricity is an essential service on which we must not compromise. With the prediction that at minus fifty degrees, utility services to our houses will collapse, Don and Jake have calculated what adequate energy and fuel each house requires to see us through these extreme winters. But will there be enough oil, gas and electricity to see us through? Our last milder winter was used to test the designs and confirm the quantities calculated, but the acid test is when we hit these extremely low temperatures for extended periods. We need a building to house a suitably large generator plus store enough oil to power all our houses as a back-up to the city's supply. The small generators inside each house would only be needed if both the electricity mains and the standby generator have failed. The cost for the stand, building and cables have been estimated. But we would need to finalize how much electricity we want, to determine the size of the generator. If it is a supplement, then it could be smaller. If we want all the homes to continue running as though they still have city power, it will need to be larger and therefore more expensive to buy. We are now seventeen families and that means each would contribute just under six percent of the total cost. This cost could be recovered further over time from future people who buy into this project.

"My second proposal or request is for us all to meet regularly, either socially or for regular project progress meetings. We need to know each other better since we have become an extended family anticipating the need to depend on each other under extreme survival conditions."

Fran as the company's financial officer said "Regarding the first suggestion, if funds were unlimited, we would have incorporated a central electricity generating plant long ago without discussion. After the subject was initially raised about whether the tunnel temperature could drop too much making it impossibly cold to walk in, Don gave it some thought. When the outside temperature is minus fifty, the tunnel would drop down to that temperature. Where could we recover lost heat from? If we have a large generator, it will release plenty of heat, some of which could be ducted down the tunnel through a long chimney running up and down the tunnel. That is an added benefit, but only if the generator is running. However, all the heat may well be dissipated before the pipe reaches the last few houses including your own Simon. But let Don explain more and then I will pick on the financial side."

Don said "Bleeding off some of each house's boiler or furnace heat along the street could be used when the generator is not running, especially for houses at the far ends of the tunnel. Less if the generator was running leaving more heat for inside each house. It will require some calculations and considerations, which we can present to you as soon as possible to make a joint decision if the majority votes to go ahead and buy a large generator now."

Simon continued with the thread of immediately installing a large generator. "Given the potential scenarios that Fran and Don have described, to me a large, stand-by generator is a must and not a luxury. I therefore did some calculations using some initial estimates based on figures Don had mentioned for both a generator and building. I am prepared to fund it on a loan basis as follows. Those who can contribute their share now will simply pay that amount. Those who cannot, I will cover and charge a bank overdraft rate plus 2% for the risk. We can work on deferred payment plans for those who cannot start repayments now."

Fran looked quite shocked and there was a stunned silence before she responded. "Having negotiated all the sales of the houses, I have a fair idea of who can afford what. Almost half the residents of Delaney Street have opted for the incremental addition of systems and resources as fast as their personal funds permit. The additional shared generator cost, even if split seventeen ways, would still be a significant additional burden, whether payments started now, or the interest was capitalized with repayments only starting after the houses are completed. As a first guess, I suspect those homeowners would have to pass now on contributing towards the large stand-by generator option. Although they may represent less than fifty percent, a majority vote would impose a financial encumbrance which I cannot support."

Simon countered "But what I am offering does not impose repayments until they can afford it."

"During which time interest is being accrued at quite a high rate" replied Fran. "And I assume loan terms would be at least as stringent as bank loan."

In a hurt voice Simon said, "I am prepared to take the risk and feel we all should have this safety feature if Polar Vortex storms will be so severe."

During the short silence, Fran saw her father Robert look at Jake, giving him an almost imperceptible nod. He did this when he saw Fran glancing at him so she knew she saw it. Realizing they would step up to assist with this finance proposal, why did they wish to remain quiet for now. Knowing her father, Fran realized that Robert wanted her to push Simon and see whether he was being altruistic but protecting his money, or if he was more mercenary as a person. Since they were now a tight group of people planning to survive in an imminent, hostile environment, knowing people's strengths and weaknesses was vital. She therefore continued with the same line of questioning. "Simon, I need to understand the terms and conditions you have in mind. If T&Cs are like a bank loan, there will be a finite time in which to pay it off even if it commences with a deferred payment period. Secondly, borrowers must sign over personal assets as loan security in the event of a default. Those that could not pay now only have their houses as assets of sufficient substance for surety and they would stand to lose their homes. That is a heavy burden to impose on them. Imagine if they lose a home to you, where could they go? And if the ice age has descended, that could be a death sentence."

Simon had not considered this reaction to his proposal and could feel general sentiment becoming antagonist towards him. He quickly backtracked to try and reverse this trend. "Fran, you are right, and I must admit that I never thought it through. I was focused on how essential a

117

generator is for our survival, which was the incentive for my proposal. These downstream, potential financial problems were never adequately considered."

Skeptically Fran replied "Okay, but then you need to revise your model and present it for everyone to consider. I need a unanimous vote as I intend protecting everyone in our extended family and will not entertain any possibility of an eviction because we have imposed some financial hardship on them."

Before Simon could continue trying to redeem himself, an irritated Robert spoke up. As an old school gentleman, he did not intend slating Simon or his proposal and simply said "I am prepared to offer the following. I will pay for the generator and building, welcoming any other contributors now. It would be appreciated if those that can afford a seventeenth share put in their portion up front. For the forty percenters, I will carry them interest free and if anyone else wants to share in this expense, it would be welcomed."

Jake interjected "I am in Robert."

Simon felt that he needed to do some serious disaster management because of how badly this went and said "If three of us are carrying the forty percenters, we would each bear about thirteen percent and less if there are any more offers to help. On that basis and acknowledging that we are an extended family, I am also volunteering to contribute proportionately to your proposal Robert."

The tension in the room of the forty percenters who had become quite apprehensive, started abating. They would still have to pay their shares but not under any time pressure, nor carry an additional interest burden. Ownership of their houses would not be threatened and they would benefit equally from the generator.

In a more upbeat voice, Fran then said "Thank you guys for your generous offer. I am sure we will now proceed with the generator and building for it, which will be a vital component in our formula for survival. This is the best time to implement additional building work while the contractors are on site. As per Simon's second suggestion, I agree there should be women's and men's committees for joint planning of other issues such as how we are going to occupy ourselves and how to respond to various emergencies. Given the Corona virus lockdown, we went through, it gave us a taste of what living at home without respite for extended periods is like. The men will be plan how to respond to problems, help calls and perhaps even attempted incursions into a home by desperate people looking for food between storms. And we will need a reliable, independent communications system."

William said "This is my field. We need video conferencing and two-way radio communications by setting up a VPN or virtual private network between the homes. The cables would be run in the tunnel to protect them from the elements. If the mobile phone and data network collapse, this will still maintain our communication with each other. I will design a communications network and discuss it with Jake and Don."

Fran continued. "Thanks William. It is great to know we have a specialist onboard for such an essential service. As much as we have already done, there always seems to be plenty more that can and should be included. I will send everyone a list of our names and contact details. If there are other things to propose or discuss, let us hear them now. Otherwise please enjoy the tea and cake that we prepared for you."

"Before we start the tea," said Sybil, "I have an important suggestion. We must do bulk buying for discounts, especially for oil and I am sure we can negotiate many more things. I would like to convene with a buying group if all agree and request some volunteers."

Everyone looked quite surprised at Sybil who, not being renown for any regular business contributions, continued to propose excellent ideas. "Well, that is another great proposal" exclaimed Fran. "We will start on the generator facility and form a buying department tomorrow. Are there any other suggestions? If not, it is teatime."

Later when getting ready for bed, Fran first turned on their electric blankets before going to the bathroom. Later when snuggling in between the sheets, she wondered whether these heated blankets would be a vital item for their survival. A few minutes later Don climbed into bed besides her and she said to him "What do you make of Simon?"

"I am tired. Is this a conversation for now?" After a few moments he said, "I think he is either quite mercenary or does not think things through."

"Or both" said Fran, "I feel we need to watch him. With the number of people now on Delaney Street, I suppose there are some who will chronically be a problem."

Don said "Not thinking things through is easier to understand by the way he did a quick about turn when your dad made his counteroffer. Why do you think there could be a mercenary side to him?"

"During tea, I asked him what he did for a living. He was in finance and must know all about loans. It could have been an opportunity for him to make some money subject to quite austere terms and conditions. With this background, I do not feel his offer was a naïve one made in good faith that had ramifications he never realized."

120

Part 6

Learning survival skills

Chapter 14   ORIENTATION

Ice age shock:
'Timing is right for the next
ice age to come around soon …
but due to greenhouse gasses,
the next ice age may be delayed.'
**Prof J Renwick, School of Geography,
Environment, and Earth Sciences,
University of Wellington**

Don felt that survival training for his children was essential if there was going to be a substantial shift in climate and probably civilization as they knew it. Sean was now twelve years old and Don felt he could not wait any longer as the clock counted down to D-Day. Like his father, Don was tall for his age. Inspired by his father, Sean had been pushing weights so he had a wiry shape and was strong for his age. At ten, skinny David was still too young to receive the same extent of training but tagged along. They had all been camping and spent time outdoors for the boys to develop a sensitivity and awareness of nature. But now that Sean was twelve, Don planned to teach him other skills. More specifically how to shoot various firearms, to navigate with a compass and GPS, and other survival skills. Sean was too young to own a firearm even though the legal minimum age in Canada is 12 years. At that age, licenses are generally only given to children living on farms. However, under Don's strict supervision, he could still learn to use handguns, rifles and shotguns.

After planning a trip outdoors with Fran, Don told the boys they were going on an adventure into the real wilds. Sean's excitement knew no bounds. Before the proposed trip, Don told Sean that he first needs to learn theory and how to handle a firearm before shooting one. He would be taught about map reading, using a compass, a GPS and using signs in nature to help orientate one in the wild. Moving on to firearms, Don explained the difference between a revolver and a pistol. While Sean was learning, Fran would sit in for a refresher, and David would pick up some of the training. Don had bought a range of weapons when a police reservist and kept them with thoughts of a possible apocalyptic future in mind. They went through how to load, aim and fire the two types of handguns. He then moved on to rifles and explained three types: bolt action, lever action and semi-automatic. They had to strip and reassemble all the weapons many times until they were proficient and fast, especially reloading in an emergency. Don bought a small .410 shotgun rather than the larger, more common 12 gauge which has too severe recoil for Sean to manage and Fran to be comfortable in shooting it with her slight frame.

Don moved on to teaching how to orientate and navigate in the wild starting with Sean learning about the four points of a compass. Don would repeatedly ask Sean around town "Which way are we heading?" or point in some arbitrary direction and ask, "Which compass point lies in that direction?" Don showed him how to use his watch hands to determine south. "Point the 12 o'clock at the sun and south will be midway between the 12 and the hour hand." Soon Sean could estimate by seeing the position of the sun and checking the time. At night Sean had to learn some of the constellations, particularly the Pole Star that was above due north. Don asked, "Why should you also learn some other constellations?" Sean thought for a moment and then shrugged, not volunteering to answer. Don explained "To help find where the Pole Star would be if it is partly hidden by cloud cover."

"So, the other constellations help work out where north or the Pole Star would be if I could not see it?" repeated Sean to himself.

Then Sean learned to read a map, longitude and latitude coordinates, and how a GPS would tell you exactly what your position was. Don explained "A map of the world is dived up into parallel lines that are vertical and horizontal. The top quarter is 90 degrees, which is the northern hemisphere or the upper half of the planet. The lower half is also divided into 90 degrees for the southern hemisphere. The number for Toronto is nearly 44 degrees north of the equator. Half of 90 is 45 so we are almost in the middle of the distance from the equator to the north pole. Have a look at this globe to see what I mean." After Sean understood how one measures distance north of the equator, Don continued. "Similarly for longitude. In London, England there is a place called Greenwich where naught degrees longitude lies, just like the equator is naught degrees for latitude. Do you know how many degrees there are in a circle?"

"No."

"The number is 360 degrees. We use half of that number or 180 degrees for latitude as we only measure halfway around the earth from North Pole to South Pole. But as we have night and day going around the world, we need to use 360 degrees. From zero at Greenwich, the distance increases going east to the right or becomes negative going west. Do you understand what a negative number is?"

Sean said "Not really Dad. What is it?"

"Let me think. If I give you $10 pocket money and ask you how much you have, you will say $10. But if you want something that costs $15, I can lend you $5 and you then owe me $5. After my loan, how much do you then have as you are now in debt?"

"Well, I owe you $5. Is that written as minus five?"

"Exactly! But the idea of negative can be used other ways as well. If you go west to the left or west of Greenwich, the numbers can be written either as say 80 degrees west or minus 80. Do we lie east or west of Greenwich?"

After looking at the globe, Sean said "West."

"Correct, and can see you see that Toronto is about 80 degrees west?" Sean looked at the globe, ran his finger down the line of longitude to the equator, saw 80^0, then nodded a yes. "So, its position can be written as 80^0W or -80^0. Lots of difficult concepts and theories for young boy who I think is loving all this training." Sean nodded affirmatively again with a wide smile.

To convert theory into practice, the family would go for a walk out of town using the GPS and Sean had to take them back to their starting point using the backtrack feature. That way he would be able to return to any waypoint position that had been saved in the GPS. But all the time, Don would be asking Sean what compass direction they were walking without looking at the GPS or the military marching compass he had bought Sean, and a simpler compass for David to not feel left out.

Chapter 15   FIELD TRIP

> Be strong enough to stand alone,
> be yourself to stand apart,
> but wise enough to stand together
> when the time comes.
> **- Dream Weaver**
> **Native American**

Finally, it was time to convert all this training from theory into practice in the wild. Don selected a resort located on Lake of the Woods, between the towns of Rainy River and Morson, Ontario. Hunting of black bears, moose and deer was permitted so it was a wild area although they had no intention of shooting any animals. Don had specifically requested that the family could do some shooting. The tour operator said they had a range close to their cabin where hunters sighted in their rifles, and they could do their shooting there. The family were flying to Baudette International Airport in Rainy River. In the plane, sitting next to Don, Fran glanced at her two boys seated together across the aisle. Sean was studying something intently on his tablet while David was lost in reverie listening to music through his Bluetooth headphones. Fran looked at David's wispy, thin blond hair, cut short for the trip, lying dead straight. Sean sported a wide brimmed field hat with some of his dark brown wavy hair protruding.

Fran thought: Whoever coined the phrase 'Identical as the peas in a pod' never shelled peas. The same way peas in a pod range from tiny to large, my boys are unlike in every way. Looks, interests, temperament. Sean is a tall beanpole so he cannot be a pea – *chuckle*! They are so excited, and it is infectious as I am equally eager for all the activities that Don has planned for us. Dearest Don. Always the meticulous engineer. What a beautiful place he found. Lake, forests, wildlife, hikes, canoeing, staying in a log cabin. How much better can it get?

Fran looked at the boys' outfits, another reflection of their differences. Sean had chosen a beige, pastel shirt with cord pants and a khaki jacket. He looked like he was off on an African safari, decked for a serious outdoor experience. Sean had asked Don what he would be wearing, and Don said he still had his safari clothes from their Kenyan safari that he would wear. He had kept his khaki pants and shirts to do maintenance chores but had forgotten about them until considering an appropriate outfit. Sean wanted similar outdoor attire, so Don took him to a Banana Republic store for his outfit. David wore jeans, a denim jacket and a Western shirt checked with large red squares bordered by white lines looking more like a cowboy than a game ranger. Thinking beyond the trip, he wanted something that he could still wear when they returned home and used the opportunity to shop for new denim clothes. Fran was also in a denim outfit having long since disposed of her khaki clothes, which she never anticipated using again. Sean looked across to Fran and asked "Mom, can we swap seats for a bit. I want to ask Dad some things about our trip?"

They exchanged seats and Fran decided to engage David. "Are you lost in music or thinking about where we are going?"

"I suppose I am thinking about the trip with a great music background."

"And what are you thinking?"

With a bit of a frown, David said "A bit jealous of Sean. Because he is older, he has had more training by Dad and will be doing more things when we get to Woods Lake."

"Okay. But you can have a turn as well when you are older. This will heighten your anticipation and expectation by knowing firsthand what is in store for you." After some general banter, the stewardess announced they would be landing soon and must remain seated. Fran said "I better swap with Sean again while we can move. See you on the ground."

They were met by Harry, their tour operator. It was a beautiful road trip, running part of the way along the lake's edge. There were a myriad of islands stretching to the horizon, covered predominantly with pine trees, often clinging to rocks as their roots were unable to find soil. Happy to have guests interested in nature, Harry pointed out other trees including poplar, hickory, oak, spruce, walnut, willow, beech, cedar, fir, birch, maple, and aspen. The boys' digital cameras clicked away through the car windows at one spectacular sight after another. Finally, they reached their destination and after checking in they were shown to their cabin, about a hundred meters from the lake shore, close to the main administration area.

Sighing with delight, Fran said "What a heavenly spot! Listen to the gentle breeze sighing through the leaves. The deep blue water was lapping along the shore. The pale blue-sky canopy with its warm, soft light over the forests and lake below. Birds chirping in trees. How idyllic. And this quaint log cabin. I just love all of it."

The outside of the cabin had a front porch with a wooden table and chairs for meals. There were lounging chairs and a bench to sit on that faced the lake close by that one could see through gaps in the trees. Fran went in first and saw a comfortable, open plan living area, a more formal dining room table, kitchen area on one side and a large fireplace with a stack of cut wood in a large wicker basket next to it. There was a bedroom section behind a wall with access doorway to make the area private from people in the living area. The first bedroom had a double bed with a mattress nestling in a frame made from logs, a small table and two chairs, a cupboard, chest of drawers, all made from the same timber as the walls of the log cabin. Not her rustic taste in curtains or bedspread, but she was not fussed by the décor as she would only be exposed to it for a week. Fran bounced on the edge of the bed to test the mattress. Quite firm! The boys' bedroom had the same furniture other than two single beds. Both bedrooms had fireplaces for guests in winter.

The bathroom had a bath as well as a shower, and she imagined soaking in the hot tub after an active day to relax her muscles. There was a donkey boiler outside to heat the water as well as two large cylinders of gas as backup. "Where are the light switches? " she heard David ask.

Don replied. "Everything in the cabin is either gas or wood fire. No electricity, only at the main lodge where they have a generator. This evening, I will show you how to ignite the gas wall lamps. The refrigerator and stove with oven all use gas as well."

"How can you burn hot gas to make a fridge cold?" asked David.

"Good question and not easy to answer. Basically, a liquid coolant flows into the fridge compartment where the heat from food stored there is removed. The heat makes the liquid boil, and it becomes a gas like steam when one boils water, but at a much cooler temperature than steam. Surprisingly, the gas flame is used to turn the coolant back into liquid so the cycle can go round and round as long as there is gas to burn. But you will have to wait until you learn some high school chemistry to understand better how it works."

"Will you have a gas fridge at home if the electricity fails during one of these polar storms? asked David.

"No, there will be enough cold outside to freeze those blue gel bricks to keep the contents of the fridge cold. But those were excellent questions. I am pleased you are curious and understand as much as you do about these things. Maybe you will also want to be an engineer!"

That evening the boys were asked to make a fire so they could barbecue deer steaks that Harry supplied with potatoes and a green salad. There was a box of Zip firelighters, matches and chopped wood next to the outdoor barbeque. Don had shown the boys how to stack the wood around and above the burning white cubes of wax and left them to make the fire. Soon it was roaring, and Sean asked if he could start the cooking. Fran had poured a marinade sauce over the steaks enticing hungry boys to get started. "Sorry!" said Dad. "We need the flames to subside until they become hot, glowing embers. Flames will char the outside of the steaks and leave the inside raw. One needs patience to cook meat properly over an open fire."

"Yes Dad, and while waiting impatiently, you can drink a beer" replied David. "What can we drink to pass the time?"

"Fresh lake water?"

"Thanks, but no thanks. Anything more exciting? "

Nearly three quarters of an hour later the family finally sat at the table on the porch under a starry sky with the first quarter waxing moon crescent setting over the lake in the west. Tired and hungry, the only conversation was with David who commented on the steak. "This has quite a tang to it. Not like beef. Any idea what it is?"

Fran replied. "Harry said it is whitetail deer, which are fairly common and are therefore a favorite of the hunters who come here." Then more unbroken silence as everyone ate hungrily with only an occasional request to pass on the salt or for some more salad.

After supper, Fran made coffee and hot chocolate, and soon everyone felt revived enough to start talking again. Sean said "I came across some interesting facts about color vision in animals and other creatures. Many cannot see red so ideally, if we were stalking deer, we should be dressed in red pants with a red flannel jacket. Rattlesnakes can see in infrared and pick up the heat from mammals' bodies to know prey is near. Some creatures see in black and white as their eyes only have rods and no cones for color vision. Since we are not hunting, I chose khaki which hunters in Africa and soldiers seem to prefer. Maybe it blends with sand or wood and gives some camouflage. But Dad, can we look at the map you brought now that we are here?"

Don took out the ordnance map of the area that he had bought for the trip. They had thoroughly examined it before leaving home and were now going to put theory into practice. Don rolled the map out on the table then asked, "Okay Sean, what are our coordinates by looking on the map, then check it with your GPS."

Sean studied the map and wrote down his estimate. "It looks like about 49^0 North and 95^0 West. Let us see what the GPS says and set it as a way point." Sean switched on the GPS and wrote down the exact location and said out aloud "48^0 57' 19" North, 94^0 32' 32" West."

"Wow, well done Sean. Your estimate was as good as anyone can read off a map" raved Fran who gave Sean a big hug. "It seems you really have learned all these difficult concepts so well."

Don said, "Excellent work but I am not surprised" and gave Sean a wink. "Now store it as a waypoint in the GPS so it knows the location of our home base. Tomorrow Sean, you and Mom are scheduled to go off into the wilds to test your skills, to be able to return back here on foot. I will ask Harry to drop you off about seven kilometers away, inland in the forest. You will have a walkie talkie, compass and GPS so it will probably be quite easy. I plan to do a shoot with David on the range and then some canoeing."

The next morning Sean packed his bag using a list he had drawn up with his father. Space blanket, waterproof ponchos, map, rope, multifunction knife, first aid kit, energy bars, water, and the GPS, compass and walkie talkie that were placed on the top of the bag for quick access. They climbed into Harry's Chevrolet Silverado 4x4 truck and headed inland for about twenty minutes off and on tracks until he finally pulled up. Wishing them good luck, Harry said "Okay explorers, here we are. Enjoy your walk and see you back at the lodge in about two and a half hours." They climbed out, he did a 180^0 turn and drove off.

They watched him go, then Sean bent down to open his backpack to get out his compass. With a look of shock, he flapped the loose top and said to Fran. "Mom, it seems my backpack's one strap was not properly secured. It must have opened while bumping along the road and the compass, GPS and walkie talkie have fallen out. They probably slid under the front seat while Harry drove downhill to this spot, so I never saw them lying on the floor next to my bag." He looked up to see a shocked and panic look on his mother's face. Quickly replying he reassured her saying "But no problem. The lake lies to the west. It is nine o'clock and looking at the sun, west is over there." He pointed in a direction along the track that Harry had used.

"Why don't we simply walk back along that track?" asked Fran.

"I tried to stay orientated during the ride here and Harry

not only drove along tracks but went off-road a few times. Look Mom, let me draw approximately where we are in the sand." Sean drew a line. "Here is the shore running at an angle that is approximately southwest to northeast." He stabbed the sand with his stick and said "We are somewhere here and only need to walk in this direction to reach the shore" drawing a straight line from his stab point running northwest to the shore. "Once we reach the shore, we simply walk along it in this direction until we reach the lodge. If we need to detour because we come across a stream or a canyon, as long as we still keep our north westerly heading, we will get to Woods Lake and then home. I am not worried. I have my watch, there is the sun, and I know where the west and shoreline are. No need to panic. Without the instruments, our only change without instruments is that we may take a bit longer by not quite going the shortest route."

Fran was smiling with relief and pride. "You really are your dad's son. I am proud of you and feel quite relieved. Okay Mr. Explorer, lead the way." Sean headed off confidently in the direction he had indicated, glancing frequently at the sun's position. They walked up and down forested hills with no real view, which was blocked by the many trees around them. At the top of one hill there was a sheer drop where they could look out and Fran pointed to the lake in the distance. "Well, there you are, making a beeline towards the shore. But look, there in the distance are clouds rolling in and coming quite fast. I can feel the winding picking up already."

"Not good. Without sun hidden behind thick clouds I cannot navigate. Since we have no Internet connectivity being so remote, we could not get a weather forecast anyway. Now what?"

Fran thought then suggested "The wind is blowing almost straight into our faces, perhaps slightly to the right. Instead of the sun, we will use the wind as a reference. At what compass angle do you think it is coming towards us?"

Sean pointed at his watch's 12 o'clock to the sun and gestured with his arm. "It is just after 10 a.m., that must be south, so the wind is blowing towards us from the north. We have been trying to walk in a north westerly direction and as you said, the wind is off center to the right. If we keep it there, we will still be on track."

First feeling relieved, Fran's concern returned asking "Aren't those lines below the clouds from rain? I think we need to get out our ponchos. The temperature is also falling. Rats! This was bad planning, and I am not looking forward to a soaking as well." They took out their small, plastic poncho packs and put them on covering their backpacks as well. "This is turning into a real survival experience and not a simple hike home."

Fran set out in front, now impatient to reach the lodge and walked quite fast. The wind picked up and in about fifteen minutes the first drops started falling. Within a few more minutes it was pouring, and they were trudging through mud with wet legs as the ponchos only reached down to above the knees because of bulge caused by their backpacks.

With the rain being blown into their faces, their eyes were screwed up to mere slits with a hand used as a visor to look down and see the terrain before putting down each subsequent muddy step. They plodded on in silence feeling quite miserable in the cold, wet weather and hoped they were still heading towards the shore. Every now and then Sean would try to look up. Under a thick canopy of sycamore leaves that blocked the deluge with only large drops running off the leaves onto them, he was able to see a bit further ahead under the canopy. To his horror they had reached a cliff edge where his mother was about to step off. He grabbed Fran's arm and pulled her back. She looked ahead and saw where she had almost fallen. Feeling quite shaken she said "Thank you Sean. I was so occupied with only looking where to put the next step because of the rain that I would have gone over the edge."

Sean was peering down trying to see the bottom and in a momentary lull of the rain, he said "It's the shore down there. We have found it. What a relief. But this cliff seems to run along as far as I can see with this poor visibility. We need to walk along it until either it runs out or we find a way down." Sean turned to the right and started walking parallel to the shore slightly back from the cliff's edge with his mother close behind him. The rain let up and after about half a kilometer, the cliff took a right angle away from the shore where a stream below ran into the lake. "This may result in a long detour inland before we can cross. Otherwise, we must find a way down. After this I am sure it will be along the shore as we cannot be that far from the lodge."

They came to a spot where a large tree grew at the edge with a stout branch reaching out over the side. Fran looked down and along the cliff face. It was nearly ten meters down and would be a wet and slippery climb. "I do not want to lengthen the time to get back, but we have not found an easier way. Could we sling a rope over the tree's branch to help us climb down? What do you think? We would have to leave the rope tied to the tree."

Sean said "I am happy to do that. You also have a rope so we can join them, tie the rope around the tree that has one end tight to climb down and the other end to loosen a knot like a bow, then pull the rope down."

"Do you know how to tie such a knot?"

"Kind of, so let me try." Fran took her rope out of her backpack and Sean suddenly realized his dad's boring knot lessons were worthwhile. Almost in the middle he joined the two ropes with two half hitches, he draped the rope around the branch and fed it on around the trunk. He then tied a slip knot that could be pulled out with the loose end. Sean tested the other end was secure by pulling on it with all his weight and asked, "Should I go first?"

"Yes. No, I think I want to go first." Sean tied one end around his mother's waist using a Bowline knot. Fran started climbing down ignoring the safety rope while using both hands for grips. Sean slowly played out the rope ensuring it never had much slack. The cliff may have been a reasonable climb if the face was dry. But all the hand and footholds were slippery and cold. Fran progressed slowly but surely until about halfway down when she slipped her foot into a downward angled crevice. As she put her weight on that leg, her wet rubber sole slipped out. As Fran fell, she grabbed the rope and tensed. She fell about 10 centimeters before the safety rope that had been looped around her stopped the fall with an uncomfortable jerk. Sean had been slowly feeding out the rope that he had wound around the tree trunk where it was looped across itself. Fran's weight pulled on the loop so it could not slip further without Sean feeding short lengths through the rope's crossover. It had arrested her fall with an uncomfortable jolt, but Fran swung away from the cliff as the loop over the branch had shifted outwards with the jerk. Fran's arms and legs were flailing as she tried to stabilize her pendulum and rotating movement. However, her wild actions made it worse.

Sean's thoughts: Oh God, that`s Mom at the end of the rope dangling over a cliff! What if the rope slips? If I cannot hold her? She has panicked.

Don shouted, "Stop waving your arms Mom. Keep still."

She is not listening. All this jerking is pulling on the rope. The knot might slip. If she falls, she will …. Do not go there. What would Dad do? I am such a fool not to have closed my backpack properly. Okay Dad would really shout loudly at her. Focus. Wet rope please do not slip so she falls.

Sean did not shout but screamed at his mother. "Stop Mom! Stop! Keep still! Only then will you stop swinging". After a few moments, Fran stopped and looked up at Sean. "Get yourself steady and we will see how you can get youself back to the rock face."

Fran took a deep breath to control her panic, did as instructed and managed to slow down and finally stop gyrating. She paused again to gather her wits and looked at the cliff face about two meters away from where she was hanging. She was now scared of the descent and was stuck, suspended in space. "Sean, what do I do now? Can I try to swing forward and back until I reach the cliff?"

"No Mom, if you can build up that much swing, when you reach the cliff, you won't have enough time to grab onto the slippery surface in time and will swing out again. I need to come down and help you get back to the cliff face. I do not think I can lower you between my strength, the slippery rope and not having abseiling equipment to feed out the rope safely. I am going to secure the other end of the rope as my backup to help me reach you."

Calling up Fran shouted back "Sean, please go slow and first test each foot- and handhold. Cut a piece off the end and make a belt with a small loop so that the rope can feed through it. The rope will always be close against you in case you slip. There is no one to catch you so you must be incredibly careful."

Sean prepared a makeshift belt and loop to pass the rope through. He found a long stick which he also tied vertically to him with a bow, to use to reach out to his mother. "Okay Mom, coming now." Sean's climb down was uneventful. Quite used to clambering up and down trees, climbing up and down ropes, and if ever there were rocks around, he would climb them too. Not scared of heights either, Sean made the descent to Fran's level look like walking down a flight of stairs. He then tied his length of the rope tight around him so he was secure and pulled on the bow to release the long stick. With one hand gripping a crevice tightly, he extended the branch out with his other hand so Fran could reach it. "Pull yourself towards me gently Mom or you may pull me away from the cliff face."

Slowly Fran pulled herself along the stick until she reached Sean's hand. "Okay you can drop the stick now."

"No Mom, if you slip away and we must do this again, I will still need the stick. I will drop it once you are safe against the side next to me. Keep pulling yourself across me to the face."

Fran continued to pull herself closer to the cliff along Sean's outstretched arms until she reached the wet rock face. "There to your right is a good handhold, Mom. Then place your other hand along the same crevice. At feet level is another good crevice to get your boots into. I need you to be stable against the side before I can loosen your rope for you to continue climbing down."

Gingerly Fran established herself against the vertical rock. Was she shaking from fear or cold? She decided on both. "Sean I am scared to lose this safety rope."

"I am sure. But I am going to loosen it, cut the end to make a belt and loop like mine and feed my secure rope through the same way. You will then have it to grab if necessary." Sean wondered if Fran had the strength to grab the wet rope in a fall, stop herself and then be able to lower herself the rest of the way. He shook off the thoughts not wanting to invite trouble. When it was done, he said "Mom, it is not far to go, there are plenty of good hand and footholds, and you must just continue slowly and carefully. Do you want me to go first and check the route?"

"I don't think so. I need to get down as I am really tired and do not want to extend this ordeal more than I need to." Fran set off with Sean suggesting useful cracks, protuberances, and ledges to use and she soon reached the bottom. He then followed, doing the last few meters quickly.

Sean turned and noticed Fran staring at him. "Let's go Mom. I am sure we are not that far now. I hope Harry did not find my stuff in the back of his truck as he would have told Dad who will then be worried, and I am sure have everyone out now to searching for us."

Fran did not move then stepped forward with teary eyes and gave him a tight hug. Almost whispering she said "You snapped me out of my panic by shouting. Where did you learn to do something like that?"

"I don't know. I tried to think about what Dad would do and that is what came to me. Seems it worked."

Fran released him from her fierce hug saying "Thanks Sean, for keeping your cool and continuing to save the day. Let us get going." The shoreline was not all a sandy beach to walk along and at times they had to clamber up and around rocks, a fallen tree or where the lake was right up against a vertical section of embankment. After about twenty minutes from the cliff descent, they saw the lodge and were soon in the administration building.

Harry's wife Lorna, who acted as manager, receptionist, assistant, bookkeeper, and cook jumped up from her desk when she saw them. "Thank God. Are you alright?" A tired Fran nodded. "Let me radio Harry and the others who are all out looking for you." She picked up a two-way radio and called "Harry. Everybody. Fran and Sean have just walked in. They are fine. You can all return."

Don's relieved voice came in over the radio. "Thanks Lorna. Please put Fran onto the radio." Lorna passed the radio to Fran.

"Don, we are back, fine, cold, hungry and pleased to be here."

"How did you find your way back with no compass or GPS?"

"It seems you taught your son better than you realized. He determined south from the sun and his watch, remembered the map of the area, and led us towards the shoreline. When the rain came in and hid the sun, we used the wind to know in which direction to continue towards the shore. Then we made our way along it until we got back. But we are cold, and both need a hot shower so we will give you more details when you get back."

"Copy that. Relieved and happy you guys are fine. See you soon. Out!"

Chapter 16   BLACK BEAR

A bear lifted me up so I could see all the earth.
He said I may jump among high cliffs
and I shall never die.
- Full Mouth (Crow)

Don and Harry were soon in the cabin and had to wait for Fran to come out of the shower and dress. Sean went into the bathroom after Fran so the two men had to wait impatiently until the two had washed, thawed, and dressed in dry clothing. After debriefing Don and Harry with their experience, Don said "I never expected you guys would have to use your skills for a real survival challenge. No more incidents please. We are here for fun, not to undertake dangerous tasks. We have a few more days and they better go smoothly and uneventfully."

"I definitely endorse that," said Harry. "No more extreme experiences. Just fun ones please."

Two days later they planned to paddle in two canoes for more experience having already practiced getting in, climbing out, jumping overboard, climbing back in from the water, and how to paddle using the Indian J-stroke. The following day's focus was to learn how to fish for food. The night before Don briefed everyone about the fish that were in the lake. "Since this lake is over a hundred kilometers long, it is stocked with many different species including large fish like the sturgeon and pike. Some of the other fish are perch, bass, trout, and walleye. Each one needs a different type of lure or baited hook so one must decide beforehand which type one wants to fish for and take suitable tackle and bait." The lecture then focused on each person's fishing preference and the equipment was prepared for the next morning's fishing trip. After a quick breakfast, carrying backpacks and rods, Fran and Don left the cabin ahead of the boys walking towards the nearby shore about a hundred meters away where the canoes were beached.

David strolled a way behind his parents eating a slice of breakfast toast with peanut butter and jelly. Sean was still putting on sun cream and walked out the door by the time his parents had reached the canoes. He heard a sniffing and looked left. Through the trees he saw a black bear smelling the air, realized the wind was blowing from David's food towards the bear and shouted at him. "Bear David, drop the food and walk quickly to Dad." He rushed back inside, grabbed the spare two-way radio on the table, turned it on and called his father. "Dad there is a black bear outside and it has picked up the scent of David's toast. I told him to drop it and walk fast towards you. I'll get out your rifle." He dropped the radio back on the bed having pulled out the rifle bag from under the bed while talking on the radio. Sean unzipped the bag, pulled it out, and ran to the cupboard for ammunition.

Sean's thoughts: If in time, they can launch the canoes and paddle safely away from the bear. That leaves me alone here. Which cartridges must I choose? Dad said soft point bullets were for animals like deer, but dangerous animals require more solid bullets. I need the ones in this box with full metal jackets for maximum penetration. I hope David got to the shore okay and I need to check.

Sean slung the rifle over his shoulder so he could use both hands to open the box and get some rounds out. He then pulled back the bolt and pushed three rounds into the magazine, by which time he was out on the porch again. To his horror he saw that David had frozen with fear and was staring transfixed at the approaching bear that was now only twenty meters away. "Throw your toast at the bear and walk slowly towards me." This jarred David into action. He threw wildly and the toast hit a nearby tree bouncing back towards him. The sudden action caused the bear to start running towards David. From his gym work, Sean easily lifted the 4 kg rifle up, and sighting onto the bear's eye as it was now less than ten meters from David. He squeezed the trigger and as the rifle's recoil pushed his light frame backwards, he thought 'I did not compensate for the bear's movement. I may have missed completely.' But the bullet, missing the eye, entered the bear's neck, tore its way through the skin, muscle and other tissue until it hit the fourth cervical vertebra. The spine was pushed sideways but the speed and power of the bullet forced it into the bone and through the spinal column shredding the nerve bundle as it passed through the center and continued its destructive path through the other side of the bone. The bear dropped dead about three meters from a terrified David as Don burst through the trees, his Colt Python .357 revolver in hand. He scooped up David and ran up to the cabin carrying him. Sean passed his father the rifle asking "Do you think he is dead. I am not sure where the bullet hit it."

Don said "I will go and see if it is dead or needs to be finished off. Get the radio and tell Mom we are all alright and take David inside. I told her to get in the boat and move safely offshore." Don went towards the fallen bear with the rifle ready and saw the blood oozing from the neck. The bear did not appear to be breathing and from the position of the wound, Don knew it had been killed.

Meanwhile Sean ran inside and radioed Fran. "Mom, we are all okay. You can come back now."

She replied, "No I want an armed escort. Tell Dad to lock you in the house and to come for me."

Harry came in over the radio. "What's going on? We heard Sean say there was a bear and then heard a shot."

"It's Sean, Harry. Yes, a bear went for David and I shot it. You better come."

Everyone's adrenalin was still pumping, and David was shaking. Don was not prepared to leave him and Sean in the cabin while he fetched Fran and therefore took the boys with him to the lake shore. As they walked towards the bear carcass, Don took a wide berth and said to David. "Lucky Sean was behind you and could get the rifle. You must have been really scared."

David finally found his voice. "Dad I was so terrified. At first, I could not move. Then Sean called again, telling me to throw my toast towards the bear that was coming and coming. But it hit a nearby tree and bounced back at me. I thought the bear was going to kill me. Then I heard the shot and saw it fall. I just ran back to the cabin. I am still shivering."

Pleased that his son was expressing what his feelings had been, Don kept up the conversation to help David have some catharsis rather than bottle up this fearful experience and suffer any Post Traumatic Shock symptoms from the incident. "You are going to have an exciting story to tell your friends when we get home. And if your teacher wants a *show and tell* of what people did in the holidays, we will take a photograph of you next to the dead bear and another standing with Sean holding the rifle."

David got this wan grin and said "I bet that I will have the most exciting story in my class. Shouldn't I hold the rifle? And Dad, I am still hungry after wasting my toast."

Don stopped, bent down and hugged David. "You must be feeling better if you have your appetite back."

Fran's thoughts, anxiously and impatiently waiting in the canoe: This trip turned out to be a really bad idea. Getting lost, slipping off the cliff face, a bear attacking David. What were we thinking? Teaching youngsters to shoot, dump us in the wilderness to see if we get lost, falling out of canoes and capsizing them! Why can't we simply watch survival programs on TV? Sean just killed a bear that was about to attack David! What were we thinking? No more crazy ideas Don. And where are you? Fetch me. Now!! I cannot just sit in the canoe. Come!

Staring at the shore, Fran finally saw Don and the boys' shapes between the trees heading towards her. She paddled back to shore, jumped out, ran through the trees and grabbed David. "Are you alright? You frightened us. What a thing to happen. Oh, Sean, if you weren't there …" and she burst into tears.

"I am fine Mom" reassured David. "I was terrified, but it is all over, and I want some more toast with peanut butter and jelly since I wasted mine throwing it at the bear, well at a tree. Can I have another slice?"

"Of course you can. Let's go back to the cabin and feed you. I am so happy that you are hungry and chatty."

Don gently held Fran, then the four walked back to the cabin with their arms around each other. Don said "It seems this trip did not go as planned with the real survival challenges we have had. And we have been successful with all of them. I am proud of all of you. And I think a bit of quiet fishing later is just what we need."

Harry arrived, inspected the bear carcass, listened to everyone relating their account of the event, thought about it and asked Don to step outside with him. "This is an obvious case of self-defense and it would undoubtedly be accepted as such if there is a hearing. I know you are a police reservist and therefore should report this incident to the Ontario Ministry of Natural Resources and Forestry."

Don asked, "Surely as an act of self-defense, I do not need to take my son or sons to a hearing somewhere?"

"The youngest age one can legally hunt in Ontario is 16. Bears are highly regulated and require a license. These are two regulations which have been broken and a hearing would listen to the reasons then undoubtedly agree it was warranted."

"I do not want to come all the way back to Rainy River or Morson, wherever the local Ministry offices are and subject my youngsters to a hearing. You also seem reluctant to go through this process. What can we do?"

Harry said "I obviously do not want the adverse publicity of potential customers thinking our camp is dangerous. Bears can be opportunists looking for garbage. And as you know, we strictly ensure nothing edible is accessible to a foraging bear, so they are not attracted to the camp. We have never had a bear this close before and after examining it, may find the bear was injured or sick so it may have been looking for easier pickings."

"Yes, the inevitable publicity could deter future customers."

"This is what we can do. I am allocated three bear hunting licenses a season. This bear can be assigned to one of them. But these licenses are normally expensive for hunters when bundled in a hunting package, and I will ask you to only pay for the basic license cost. I just want to recover my outlay considering this was an unforeseen and unplanned event. The license costs $230 per bear."

"Don said, "Harry, I appreciate your offer and that is not an excessive amount. I know it is the charge of a complete hunting trip where you make your profit, which you are now having to forfeit. And I appreciate that. Can you sell the meat and pelt? That would help."

"Thanks for your understanding. I will use the meat and sell the pelt. The skin will fetch a reasonable price after it has been tanned. Don, you guys have really had more than you bargained for. You must be so proud of Sean, and a credit to you as to how well you have obviously trained him."

Harry left to attend to the bear and Don called Fran outside. He related Harry's proposal to Fran who merely nodded. "What are you thinking Fran? You are unusually silent."

"It is an excellent proposal with no real losers or serious laws being broken like poaching. But I am wondering how Sean feels about his successful exploits and am worried that it might overly inflate his ego. A young boy, not even a teenager, leading the two of us out of the wilderness, rescuing me on the side of a cliff, then saving his younger brother's life by shooting a black bear. For a novice adult's first trip to the wild, that could be difficult to process and leave one unaffected, never mind a young boy."

"Well, we need to discuss it with Sean. See what he thinks and feels and gently place it in a balanced perspective so it does not distort his self-image while building his self-confidence." Let us go back inside, sit down and chat over some drinks and cookies. After some small talk with the four of them munching and sipping, Fran asked Sean "How do you feel about what you have accomplished on this trip?"

147

"It has been amazing. This was the best vacation I have ever had. We have done so many different things. Had big adventures. And dad's training has been fantastic."

"But how do you feel inside having accomplished such pretty big challenges like getting us home without a compass or shooting the bear?"

Sean thought for a few moments. "I feel quite brave. I never panicked. Dad trained me well. I remember him telling us about some Russian who protects snow leopards. He said that in an emergency some people think while others just act. Those that think, die. There is no time to wonder what the best thing may be to do. There is a saying we learnt at school that says, 'He who hesitates is lost.' Those two comments increased my understanding of the need to act fast in an emergency and do not get lost in thinking about what options there may be. With the bear I first thought that Dad has his revolver and would come but it is a small bullet for a large, dangerous animal. So, I just acted to save David. I did not delay considering it. I just acted."

David gave his brother an adoring look and a thumbs up saying "Thanks bro."

Fran persisted. "But how does that make you feel as a person?

"Great! Not that I killed an animal. Rather because of Dad's training I am feeling confident that I can manage many survival situations."

"And how does that make you feel compared to your friends?"

"What do you mean?" asked Sean.

"Do you feel better than them? Superior?"

"Yes. No. I don't know!"

Slowly Fran said "It is important to know that you are not superior. You have been lucky to have a father who could give this kind of training, take you into the wild to test what you learnt, and have the adventures that we experienced. There are other boys in your age group that could probably do what you did if they were given the same training and opportunity. If you set yourself apart from them, you will become separated as your friends will feel that you think you are better than they are. You do not want that. Do you understand?"

"Yes Mom, I know when anyone of my friends think they are superior for whatever reason, we get irritated and cut them out. I do not want that for me and will not act like a pompous snob."

"Good, but at the same time, do not feel apologetic and pretend this trip did not happen. Just say how thankful you are and not how better you are."

"Isn't that what humble means?" asked David.

His parents stared at him. Don asked, "Where did you learn that word? Yes, it does mean to be humble."

"Our teacher spoke about it and told us about famous people like Gandhi who got India's independence from the British without a war and stayed humble about it" explained David.

"Do you think it is a good way to be or if you are better in some way, let everyone know?" asked Fran.

After thinking for a moment, David said "Other people do not like feeling anyone is better than them. It is a good way to lose friends."

"Exactly. I am impressed you both understand the idea of humble so well" said proud mom smiling broadly at her sons.

After David did his `Show and Tell' about their trip, word about the twelve-year-old pupil who shot a bear to protect his younger brother quickly spread around the school. Sean was asked by his class to do a `Show and Tell' as well. He spoke about their wilderness trip and projected photos they had taken including of the bear. Sean was particularly sensitive about not coming across as haughty and emphasized how lucky he was to have had this opportunity, which he was sure his peers would have equally handled the same way. However, his teacher was so impressed that she then asked him to present to the same grade class in the next-door classroom. Before Sean reached home, Fran received a call from the headmistress.

"Hello, Mrs. Whitely. This is Mrs. Spencer, the school's headmistress. Congratulations on your brave son. We would like Sean to present to the school during the hall assembly on Friday. I also know someone at the local TV station …"

Fran interrupted as Don walked in and she indicated for him to listen. "Thank you, Mrs. Spencer, for that but I need to explain a few things. The first is that we are concerned Sean remains balanced and does not consider his recent, brave exploits a reason to feel superior in any way. Singling him out this way will feed his ego, which at twelve years old, would not be easy to manage. Although Sean shot the bear in self-defense, he is below the minimum age to be able to hunt. We do not need to fly him up to the town of Rainy River for a hearing with the Ministry of Forestry and Environment, where it would undoubtedly be accepted as an act of defense. But it would be a real pain to trek there, to be interrogated just to be exonerated. Finally, do you know why we went to Lake of the Woods?"

"My understanding is that you and some like-minded people believe there is an impending ice age and Sean and David were being given some survival training."

"That is correct Mrs. Spencer and although this concept is finally gaining traction as the winter Polar Vortex storms increase in intensity from year to year, we are still a minority voice. We therefore keep a low profile and definitely do not want to highlight this on television or radio. Therefore

150

for a few reasons we must decline your kind offer. Knowing these extra dimensions, I am sure you agree it is not in Sean's or our interest for him to go public with these experiences. I know Don shares my sentiments and would concur." Don nodded his head.

"Yes, it places the situation in a different perspective, and we will leave it. Thank you for explaining your position. And well done on training Sean. He is a well-adjusted, popular boy and your concern to retain that balance is commendable."

Chapter 17   SURVIVING MINUS FIFTY

Don convened everyone early in the fall to brief and remind people with what to expect in ice age weather plus various dos and don'ts. Would this be the year of the ice age descending? A barbeque lunch was organized on Don and Fran's lawn with everyone bringing their own food and sharing salads and desserts. It was a cloudy, lukewarm day with no breeze. A few complained about the heat while some of the older people wore thin sweaters. Children were running about on the grass and playing on Sean and David's swing, small slide, and other garden toys. The men, beers in hand, hung around the fire while Don and Lucas slowly turned the meat and corn on the grill. Conversation centered around sport, work, the economy, politics, and survival systems in their houses. The ladies were chatting about children, shopping, and clothes. One of the biggest complaints was buying cooler clothes for global warming if an ice age was expected.

After lunch, tea and coffee were served and Don launched into why he had requested everyone's presence. "Thank you all for coming and sharing your food. These gatherings have helped us to get to know one another better, especially if we have any emergencies and must rely on each other. I want to share with you what we know about surviving in the extreme weather conditions we anticipate coming soon. Many of these facts were told to you when you were considering joining us, but the repetition is important to ensure you have all these particulars at your fingertips. First some refresher background. The coldest occupied village in the world is Oymyakon in Russia's Yakutia region. Temperatures can fall to below -70°C.

As you know, our concern about global warming is that this heating allows storms normally contained in the polar regions to break out of their vortices and blast freezing air towards the equator. We are here because we want to survive lengthy storms with wind speeds up to 100 kph. Please interrupt with any questions as it is vital that we understand everything if we wish to survive.

"I want to tell you how people have described these extreme climatic conditions, so you know what to expect. Down to around -20⁰F or -30⁰C, we function reasonably well and most if not all of us have had experience with these temperatures. Some people will even dash outside to do something quickly, especially if it is done faster than it takes to get togged up. With our existing experience, we know what to expect.

"But as temperatures fall below that, the situation changes dramatically. By -30⁰F or around -35⁰C the sensation is no longer one of cold but initially of burning pain. This quickly develops into a deep ache in your bones. High wind speeds at these temperatures make it far worse with the wind chill factor so that any exposed skin feels like it is being burned with hot oil. As the temperature falls further to around minus forty where Fahrenheit and Centigrade are the same temperature, the sensation becomes excruciating, perhaps like fire."

"If people in this town of Oymyakon live at temperatures even lower, do they never go out when the temperatures are that low or do they have suitable gear to function outside?" asked Jacob.

Don said "I have almost no information about how they live and whatever is documented is probably written in Russian. But I read a book called The Tiger by John Vaillant which is about the Siberian Tiger and is the largest of all the cats. The remaining few live in an area called the Taiga on the eastern side of Russian which is remote and freezing. Vaillant says at temperatures of minus forty and below, spit will freeze before it hits the ground, and trees become so brittle that expanding sap can cause them to explode. Everything is frozen solid so there is nothing to absorb sound. It therefore has a sharp timbre that is percussive. But it is generally completely silent unless there is a storm. Everything is as still as outer space, and almost as cold. Vaillant relates stories of hunters who are often hunted in turn by these tigers. One called Khomenko would tramp through snow hearing only the sound of his breath and footfalls crunching through the snow. Eventually a tiger did take him and when they found the body at minus forty, it was as rigid as a shop window mannequin. Another hunter Kaplanov would be out at temperatures of minus forty-five, even in blizzards. These people can function in such extremes, which is why they were mentioned. But I doubt any of us would be able to withstand such frigid cold. In a forest it is easy to become disorientated. But with snow and strong winds making it worse, one would not have a chance. And the ground freezes solid to a depth of a meter."

"I am scared of what is coming" commented Miguel half under his breath. When people turned towards him expecting him to add a question, he qualified his comment by saying "Coming from Brazil where we have never even seen snow, this sounds like another planet." Miguel had the swarthy complexion of a Brazilian, appropriate for a climate enjoying substantially more sunshine and heat than Canada. He could have looked incongruous, but Canada had become quite cosmopolitan with citizens from all over the world. The Brazilians therefore merely contributed to a society that had become quite multicultural. Miguel's wife Beatriz, their friends Enrique and Gabriela who lived next door, and their respective children were olive-skinned. All had black hair and eyes and seldom bothered with protective sun cream in summer being endowed with copious, natural melanin pigment for skin protection against ultraviolet radiation. Miguel turned to Don and asked "Originally living in a country where temperatures can reach into the forties, I wonder what people experience when the temperature falls to the minus forties and fifty centigrade? This extreme is too far outside our range of experience to even vaguely contemplate."

"Yes, having grown up in Canada, I also wonder what it must be like to experience such cold, and more. This scenario is for another twenty to thirty degrees Centigrade below my experiences of only down to a minimum of around minus twenty," said Don. "Like the people in Oymyakon enduring temperatures of -70^{0}C and lower. I hate to sound like some doomsday prophet describing hell frozen over, but as you hear from these descriptions, we need to know what to expect and how to prevent exposure to such extreme cold."

The normally quiet Harper decided to contribute. She was a born and bred Canadian with more snow and cold experience than the Brazilians but was equally concerned about an ice age. "Back in 2019 when I was researching this impending ice age, The Guardian had an article about the coldest jobs in the world. One was a horse breeder in Oymyakon who had to go out daily to feed his horses. The coldest day he experienced was minus sixty-seven degrees Centigrade. If they cannot start a car, the children would be taken to school by sleigh."

Don said "In the book The Tiger, he describes how people living in other extremely cold parts of Russia either run their vehicle engines all night or drain radiators if they cannot get antifreeze, which is most of the time. In the morning, they must thaw ice to refill the radiator."

"What about pogonips?" said Amelia.

"What are pogonips?" asked Sophia.

"We would get them in valleys in Nevada and Idaho when it was extremely cold. The mist would be frozen into ice particles, also called ice fog, and if inhaled, cause pulmonary problems. Now that extreme cold is expected here, could we expect pogonips to extend to Polar Vortex storm areas as well?"

"That is definitely another problem to be concerned about if one is forced to go outside" said Mary wearing her nurse's hat. "Freezing one's alveoli tissue by breathing in icicles would prevent oxygen and carbon dioxide transfer through the membrane and probably do irreparable damage to these gas exchange sacks. This is all terrifying."

Harper nodded and continued with her Guardian article. "A woman living in Alaska who was interviewed said she had endured cold only down to minus forty-five. They live off the land fishing, hunting and trapping. This lady Renae said as they cannot grow anything, their diet is primarily protein. To survive life in the frigid wastes of the far north she spoke about how their clothes are made from the furs of the arctic animals caught in their traps."

Prompted by Harper's clothing comment, Don moved to the subject of appropriate clothing for them. "Everyone needs to buy their own set of survival gear as I am sure no one wants to make their own fur clothing. I bought Fran, the boys and myself complete frigid weather outfits to test during winter but have not flown up into the arctic circle to check them out at temperatures of below forty or fifty. It is what is recommended by a company that takes people on expeditions into the far north to see the Northern Lights in mid-winter. The principle is to wear multiple layers of clothing, thereby providing sufficient insulation, helped by the retention of air in and between the fabrics to increase the total cold protection of the outfits. Multiple layers also enable one to easily add and remove garments as required. Let us move inside to my dining room where we have laid out the items on the table.

After everyone had squeezed around the dining table, Don continued his explanation. "First there is a base layer of close but loose-fitting garments that will also draw off any perspiration by capillary action. Merino wool underwear is considered the best. Long underwear is usually synthetic material or merino wool and can be treated with some anti-bacterial product to prevent odor if unable to wash them frequently. This includes long sleeve vests and *long johns.*' The middle layer has a shirt, sweater, and jacket. Zips with draw strings allow one to easily open and close jackets to adjust for changing environmental temperatures. Pants are either moleskin or synthetic material. Moleskin is made of cotton and is only called this as it looks like a mole's skin. Pants must be loose, not tight. Finally, there is the outer layer which must be wind proof. We all know about the wind chill factor that effectively will make the actual temperature feel tens of degrees colder at minus fifty. The outer shell does not need to be waterproof at the temperatures we are preparing for as water is either ice or snow and not liquid rain. These parkas or anoraks can be synthetic or down filled. Then there are head, hands, fingers, feet, toes and ankles, wrists and neck. Here are examples of gloves, balaclavas, socks, goggles, and boots. Any questions?"

Miguel asked "In an emergency, won't this take at least five minutes to kit up? If someone is in trouble, that length of time may not be a luxury we would have."

"Yes" said Don. "But first, we have no option or someone responding with inadequate protection will be in trouble themselves within seconds more than minutes."

"Then we need to practice and leave a complete outfit laid out, ready to put on as quickly as possible" replied Miguel. "Like firemen do when they are called out. And I assume when we move around, no spot can be exposed at all, so we need to be completely enveloped in our outfits."

Fran said "There are web sites worth exploring for details on the hows, whys and what to wear. One called Cool Antarctica has a wealth of information and examples of all the clothing mentioned. We can either standardize, or everyone can choose their own preferences. Ideally, we should all do one of their arctic trips in full gear to experience more severe conditions that we currently experience in Toronto."

There was a silent pause while everyone reflected on what could not be described as a chilling orientation since there seemed no words to adequately express the kind of cold they were expecting. Finally, Amelia broke the silence by saying "Okay Don, we all get the picture. Now tell us how to survive outside in such extremes."

Don gathered his thoughts and continued. "The descriptions are realistic and were designed to ensure you are all serious about what to expect, what will be confronting us and how to survive in those conditions. Since people living in Oymyakon and elsewhere do live in such freezing winters, we know that it is possible to survive temperatures well below what we are experiencing. And we must get it right before the first onslaught as we will not have time to modify or adjust anything. But we can only go outside when there are no storms and not during a Polar Vortex assault."

Ella asked everyone "Has anyone seen the 2018 movie called Arctic?" A few hands went up including Fran's, which she quickly dropped but Don had already noticed as Frans' glance revealed this quizzical look on his face.

Ella continued "It is about a man whose plane crashes in the Arctic and his compatriot is killed. It shows how he struggles to survive in the cold with only the limited resources found in the airplane. What did you get from the film Fran?"

With a worried sigh knowing how upset or angry Don was likely to be, having watched it and not said anything to him, Fran answered. "Although the movie showed the bleakness of incessant, freezing cold, I did not find anything in the story relevant to our situation or any tips for survival. I therefore never promoted it to anyone as something worth watching."

After Fran's pause, Ella said "I agree and what I used to find beautiful, a landscape covered in pure white draped over the icy mountains, the film made the snow feel ominous and foreboding. But I still feel there is some merit in watching the movie as it does highlight the challenges of cold, which we are anticipating."

Fran added, "Yes, we need to be sensitive to such extreme conditions and the storms in the film were not as harsh as we are expecting. He survived being outside, which we would not do during a Polar Vortex storm. However, the stories we have heard about now are at temperatures of fifty and below. But people are never voluntarily active outside when there is a Polar Vortex storm with gale force winds blasting them."

As soon as they were alone, Don asked Fran "Well! Why the big secret?"

Fran looked straight at Don. "I could have mentioned it at the time, and I apologize. But I was also worried about Sean and any future children?"

"I don't understand. What do our children have to do with it?"

"When we were still researching about ice survival, I came across the movie, downloaded and watched the film. As I said to everyone, yes it

159

showed the saga of someone struggling to survive arctic cold. But it had no relevant message to help us."

"Again, what has that got to do with our kids?"

"My concern is that you might have wanted them to see it as part of your ongoing orientation and sensitization as to what is coming. But it is not age appropriate for children like say a TV documentary about the Arctic. Watching a frost-bitten foot with missing toe, dead people, helicopter crashing, falling through ice into a cave and sustaining a bloody leg injury, a woman with a slit belly that becomes infected, attack by a polar bear. It would be too much, and I did not want to expose our children to such sights."

After a few pensive moments Don said "I am concerned and upset that you think I may not have been more sensitive. Or if I suggested they watch the movie, that I would not have listened to or heeded your wishes."

Fran said "Again I am sorry but as it did not have any material of substance for us, I never to bothered to tell you about it or so much of other Internet material we have both found and also dismissed. You had been talking about sensitizing our children at that time and I did not want you to consider this film as appropriate for youngsters."

"Maybe, but I would have liked the opportunity to also decide, what is and is not appropriate for children to see or know about. We are heading for tough times and sooner or later our boys will be exposed to disagreeable situations. Some prior sensitivity through discussion may help them rather than find themselves in a terrible position that they may or may not cope with. I think I better see the film and then discuss the merits with you of letting children watching it."

After watching the film Don said to Fran "I must admit I may have wanted to show such a film to Sean when he was older. But you are right that they would be too young for a while and our situation is different to the survival situation portrayed in the film. You still should have told me about it."

"With hindsight yes and I said I am sorry. I do not think I have withheld information about anything else so we should close the chapter as having been a once-off and move on."

"Alright, but nothing more to be hidden please. From either of us."

PART 7

The arrival of Armaggedon

Armageddon, referred to in The Book of Revelations in the New Testament as 'The end times.'

From Ancient Greek Ἀρμαγεδών; originally from Hebrew words הר מגידו (pronounced Har Meggido,) which means the 'Mountain of Meggido' in northern Israel.

According to the Book of Revelation in the New Testament, it is the location of the final battle during *The End Times.*

Chapter 18 THE ICE AGE STRIKES

The polar vortex is this living creature.
It's affected by waves created at the surface of the Earth,
which get excited by things like flow moving over mountains
or flow moving over land and sea.
- **Aditi Sheshadri, Assistant Professor**
Earth System Science,
Standford University
Weather can kill you so fast.

Javier felt a separate meeting of the men should be convened. "We need to discuss how to handle dangerous emergencies. Those where we would prefer the women not to respond, unless one was particularly adept in a particular situation or really wanted to be included. And I would like a refresher to better understand the systems that have been designed since our lives are dependent on them all working."

A few days later the men gathered at Javier's house, he made a short introduction about why they were there, then handed the subject across to Don. "I will first ask Jake, also being an engineer and involved in everything we designed and implemented, to talk about how we need to relate to these systems."

Don nodded at Jake, who picked up the thread saying "I am not going to describe any technical, engineering designs. Rather what we did and why. First, we simulated power outages, checked the communications systems, tested the various heating and electricity generation systems and measured the efficiency of the heat insulation by measuring temperatures both outside and inside rooms deliberately left unheated. I feel what has been refined is stable, works well and only needs to be tested live at the extremely low temperatures we are anticipating. These systems run automatically and normally require no intervention."

Don continued by saying "For the inside systems, if we remain indoors, we can work on them. But if there is an external problem, we cannot attend to it as the cold and strength of the Polar Vortex storms will be more than we can be exposed to or in which we can function. Our designs are sound and one of these winters we will be tested. So please, no heroics to try anything alone. We are a team and are here to help each other."

Jake continued. "Call for assistance even when doing any potentially dangerous repairs or maintenance work inside so someone can be with you. In lockdown, I suspect we may be bored, and you will probably end up with too many volunteers looking for a distraction and a challenge. Again, no heroes please. There are no posthumous awards being given. And if someone gets hurt, they will not be able to go to a hospital for medical treatment."

It was a day that no one will forget. The day the prophesies and alarmists' predictions came true. There was a massive outbreak of freezing Polar Vortex air. It was far more than the usual spillage due to the influence of progressive climatic warming that could no longer contain the freezing air in the arctic. The resulting Polar Vortex storm exceeded anything previously experienced in temperature and strength with winds lashing Canada, the USA, and Russia, particularly from the central to eastern parts of the two continents. The worst winters anyone in Toronto had experienced were like a gentle, mild spring drizzle compared to the fury that lashed the city without any compassion or mercy. The intense cold was blasted in with gale force winds, intent on destroying everything strewn across the innocent landscape. Buildings were buffeted with the freezing fingers of death, seeking to strangle any warmth to which terrified people clung with desperation. The icy air blast quickly froze people to death who were not adequately protected. Those were the lucky ones as others exposed to the storm that were only partially sheltered soon developed frostbite and died more painfully. Conventional homes that were insufficiently robust were damaged by the high winds blasting freezing air into them.

The call came in on the fifth day and Don answered the telephone. "Is this Mr. Whitely?"

"Yes."

"My name is Janet Muldoon and I work for the CNN News Desk. I believe you built houses to withstand this terrible storm and would like to interview you."

"About what exactly?"

"What you believe is happening, how long the storm will last, what we should do if it gets worse, and any other tips that would be useful." Don was hesitant, not particularly wanting to be in the limelight. Janet continued. "Mr. Whitely, ..."

"Please call me Don."

"Don, there have been, and I am sure there will be more serious consequences for many people. I feel you could help them and therefore think this is potentially a really important interview and opportunity for you to help those who were skeptical and are now in trouble, having found themselves in serious difficulties."

"Well, I suppose I have a civic responsibility to assist where I can. But before you play the interview, you need consider its content as it could create panic."

"Isn't *panic* an exaggeration? We will of course first review the interview's content before airing it. Can we start now? Do you have some free time?"

Laughing, Don said "Well I cannot go anywhere in this storm."

"Alright, I will start with a brief introduction and ask various questions and you will reply. Okay?"

"Sure, let's go."

"On today's show we have Don Whitely, a Toronto civil engineer who predicted this terrible storm and has built specialized homes to survive such weather extremes. Since many of us are struggling with the severe cold, Mr. Whitely, Don should have some invaluable information and advice for us. Don, how much longer do you think this storm will last?"

"I am afraid these storms, and I am sure there will be more this winter, are each likely to last three to four weeks."

"What? I do not have food to last that long! I am sure many other people also do not have adequate provisions to feed themselves and their families for such a long period."

"People need to review their stocks and ration their eating immediately. Perishables must be consumed first as it is vital not to waste anything. Check online what our RDA or Recommended Daily Allowance is of foods like proteins, carbohydrates, fats and nutrients, especially vitamins. This will determine what one's minimum daily intake should be. If one does not have all these nutrients for the rest of the storm until we can stock up with them, at least try to have sufficient daily calories to survive. The time is not long enough to develop serious vitamin deficiency diseases, but it is long enough to starve."

"This is frightening. Are you sure? What about the radically cold temperatures we are experiencing?"

"No, Janet, I am not sure for exactly how long, but I seriously think the storm will last for weeks. Regarding the cold, there is a particularly serious problem to consider."

"What's that?"

"This severe storm will damage many services, so some people will lose their electricity supply or gas. The utility companies will not be able to send out technicians to repair them until the storm abates and those affected will not have energy for heating, lights and cooking."

"Ohhh … That does not sound good. What about other emergency services?"

"No one can go out in this storm. No medical, police or fire help. No food deliveries. No repairs and maintenance. Communications will probably collapse. Mobile phone cell towers could be damaged or lose power. Many telephone poles and lines will be blown over. We are unaccustomed to such severe weather conditions and our infrastructure is not designed for such harsh weather."

"This is all most frightening. If we lose heating, then what?" asked a now concerned Janet in a tremulous voice.

"Years ago, we had wood and coal stoves in homes, but it caused pollution, smog and acid rain in large cities. They were therefore banned but ideally that is what people need now. If things become desperate, you would have been able to burn your furniture in one of these stoves."

"If one is desperate and must have an open fire inside their home, what about the smoke in a confined space? Open a window slightly?" suggested Janet.

"No, the force of the storm will blast in subzero air at around minus fifty degrees. That will counter any warming from a fire in seconds. Of course, making a fire inside has other dangers so extreme caution would be necessary. If you must vent smoke, ensure any outside air comes from the lee or sheltered side of the storm. The wind speed should then be less and easier to manage. In a house, since only a small area should be inhabited to minimize the extent of heating required, other rooms could be used to vent the smoke into instead."

"How?"

"If you have a fan and electricity, that could force or suck the smoke out. A hair dryer is also an option. Smoke inside is a serious problem, particularly any carbon monoxide if there is inadequate oxygen for combustion."

"What specifically about carbon monoxide?"

"Well, it fixes irreversibly onto hemoglobin so your blood cannot transport enough oxygen around the body. Combustion in confined spaces is a common cause of carbon monoxide poisoning. Symptoms include blurred vision, dizziness, nausea or vomiting, shortness of breath, confusion, dull headache, weakness, and loss of consciousness."

"If we are not too confused and realize the problem, what can we do?"

"Leave the room immediately, briefly open a window, do anything to inhale fresh air. But carbon monoxide irreversibly damages hemoglobin and is therefore an accumulative poison. A few breaths of fresh air will therefore not reverse the problem. If you are lucky enough to identify the condition, continuing to use a fire in a confined space becomes a life-threatening option on top of the freezing cold problem."

"Don this is all very bleak. I was hoping for some positive tips and an encouraging report as to how we can weather the storm. Instead, this is all doom and gloom. Did you foresee all this and set up what people need to survive?"

"Yes, we spent years debating many scenarios and possibilities. Therefore, we were able to anticipate what has happened so far and what still is expected to come."

"What are some of the things you did?"

"First, we designed and built homes that had increased insulation adequate for the far lower outside temperatures we are experiencing now in this Polar Vortex storm. The homes have adequate heating with minimal wastage and maximum heat recovery. We are self-sufficient with adequate food stored, have a shared electricity generator, oil and spare gas cylinders storage, plus local telecommunications between the homes. And there is an underground tunnel connecting everyone so we can reach each other in emergencies."

"That sounds like quite an investment for a speculative situation to develop given the global warming trend."

"Yes, and with it came derision with people scoffing at us to consider an ice age when the planet has been heating up. But although we now have been vindicated, it is a Pyrrhic victory to see so much suffering and fatalities."

"Thank you, Don. We have run out of time and wonder if you have any final thoughts or suggestions?"

"Not really Janet. People need to be creative and use whatever resources and skills they have until the storm passes. Then afterwards, depending on what may be available in those shops and stores that open, prepare for the next storm."

"Well, that was a most sobering interview, and I can only wish everyone the best of luck to survive this cataclysm." After a slight pause as Janet tuned off the recorder, she asked "Don before you go, may I ask you something off the air?"

"Sure, what is it?"

"I am stuck in our offices having been caught here when the storm struck with eight other workers. We have no clean clothes, the building's heating is struggling to make the offices bearable and from what you said, we are likely to run out of food and possibly utility services. How do we survive?"

"It may be good news or bad news to be stuck in the building depending on what is in it. Let's start with food. You need to determine what there is to plan on rationing whatever food you can find. Assume this storm will last for a total of at least four weeks to base what daily quantities you can each eat. You must have a canteen with food."

"Yes. We were here for a large evening function that never took place because of the storm. However, there was food for a finger dinner and so far, we have been living mainly off that food. It is almost finished and has become boring being so repetitive."

"You need to scour the building. Other offices should have food, even if it is primarily snacks. But anything that provides calories will do."

"Okay we will go out in groups but will have to break into the other offices."

"No one will respond to any alarms that may go off. Just find food and any other resources that could help like warm clothing and blankets. You are not likely to find such items, but you never know."

"From what you said about services failing, I am worried about a failure of our central heating system."

"Go to the basement and investigate what source of power the heating system is using. Is it gas, oil or electricity? If it is oil, there will be a storage tank, but gas and electricity depend on outside supplies."

"Because of the TV studios, we have a standby generator so that will surely help?"

"With lights but not necessarily heating if you don't have electric heaters. The generator will be diesel but may also run on the heating oil. Otherwise, there is plenty of office furniture to burn in the building but be careful of the smoke."

"It is all very bleak. I hope we survive" muttered a worried Janet.

"Yes, there should be enough resources in the building, so it is probably a better place to be than alone in your apartment."

Chapter 19   EXHAUST FUMES

The first priority of survival is
getting protection from extreme weather.
- Bear Grylls, Discovery TV survival expert.

The storm continued for three and a half weeks before abating. Listening

to the screeching wind, initially Fran and the boys were terrified. The feeble

attempts of day to encroach on the somber grip of winter nights lost its

battle. The dense clouds of the Polar Vortex assassinated any frail attempts

of daylight to seep through. The bleak blackness of the unyielding night was

not overnight but for weeks. It was relentless and dark outside all day long.

After a few days, everyone became accustomed to the almost hurricane-

force gale and had to speak loudly above the din to be heard. Although the

first week went by with the Delaney Street homes coping well and the utility

companies' supplies continuing, Don kept calling to confirm every home was

managing and Fran spoke to the wives regarding whether they were coping

emotionally.

The first utility service to fail was electricity and the large, stand-by

generator automatically kicked in. Some of the residents of Delaney Street

did not even realize they were being fed by the back-up system as the

transition only took about a half a minute to automatically start up. So far

no one had used the tunnel. Nobody felt like socializing, there were no

problems or emergencies and all systems continued to work as designed.

But at the end of the second week Don said to Fran, "Even though I can

monitor the generator remotely and all seems fine, it does require an onsite

visit. Something small like a leak would not show on the computer app dashboard. Everyone in the street is relying on our systems to survive the storm, and more storms that will follow this winter."

"You said nothing should be done alone. Please request a companion then call in every few minutes on your two-way radio telling me where you are and what you are seeing and doing."

"Of course," said Don as he picked up the two-way radio to call for a volunteer. "Don here. I want to inspect the generator room and as per our policy not to do anything alone, I am looking for a companion.

Oliver was the first to reply. "Sounds like a good excuse to relieve the boredom and a chance to test my arctic spec gear. I will call you when I am ready to enter the tunnel."

Don started dressing into his survival clothing and said to Fran "After checking the generator building, we will do a tunnel inspection and walk along its full length as well."

"Will the walkie talkie reach you as you get further away along the tunnel as it is quite screened with all the ground, concrete and distance?"

Smiling, Don explained "In the tunnel, with William's design, we installed a series of boosters. It is like a Wi-Fi repeater that relays the signal at full strength. So, there is coverage the full length of the tunnel. The repeaters are powered by an almost insignificant amount of electricity fed from some of the houses along the tunnel. We had the system installed when we set up our virtual private network. There is also a repeater in the roof of your parents' house so radios above ground from one end of the street will reach the other end. A radio signal in the house would not have reached into the tunnel without the booster network for the radios to communicate the full length. I will tell you when I start the tunnel inspection for you to test the radio system."

"Will do."

Don headed into the tunnel to meet Oliver. During their uneventful walk to the underground entrance of the generator building, Don did a cursory inspection of the services running along inside it. The wall looked like a typical basement or factory with steel pipes, plastic tubes, and electric cables mounted along it. The large diameter metal pipe venting the generator's exhaust fumes ran along the tunnel to warm it. The pipe was mounted close to the floor as warm air rises and this position gave the best heat distribution. Above that ran a bank of colored pipes to carry oil and gas. The next row was a cable tray with both power and communication cables, kept apart from the power cables to minimize any interference from electromagnetic fields around a flowing electric current. There were periodic wall lights mounted in waterproof bulkheads. The occupant's name of each house was stenciled above the doorway into their basement with an intercom mounted on the side of the door frame. On the facing bare wall, each person had been encouraged to decorate it with whatever they wanted. Fran's boys had painted a deer and bear with a forest background reminiscent of their Lake of the Woods adventure. Fran painted an African savannah scene reminding her of their Kenyan trip to contrast the frigid environment and Don painted a tropical, coastal village scene with its buildings reflecting his civil engineering background.

As Don opened the generator house door, the smell of exhaust fumes hit him. He immediately slammed the door closed, not wanting to flood noxious fumes into the tunnel. 'Now what?' he thought. He called Fran radio on the radio. "Calling Fran. Fran come in."

A moment later she replied, "Fran standing by."

"The generator building is full of exhaust gas. I cannot go in to inspect it as we do not have a compressed air tank with breather mask. I will need to shut it down with a computer. Being covered ion deep snow, I cannot open the ground level front door in the storm to flush the fumes before going in and need to discuss the problem with my dad. Call everyone to say we will be shutting down the generator and they must all check that their individual, standby generators automatically switch over to auxiliary power now. If anyone's home generator does not work, they must radio in before I do the shutdown. Please ask my dad to come to the house so we can plan how best to investigate and fix the problem in case he has not been monitoring the radio."

"Copy. I will contact everyone now other than those people monitoring this call. How long Don till shutdown?"

"I will do the remote shutdown in about a quarter of an hour If no one reports a faulty generator. Please will anyone who has heard this transmission, call in to tell Fran so she knows who else must be contacted."

After Jake arrived at Don's house, they reviewed options as to how they could flush the inside of the generator building considering they were completely snowed in. Jake said "The openings into and out of the building are the tunnel door, ground level outside door, air inlet, and exhaust outlet. The front door is snowed in and we cannot go out in this storm to clear it. Venting into the tunnel is too dangerous an option. Any ideas?"

Don had also been thinking about the problem and suggested "Then we only have the air inlet and exhaust outlet to vent through. Cutting open the exhaust pipe and setting up a fan to push fumes through is not possible with what equipment we have and the time it would take. There is a cover plate to access the air inlet filter that can be opened quickly and if we

175

pressurize the room with fans blowing air in from the tunnel, after a while it should clear the fumes. We can then go safely into the generator room to see where the leak is coming from and try to repair it."

Jake said "I suppose so. But in a worst-case scenario, if we cannot repair the leak and it is safe to continue using the generator, we can leave it running until the storm ends."

Don added "Yes if we have to wait, and I am not prepared to go in while holding my breath as it will not give me enough time to survey the area adequately."

Most concerned, Fran said "I don't want you passing out from carbon monoxide and carbon dioxide fumes. Even if you think you have fully vented the building, you still need to tie a rope around you so you can be pulled out if there are still residual fumes. Some of the others need to be there too, to help if anything happens."

Thinking out aloud, Don said "You know I could remove that flexible pipe we have that connects the tumble dryer to the hot air recovery duct. If I fashion some form of mouthpiece, I can breathe through it like a diver, sucking in fresh tunnel air. That way I can safely breath while removing the air inlet filter plate."

Looking marginally relieved at this suggestion, Fran said "Simon wants to join you and is on his way. Do you need more than Jake and him to assist?"

Don said "No, two men should be enough if I need to be pulled out. Dad, remember these gases are heavier than air so they will start flowing down into the tunnel as soon as the door is opened. There is already a smell of smoke from when I briefly opened the door. The door needs to be sealed as much as possible with wet towels while I go in."

176

"Yes" answered Jake, "But the gases inside the generator building will be much warmer than in the tunnel. The exhaust fumes seepage will therefore be less as the denser, colder air below will reduce the rate of gas exchange with the warmer exhaust gases above. After you come out, we will use a fan to force air into the generator room's air inlet duct through your flexible breathing pipe and force out the fumes. Fran, I think at least two more men should be on standby further down the tunnel so please recruit two more volunteers. I would rather be over cautious than sorry."

Jake ran an extension cord from the house at the end of the tunnel to a portable fan which sucked in fresh, cold outside air. At the same time Don temporarily wired another fan to an extension cord from his house next to the generator building. He had fashioned a plastic bag in the shape of a funnel around the fan's wire safety frame to one end of the flexible pipe so the fan could force air into the flexible pipe.

While Don was getting ready to enter, Fran thought: Here we go again. Don rushing off into danger to save everyone. Why can't someone else go? I know, I know. No one else other than maybe Jake can assess the situation and find the problem. But he is probably too old. What do they say about thinking you are indispensable? Well Don, you are to me and if you get gassed ... Shit!
Stop these thoughts and just monitor the radio to give them efficient back-up.

The tunnel had been cooling down without the hot exhaust fumes flowing along the extraction pipe and the icy, outside air being drawn in by the one fan was cooling down the tunnel quickly. With their artic clothing, it was still bearable. All the tunnel doors into basements were checked to be closed in case fumes leaked into the tunnel. Don fitted his swimming goggles and clip onto his nose, picked up the other end of the ducting pipe and inserted the modified snorkel he had made into his mouth. Jake turned on the fan at the other end of the flexible pipe, opened the generator room door and Don went in, pulling the safety rope behind him.

Two volunteers, Noah and Michael were on standby in the tunnel as Don went in breathing through the flexible hose. The tunnel door was ajar because of Don's breathing pipe blocking it, and Jake and Simon draped the opening with towels resulting in minimal fumes leaking into the tunnel. Don quickly unscrewed the air inlet filter cover plate in the building's wall without any difficulty having brought the right size spanner. He then pulled out the air filter to enable fumes to be pushed out with no restriction. Don hyperventilated and took a deep breath. He then removed his mouthpiece and pulled it off the ducting pipe, which he pushed into the opening near the air inlet and draped a towel around it to seal the pipe. This only took seconds and he returned to the tunnel door immediately while still holding his breath. He burst through the door and gulped in fresh tunnel air. Don was out after being inside only two minutes.

Simon held his breath, opened the door wider and ran up the steps to place the fan near the top of the stairs up to the generator room. From that position, the fan would suck in air from the room. The door was marginally ajar because of the fan's thin electric cable. This small gap was left for air to be sucked in to replace exhaust fumes that the fan blew out through the air inlet vent. The plan was to leave this set-up running for a few hours so most if not all the fumes would be cleared. A few fumes would leak back into the tunnel, which is why Jake had placed the second fan in the tunnel blowing in freezing fresh air.

Afterwards all the volunteers convened at Jake's house who said "I think we should wait for at least four hours before checking if the generator house is safe to enter. It is probably double the time we need but I would rather be safe than sorry. I am going to remove my house smoke detector and put it in the generator room to see if it is triggered as an independent check rather than only trying to smell if the fumes have been completely sucked out. Carbon monoxide is odorless so we can only smell other gases. Meanwhile Mary will make coffee and dig out some cookies."

Four hours later, the five men went back down the tunnel, which was now much colder with no heating and the outside air still being drawn in. Don went into the generator house first carrying the smoke detector. Neither Don nor the detector detected any exhaust fumes and he called Jake and Simon to come into the building over the radio. With Fran and probably everyone else monitoring transmissions, they would all know what was happening. Within a few minutes of inspecting the exhaust ducting, the leak was found in a chimney joint and the engineers decided it could easily be soldered with a blow torch. Jake went to his workshop and brought back a gas blowtorch, solder and flux. Don melted the solder into the joint, which quickly solidified and announced he was ready to turn on the generator to test the repair. The filter was replaced without the cover plate being bolted into place in case there were more problems and they had to repeat the gas extraction process. Don said "In case any more exhaust fumes leak, we need to return to the tunnel now. If there is still a leak, it will take a while to build up before reaching a dangerous level so I will briefly stay inside to monitor the repair." As no one was prepared to leave him, Don manually started the generator from the control panel. No fumes escaped from the repair and there were no other leaks. As the diesel engine was noisy, Don indicated to Jake and Simon that they should all leave. He replaced the air filter, bolted the cover plate back and left the room. In the tunnel he said "You are all invited back to my place, this time for a celebratory drink since it was the end of the day, or tea if preferred. And this invitation is for wives and kids too. It is time we gathered for something positive and to review generally how we are doing now that the ice age has finally hit. I feel vindicated with my prediction and our houses are functioning well. I assume no one else has had problems as I am sure Jake or I would have heard about it. I therefore want to celebrate with my family and like-minded friends."

In Whitely's house, Simon tapped the side of his glass to get everyone's attention. "First a big thank you to Don and Jake for sorting out the exhaust fumes problem. Second, I would like to explain that one of my reasons for buying into this development was that the developers committed themselves to live in one of these specialized homes too. This was a major reassurance for me. And as they are both engineers, it meant that they were better equipped than most to handle problems such as the one resolved most professionally and quickly today. We have developed a comradery that makes me feel proud to be a member of this extended family. I am sure there may be more serious challenges that will confront us and as there is always strength in unity, we need to continue working together. I personally feel that for any hard times ahead, as a team we will prevail."

Simon's initial words elevated everyone's feelings but having ended on a more sober note, the room remained quiet. To break the silence, Fran said "Thanks Simon. I am sure you spoke for all of us and yes, we will be confronted with unknown challenges in the future. But we need to remain as upbeat as possible, especially for the younger ones who are less able to cope with pressures that the School of Life has taught us older ones about survival in the face of adversity. I think we should have a games evening tonight, preferably ones that will make all of us laugh. We bought a host of suitable games just waiting for a moment like this. All who want to participate, please come early at say six thirty so children can also participate."

Later that evening after climbing into her electric blanket warmed bed and cuddling up to Don, Fran said "Simon is an enigma. He volunteers, is helpful, but somewhere can also be contentious and tries to be controlling. What do you think about him now that we are getting to know him better?"

"I like his strong points and feel in a crisis, he can be relied on. But in a debate, a decision, a discussion, he is pushy. In his business world where he would have been an expert, it may have been more appropriate. But our environment is technical and physically challenging, including threats by intruders. I do not consider him to be an expert or experienced in these fields and I assume his behavior may need to be managed at times, occasionally with some stress all round. These situations cannot be compromised so we must not pander to either his ego or ignorance and will need to be firm if he challenges us."

With a sigh, Fran concluded "Strong people are always at one or other extreme. Good points are great, but generally they do not acknowledge their weaknesses, which can cause all sorts of complications. In extreme situations I hope this does not become a problem."

Chapter 20   AFTERMATH

> Low-income people everywhere will be at risk of food insecurity
> due to loss of assets, absence of alternative livelihood options and
> lack of adequate insurance coverage from extreme weather events.
> **- Jacques Diof, DG, UN, Food & Agriculture Organization**

The second storm lasted four and a half weeks, devasting what was left of the city. Utility services, television and the mobile phone infrastructure were all damaged. Pockets of Internet access continued where there was not too much damage. Mobile data using 8G wireless not reliant on above ground wires was still functioning in some more fortunate areas. For those who had satellite Internet links or satellite dishes for TV could receive international news but local news was nonexistent as the few reporters and staff who had survived were stuck indoors during the storm. Fran found the roar of the storm disturbing, the relentless darkness of incessant night claustrophobic, spending much of the day teaching, feeding, and entertaining the boys, all to be emotionally drained.

Fran's thoughts: We are in prison. Covid sucked. But this! Isolation to a new level. Yea, yea. We have heat, comfort, food, and support. Am I ungrateful to complain? No, but our lives have shrunk to living in a few rooms. I want more from life and do seem thankless, which I am not. But we are cooped up. I must stop these negative thoughts and count my blessings.

After the storm finally passed, snowbound streets could not be opened with snow ploughs as there was no one to drive them. The first reports trickling in were of devastation with many more people freezing and starving to death in their homes during the second storm. Another group meeting was organized by Fran the day after the storm had abated to review the grim news. Most of the residents of Delaney Street preferred to use the tunnel to get to the Whitley's house as it was much warmer than outside that had barely warmed since the storm. But a few had felt so claustrophobic that they needed some icy, fresh air and trudged through the snow instead of using the tunnel wearing their arctic survival outfits. Don had installed multiple rows of hooks in the entrance hall for anoraks and parkas but with forty-four adults and children, there was still not enough space. Some piled jackets on a bench in the entrance hall whereas others held on to them or draped them over chairs once inside. Following on from Sybil's suggestion for bulk buying, most of the gear came from the same supplier. After the first winter meeting, there was much confusion afterwards as to who owned what with all the clothing being duplicates in styles and color. Name tag labels were immediately bought and sewn onto all the clothing, so people were able to stack jackets and find them afterwards. With limited space, only ladies and a few children could sit inside so these gatherings were always a squash. Finally, everyone arrived, the open plan lounge and dining room into which the crowd had spread out, it was warm and people were chatting to each other, happy for direct contact with other human beings. And of course, just being alive.

While people were arriving and squashing into the limited space available, Fran had this wave of regret about calling everyone to discuss what responsibilities they may have towards struggling survivors.

Fran's thoughts: I am always the one to broach the elephant in the room. I hate it. Do they hate it? Do they hate me for shoving their noses into the mess they do not want to smell? Do I want to be the bad person all the time? Come on Don. Your turn. Why are you not telepathically picking up this message that I am beaming to you? Tell them we cannot save the world. This whole project has been to save ourselves. If I say it, they may think I am callous and insensitive. That I do not care about anyone. Of course I do, but family comes first.

Reluctantly Fran tapped on a glass to get everyone's attention. It was going to be a gloomy and sobering discussion and she wondered whether children should be present. But then this was the new environment that they were also in and she commenced in a serious voice. "There are few important things we must consider that I wish to highlight. We need plans and direction going forward rather than find ourselves confronted with anything untoward happening that could have been avoided. First, although the latest storm has passed, it will be a while before some structure and services are restored, especially the supply of food. Some stores will hopefully open but will only have whatever is still on their shelves. We have no idea when and how any fresh supplies will reach Toronto and other devastated towns and cities. The next problem will be desperate people turning to theft, breaking and entering, pillaging and looting to survive. How many of the senior authorities in the city have died? The police and other essential services may be leaderless for a while. I do not want to frighten people or be some harbinger of doom. But Don and I have considered some of these scenarios to try and be prepared for them. The provisions list we handed out were based on repeats of these storms occurring during a winter. If you stocked up as recommended, you should see through an extended winter although meals may become quite boring, based on dry goods, canned and frozen food.

"After the challenge of replenishing provisions, the next matter I would like to discuss is whether or who should volunteer to go out and assist people. This runs various risks of being assaulted by marauding bands if law enforcement has collapsed. If we find people in trouble and assist them, we will deplete our precious supplies. Will we feel compelled to give a safe haven to such people, which means we could soon have many refugees in our houses, and they will quickly consume our provisions. This point requires a hard decision. If we exhaust our supplies, some of us will not survive the winter, which defeats the purpose of having prepared to save ourselves."

Mary had been itching to speak and expressed her sentiments on the subjects raised by Fran. "Our stocks are based on seeing two or more people with children through the winter, but not with any additional, unforeseen boarders. As Fran said, if we use all our supplies, we will not survive the winter. Helping others has been our credo and I feel represents the Christian values of our country. If there is a high risk, we will be endangered. I am no hero looking for a medal for dying like a martyr. This may sound selfish but at my age, I fear reckless bravado. Finally, I am also scared of an incursion by intruders looking for food and shelter who would be sufficiently desperate to injure or kill the owners and even commandeer their home. I therefore feel we should sit tight and set up some sort of vigilance of Delaney Street plus a quick response team in the event of anyone being attacked. We chose to ensure our survival in the event of this ice age scenario and there was plenty of public discussion and information debating it over the last few years. Others cannot say they knew nothing about it even if they chose to ignore this possibility. This is the same pattern that led up to the Corona virus pandemic where there were many movies, reports and discussions about a possible virus attack on the world long before the outbreak. People did nothing to prepare for that virus incident and again now, when the possibility of an ice age became increasingly apparent, few people did anything. We took proactive action and therefore found ourselves in a safe position. It would be stupid if we then got ourselves injured or killed after the storms by being excessively zealous good Samaritans and lose what we built up to survive. What do others feel?"

Sybil responded. "We are all compassionate people who consider others. But whenever we may have been altruistic in the past, they were not life or death situations whereby in helping others, we would be jeopardizing our own lives. We are all here having planned to survive an ice age onslaught, so I am not going to feel guilty and endanger my family's lives. I am not being callous and am fearful of the scenarios described by Fran. I sense many, if not all of you feel the same."

After a protracted, uncomfortable silence, Fran spoke again. "With no one contradicting Sybil or Mary, let us assume the consensus is that everyone wishes to survive and not take unnecessary risks, however guilty it may make us feel. I am now the mother of children and have been wondering how wise it was to bring children into this apocalyptic world. And we have only just begun the ice age. Where it may go for all of us, I shudder to think. I do not want to turn this meeting into something depressing, which it easily could become. Rather let us count our blessings and do some practical planning. Don?"

"Upping our level of security must be our first priority. You all know the TV monitoring systems we installed. Now we must start using it constantly for what it was designed. Our communication system between houses must always be on in case we urgently need to call for help or hear anyone else calling. As CCTV cameras can be monitored by everyone, I will compile a roster, to ensure someone is always watching, looking for any suspicious people entering the area. I hesitate to say this, but we should all keep a firearm handy and not inaccessible in our firearm safes. Those that joined a shooting range to obtain a handgun license should always carry them other than when we are locked down in a vortex storm when no one is about. I will set up a chart describing how to respond to various scenarios when on monitoring duty if there are incursions; if anyone is seen breaking

186

into a home; forced entry into your own home; and how to respond when called to help. The purpose of this meeting was to decide what we should do going forward considering the dangerous position we are now in to survive with our resources that will tempt others. Since we have decided to remain locked in and need to protect our position, they are appropriate strategies to defend ourselves and our homes. Any additional comments, suggestions, points to debate?"

After a few moments of silence, Don continued "Well it looks like we have consensus and will implement this immediately. Fran, please man the monitor for the next few hours during which time I will compile the roster, get the show on the road and feed the boys. Thanks everyone. These are difficult times and could become more troubling as winter continues. I am both pleased and relieved that we are a cohesive unit with the same survival objective, which makes it simpler to go forward together with everyone pulling in the same direction."

Chapter 21 COMPASSION

Shortly before the third and last polar vortex storm of the winter, a call came in at about 6 a.m. from Lucas who was on monitoring duty. He called over the radio "Lucas to Don and everyone else. Two suspicious individuals scrutinizing the houses. Please be on maximum alert. They are checking out each house as they slowly move down the street. Their intent is obvious." In the homes monitoring any transmission, there was a flurry of activity as those who were not carrying a sidearm quickly went to retrieve a handgun, rifle or shotgun, depending on what they had or preferred. Most without handguns who had a choice took their shotguns.

Don quickly broadcast "The two men on back-up standby, be ready to move into the tunnel and proceed to whichever house may be intruded. I am getting ready to join you."

After about four minutes during which time the response team were quickly donning their freezing weather gear, Lucas's voice came in over the radio. "Looks like they are planning to enter Evan's house.

Don replied "Okay, we are on our way. Lucas keep feeding us the moment-to-moment movement of these guys that you see on your screen."

Lucas's voice continued over the radio. "They are going to the front door. Damn! Looks like they are trying to break into Evan's house."

Don "We are entering Evan's basement from the tunnel. Evan and Lily, go upstairs and lock yourselves in the bedroom. By coming up from the basement, we should surprise them. I hope you have left the basement door into the house open as per our protocol."

A frightened Evan replied "Yes, it is open. We are going upstairs with my shotgun and I will lock the bedroom door."

Don said "Keep away from the door in case they get to it before we do and try to shoot through the lock. But we have arrived and are going in."

With James and Mason who were the men on the roster scheduled to respond to any incursion or emergency call, Don went in from the tunnel, crossed the basement to the stairs and went up. At the door into the ground floor of the house, he opened it carefully having indicated to his support team to remain at the bottom of the stairs in case bullets started flying. The intruders seemed to be unarmed as they were still fiddling with the lock from the outside.

Don thought: Should we merely open the door showing our arms and tell them to depart or be arrested? Or wait for them to break in and arrest them? I feel we must take a more compassionate approach. I just hope they are not armed as the door suddenly opening may make them pull triggers in a panic reflex. If I announce that the door is about to be opened, at least they will know it is about to happen and not be surprised.

Don shouted "Stand back. I am opening the door." The two men adopted an aggressive stance but when they saw three armed men, their resolve instantly dissipated. Don said "Bad choice guys. I am a policeman. But I do understand that we are all struggling to survive. I am therefore going to assume you are not habitual criminals and are merely trying to stay alive. What's your story?"

The one man answered hesitantly with his eyes welling up with tears. "My daughter is close to dying as she is starving to death. The rest of us are not far behind her. I did not know what else to do. All the phone lines to any possible authorities that may have been able to help us are dead or are not being answered. We are desperate. Please help us."

Don had this wave of compassion pass over him feeling terribly sad for them. "Okay, I was correct in thinking that you were desperate. We are going to organize some provisions for you, but as a once off as we have limited stocks and also need to survive. I am sorry but it is the best we can do." Half turning to his support pair he said "Radio and tell Evan that the place is secure. Everyone in the street will be monitoring so it will reassure them too. Ask for any food donations so we can give these guys some provisions considering their plight. I am bringing them inside for hot drinks and some food while we collect any donated provisions." Turning to the two men he asked "Are you able to use a cellphone to call home? I would like you to say you have found some people who are giving you some food and will be coming home. I am sure they are also worried and waiting on either a call or your return."

"Thank you, sir. Thank you" said the man in front. Everyone is desperate and your generosity in these terrible times is incongruous with what most survivors are prepared to do."

Don ushered them in repeating his statement that "I did not think you were criminals, rather desperately trying to survive. Seems I was right, but again whatever help you receive now cannot be repeated as we have limited rations to survive on. What are your names?"

"I am Bill Wheatley and this is my brother-in-law David Saunders."

"I am Don Whitely; these are James and Mason. Here comes Evan and Lily down the stairs whose house this is. What do you do?"

"I am an English high school teacher. David is an accountant. You are … a policeman?"

"Well just a reservist. I am an engineer as is my father and we designed these specialized houses here."

"That is why we chose this street" said Bill. "Your concept was originally considered unrealistic by most people with the global warming trend and constant warnings about the planet overheating. There were a few projections indicating it would tip into an ice age and most people thought you were all making a foolish investment. Now look at who has survived and how it has reduced honest citizens like us into criminals." Bill sat down, buried his head in his hands and started sobbing.

David moved next to Bill, placed a comforting hand on his shoulder and turning towards Don said. "Bill feels he has let his family down and is terrified at the thought of losing them, especially my niece, his young daughter. We are all scared. You must know how desperate we must be to try and steal food. Who would have thought we would be reduced to this? I cannot thank you enough for your understanding and generosity."

Bill found his voice feeling the need to endorse David's words. "Yes, thank you again for having such a kind and understanding, humanitarian attitude towards us when your own survival is paramount. Whatever you kindly donate will bring us a short reprieve. And then …?" He became too emotional again to continue for a few moments. Everyone waited patiently, then he went on. "Even if we embraced your belief of an imminent ice age, we could not have afforded one of these expensive homes. Teachers earn modestly but perhaps David could have."

Don said "For that reason, we had entry level houses that did not have all the survival equipment and systems initially installed. They were then added slowly over time according to one's budget. About forty percent of our homes were bought and retrofitted over a period of a few years at whatever rate each owner could afford. We were therefore sensitive to this barrier, but it did require a person to share our belief and make the commitment to investing in a survival home."

Chapter 22   FREEZING TO DEATH

People were arriving in Evan's house with their donations and were curious about who they were, why they had come, and what it was like outside their neighborhood. It was also an opportunity to be with their neighbors and socialize. Fran arrived and first stared at the two men trying to obtain a reasonable first impression.

Fran thought: They do not look like regular thieves, whatever that stereotype may be. The older one seems to have a cheap Walmart jacket, worn pants and old boots. The younger one is better dressed. The radio message said Evan's house is secure with a request for any donation of provisions. Has Don gone all soft again on possible criminals? Seems any conjecture in reading the situation is pointless so let me just ask them.

Fran said, "I am Fran, Don's wife, and you are?"

"I am Bill and my brother-in-law David."

"I gather you are in trouble, which is what brought you here. Please tell us what has been happening out there."

As the older and therefore more senior one, Bill answered. "When the first Polar Vortex storm hit with such vicious and merciless cold, we struggled to maintain warmth in the house as it was never designed to withstand an additional thirty degrees colder than our worst winters. We ended up in our bedroom most of the time so only one room had to be kept warm and only left it to use the bathroom and kitchen. Our water supply soon failed with the pipes first freezing and then rupturing even though we left the faucets dripping. We could chop out some ice to melt and drink, but the toilet became a problem. We did not have water to flush them and the sewerage pipe froze, blocking the inlet and outlet. In the end we resorted to plastic bags that were thrown out to freeze. Fortunately, our gas supply continued to work but our electricity failed after three weeks into the first storm. When it finally subsided, David and I went out to try and find provisions, fuel as back-up and luckily we found a wood stove and pipes to fashion a temporary chimney."

David continued to describe their ordeal. "I live two houses away from Bill, but it could have been on the other side of the planet because we were locked down by the storm. After the storm I therefore moved into Bill's home so we could share resources and I would not be isolated. I also brought things like dining room chairs to burn. We were better prepared for the second blizzard and that is when the gas supply failed. Luckily, it was towards the end of the vortex storm and we had the wood burning stove. We had a makeshift chimney rising inside before bending out of the top of a window to obtain as much heat as possible. It was grossly inadequate but kept us alive in a room that we could barely warm above freezing point. After the second storm ended, we were unable to find provisions as most shops had been unable to restock after the first storm. There were branches, broken by the weight of snow and intense winds so we were able to replenish some of our wood."

David paused, thinking about one or other of their horrors they had experienced. Lily arrived with two mugs of steaming coffee, milk and sugar on the side, a pile of cookies and two slices of cake. They could see the voracious hunger in their eyes but Bill said, "We will each eat a biscuit but do you mind if we wrap the rest of this luxurious treat in a paper napkin to take home?" Eyes started watering and Lily nodded affirmatively, also feeling quite choked up and unable to speak.

Fran started in a croaky voice, "Bill, how old is your daughter?"

"She is eight."

"Does she have adequate clothes for the extreme cold?"

"We were all cold. Freezing!"

"I am going to bring you one of my boy's parkas that he has grown out of. It may not fit perfectly but will still be additional insulation against the cold" said Fran. "Please do not leave before I return from my house."

Quite bereft, Bill said "You are all too kind. I feel guilty that we tried to rob Evan's house and wonder how much worse this is going to get before either our lives or winter is over. And what will be left of our society?"

Fran descended into the basement to run home down the tunnel while the two men turned to look at their gifts. A pile of various foods had been placed on the coffee table that included rice, canned Vienna sausages, some tins of tuna and sardines, a box of cookies, a packet of polenta and other treasures for the men to take home. Bill and David got up after gulping down their coffee, opened their backpacks and started filling them. Don said "I am concerned that you may be attacked, and your bags stolen. How do you plan to get home safely? How far away are you?

David answered, "We are about three kilometers away and as it will be dark soon, perhaps we should wait until after sunset?"

Don replied, "That may help. Ideally you should take half now and do two trips to minimize any loss if anything is taken from you. Also, perhaps you should walk separately. The one behind could then drop his bag if he sees trouble ahead and run forward to help. It is best to plan ahead to minimize the downside and hopefully maintain an upside."

Bill shrugged his shoulders. "I do not think we want to come this far in the cold again to collect the balance of what everyone has kindly donated.

We did not appreciate the distance and it was quite grueling considering how undernourished we are. But we could walk apart although together it would look more formidable if a single person wants to accost one us. What do you think David?"

"If we are too far apart in the dark, the one behind may not see the one in front. If we are too close together, it defeats the purpose of being split up. "

Don suggested "You should walk apart and vary the distance according to the terrain and if any streetlights are working. Just be flexible and careful. Perhaps you should use side streets?"

"Side streets may not have stalkers waiting for prey" said David. "But opportunists who do not live on a main road may just happen to be walking there when we pass through. With less chance of being seen on a quiet road, they may feel more comfortable in confronting whoever is in front. There are pros and cons for every option being considered."

Bill made the final decision. "We will stick to the main roads to make the trip shorter. Keep some distance apart but the one in front must periodically wait for the follower to catch up. Constantly checking each other are okay. David, would you like to go in front being younger, taller and stronger?"

"I suppose" said David. "I think I will put the tinned foods in the inside pockets under my parka in case the backpacks are taken so we still reach home with something."

Fran had returned with the parka for Bill's daughter and the two men packed away their precious gifts in pockets and backpacks. They profusely thanked everyone again and said their goodbyes. For a few moments there was silence after they had left until Fran broke the silence. "When we spoke about helping people, it was merely an intellectual debate. But meeting suffering people firsthand has much more emotional impact. I feel terribly sorry for these two men and their families. I am pleased we did something albeit only enough for a short respite."

"Yes, the reality of suffering" said Sybil, "is so much more vivid than we can imagine even if poets try to express it emotively in words."

That night when they climbed into bed, before turning off her bedside lamp, Fran asked Don "With a background as an enforcer of the law and a practitioner of martial arts, you can be so compassionate and generous. The opposite of the tough stance of the police to uphold the law versus being understanding and lenient is somewhat incongruous and are perhaps incompatible beliefs. How do you reconcile these opposing stances?"

Don first pondered Fran's question. "I have not thought about it that way before now, so I am just going to let my thoughts flow. The subject of punishment is a complex one and something I am personally not cut out for. I am too soft to mete out extreme punishments that judges must make. For the same reason I would like to think I am too passive to be able to perpetrate the terrible deeds some people do. As I feel our prison system is not adequately structured for rehabilitation, my knee-jerk response is not to try and arrest someone without a better understanding of their motivations. Prison is generally not a constructive place to enable people to understand the driving forces that may have possessed them to perform some appalling deed. I am sure that only a few prisoners who may have committed a once-off act can be taught through therapy to understand their motivations and how many have the luxury of such intense rehabilitation once locked up? They may not intrinsically be criminals who then become subverted within jail and eventually become corrupted by the time they are released. These ex-cons may then be more dangerous to society than perhaps they were

197

when initially incarcerated. If I feel people like Bill and David are desperately trying to survive, I cannot view them as criminals and treat them that way."

After another moment of thoughtful silence Fran said "You know the Biblical *eye for an eye* is not literal as the remedy is monetary compensation for whatever income losses an injured person may sustain through a loss of ability to continue their work. Examples include the loss of an eye of a scribe or the limb of a farmer. These people must be compensated financially for whatever their compromised ability to earn a living becomes after healing from an inflicted injury. But I feel *a tooth for a tooth* does have an appeal in certain instances as it suggests that someone who commits some heinous deed should at least be subjected to an equivalent punishment if not more to learn a lesson and ensure fair justice is upheld."

Don said "Both arguments have merit. I suppose Western prisons are substantially better than they were a hundred and a thousand years ago and hopefully continue to improve as our understanding of human behavior advances. But I suspect we still have a long way to go before detention in prison becomes a constructive opportunity to gain control over one's aberrant behavior."

Fran snuggled up to Don and said "I am pleased and relieved you first gave Bill and David an opportunity to explain their desperate position. Everyone's generosity in helping them shows how we were all touched by their distressing circumstances as no one thought of them as villains needing to be locked up. Your appropriate response to their attempted breaking and entering is just another reason why I love you so much, my tough but thoughtful and compassionate husband."

Chapter 23　FIRST SUMMER

*The winter may pass
and the spring disappear.
But I know for certain
you will come back again,
and even as I promised,
you will find me waiting then.*
**- Composer Edvard Grieg
Solveig's Song**

Since spring arrived late, the paltry summer would only be a time of mediocre recovery. Traditionally it was when life would be renewed after slumbering through winter. But winter was no longer merely a hibernation. It was a death. A demise of the old paradigm. Life as one knew, would never blossom the same way again as the days struggled to warm. The icy ice age bite would barely open its powerful jaws to permit any heat to permeate the country, the continent, and the world.

The mortality devastation of minus fifty degrees left many families dead in their homes. Authorities were denuded of numerous senior staff. The inexperienced juniors who were drawn into the vacuum created by the extreme winter toll struggled to manage the services of their respective departments. But the biggest challenge was what to do with the enormous number of dead who had not survived the winter.

Companies whose owners and workers survived tried to revive their trade but stocks were hard to come by. There was a desperate attempt to find suppliers in those parts of the United States that had not been hit by the Polar Vortex storms to supply food, groceries, medical and other essential products. However, American allegiances were first to their own citizens before considering Canadians.

No one knew how extensive the problem was. Some TV stations started up again but only stations using satellites could transmit as land-based transmitters' cables to them or their electricity supply had been damaged. Don and Fran's group were glued to their TV's, thankful every day for their resilient houses but concerned about the collapse of services. They were extremely worried about how they were going to replenish their stocks before the next ice age winter descended, possibly with even more fury as the world slipped deeper into this new climate catastrophe.

The group had agreed that every day, in groups of two men, they would drive off to forage for food, fuel and other items on a list of items requiring replenishment or things needed for maintenance. During one of the regular meetings to check their procurement progress, Evan said we are now in that post-apocalyptic period aptly described by Russian President Nikita Khrushchev in 1979 when `the survivors would envy the dead.' "

Mary said "Yes Evan, no one can dispute that thought but it is not a place we can afford to go to. Please do not put such depressing and pessimistic thoughts on the table since it contributes nothing towards us maintaining some semblance of essential optimism. As a group, we need to survive what has descended upon us by remaining in an appropriate frame of mind to cope with the challenges we now face in a dramatically changed world."

Across the city and the country, spring was frenetically spent by people trying to retrofit their houses with additional insulation. Depending on what they could buy, scavenge, or cannibalize from empty homes where all the occupants had died, many makeshift panels were screwed or hammered onto walls on either the inside or outside of their homes. Some windows were also closed off, especially single glazed glass that had resulted in enormous heat loss. Authorities turned a blind eye to the scavenging of houses where all the occupants had died, accepting that insulating survivors' houses was essential to reduce the number of deaths during the next winter. TV programs covered DIY techniques to install panels, boards and whatever else innovative people had managed to scrounge. The city's housing soon looked like patchwork quilts with various rectangles attached to the sides of homes. Apartments were lined on the inside with panels even if they were merely pushed up against an outer wall like a vertical carpet. Those that could, would bolt in or try to use a film of adhesive to fix the panels to walls. There was a run on carpets to provide more floor insulation. Storage tanks for more oil and additional gas cylinders were purchased and installed by those who could afford it, if they were fortunate to find anyone with stock. With the high mortality rate, many businesses collapsed, leaving people out of work. But those that were trying to re-commence operation were hiring replacements of lost staff, offering job opportunities to unemployed people whose organizations no longer existed. In some instances, staff tried to keep existing businesses going where the owners had died.

The United States had its northeast quadrant hammered by the Polar Vortex storms. The rest of the country had a winter that was considered intensely cold but not as extreme. After satisfying local needs, eventually America was able to export vital goods to Canada including food thereby relieving some of the shortages.

TV talk shows aired comparisons between the effect of the sudden ice age to the impact of the Covid-19 virus on the economy, if any comparisons were possible. The other topical subject was why most climatologists missed how global warming could tip the earth into an ice age and why the few who did warn people were ignored. One comment circulating was that as an autopsy on a dead body can be a waste of time. Rather focus on how to heal the sick and stay alive.

Those of the authorities that had survived tried to prioritize what was needed to prepare for the next winter. The dead were found by going from house to house or apartment to apartment. The gruesome findings had to be buried in mass graves. They tried to keep records of unidentifiable bodies found by listing what was on record at a particular address. There was no time or resources for people to interrogate neighbors for names, especially as they may have also frozen to death.

The worst hit areas of both Canada and the United States were the central to eastern sides of the continent. Unfortunately, the west side of the continent was not much of a breadbasket and the historical areas of major crops that were decimated were not resuscitated during the pathetic summer. Both countries were therefore under pressure to find adequate food for their populations, as were parts of Europe and Russia. As Don and Fran had discussed, these governments sought Third World suppliers who were limited in their ability to ramp up their agricultural output adequately to satisfy this sudden, massive demand.

Many farmers did not survive the storms and the summer was both shorter and colder than average. A one-degree Celsius change in average seasonal temperatures is enough to disrupt the yields of traditional crops, which is what happened. Some published figures stated that wheat crops would decline by 6% for a 1^0C change in average seasonal temperature. With everyone only considering global warming, yield reductions due to falling temperatures were never considered. Irrespective of the actual quantity, these figures were still indicative of the magnitude of possible yield changes. Rice was 3.2% per degree, corn 7.4% and soya 3.1%. This summer, average temperatures were nearly ten degrees colder than anything in recorded history. Despite the colder, shorter season, farmers managed to grow some crops. As the enormous mortality rate reduced the number of people in North America, less food was needed. The collapse in infrastructure meant that there was limited data, so statistics were virtually impossible to compile. Towards the end of summer when more food and groceries became available, fortunately everyone in Delaney Street were able to stock themselves with sufficient provisions for the next winter. Whatever surpluses they could find were bought fearing that in subsequent years, finding goods would become increasingly difficult. Don and Jake also bought many hardware items anticipating increasing shortages of basics needed for repairs and maintenance.

Chapter 24   A SECOND WINTER'S TALE

As the poor hint of summer progressed, a semblance of normality returned. The boys went to school and played with friends. Don and the other men performed maintenance and modifications to their homes based on the experience of the horrendous winter. Understandably, *nIce Age* had more orders than they could fulfil. The lucky customers were ones who had their names down before the ice age struck and the company struggled to complete the houses before the next winter. Some of the contractors had died and various materials were not available. Still, eleven new houses were built during the short period of that was more clement winter weather than a summer. The number was almost trivial compared to the dire need but it still represented eleven fortunate families who would survive the next winter comfortably.

With time, during the calendar indication that it should be of summer when it remained wintry cold, many businesses were slowly resuscitated so more basics became available and farms grew some crops so there was fresh produce in those shops that had re-opened. Those canicular days of summer were now extinct and the early advent of winter was viewed by Fran with trepidation. Within the group she felt reassured that their homes and support systems would enable them to survive another extreme winter. But entering the long, tunnel of darkness with its banshee storms was a depressing anticipation. Fran decided to replace photographs hanging on the walls of winter scenes where the family may have been playing in the snow or landscape shots of the Canadian Rockies covered in snow. These were replaced with summer pictures of wildlife from Kenya and their Masai as well as the Lake of the Woods trip. But no pictures of the dead bear with the boys next to its carcass feeling it would be tasteless and insensitive. Fran wondered whether they would ever experience such hot weather again and although a depressing thought, she much preferred the bright warmth of the scenes to the depressingly cold ones she had removed. Fran constantly asked Don questions such as:

"What do we do if someone requires urgent medical attention during one of the long storms as we cannot get them to a hospital," or

"I am concerned that although survivors have added additional insulation to their dwellings, will it be adequate?"

or

"The deaths of more of the population would further reduce the country's ability to recover the impact of these devasting blizzards."

One evening as the sun was setting earlier and earlier with the encroaching winter, Fran's gloom increased, and she admitted to Don "I am anticipating being confined to our home for even more severe snowstorms bouts than last year's with serious claustrophobic angst. Winter is no longer just another season but a gauntlet being run with death the result of not successfully completing the challenge. Life has changed far more than during the Corona virus period during 2020 to 2021 when the whole world had felt the devasting effects of widespread death and living under lockdown. As usual, I am so worried about what kind of a world into which we have brought our children. I wrote this down yesterday when trying to elevate my spirits. This technique has helped me in the past, but its content shows what I really am feeling." Fran handed a piece of paper to Don who read it.

Time is a capricious partner.
When we are impatient, it develops leaden boots.
But if we want a moment to last forever,
time accelerates, rushing to end it.

The ever-pragmatic engineer tried to reassure his anxious wife by expanding her perspective about the melancholy situations she had described. "Chaucer wrote 'Time and tide wait for no man.' Even he felt what you described about the relentless movement of time. If you excuse the pun, we all do at *times* in our lives. Regarding the imminent winter, I have seen people emigrate from hot to cold climates or cold to hot climates. Invariably they miss their roots including the heat or cold no matter how long they have lived in an opposite climate. Our boys know what they are being exposed to and this becomes their norm. It is not your childhood experience of winter and you, no we, are baulking at the new extreme. Do not see it through your eyes but through theirs. They will not have a childhood with as much skating, skiing, tobogganing, ice hockey and other winter sports as we did growing up. This will be how they expect winters to be. Remember there are people living deep within the arctic circle in North America, Northern Europe, and Asia. Siberians never have the milder winters we enjoyed and are now pining for. The boys will expect winters to be this way."

"Maybe" replied Fran. "But we know life can be different and perhaps we need to think about moving. Not to Kenya but further south on this continent. And if we do decide to move, it needs to be this coming summer as I would not like to delay setting up a new life in a more temperate climate more than necessary."

Winter's icy hold clamped itself on the country. But it was the next breakaway polar vortex that strangled the land. Even in daylight hours it was dark as night. Once again the relentless screech of the wind unsettled everyone as the houses were buffeted by the storm. After the noise of the previous winter's storms, Fran had bought foam earplugs for everyone, but they ameliorated the audio invasion insufficiently to bring any semblance of real relief. They took to wearing Bluetooth headphones that also reduced the ghoulish howl of the storm and laid pleasing music over the blaring blizzard's bellowing roar. Energy-saving lights were left on to reduce the dismal gloom of the inexorable days as dark as night. Fran and Don were challenged to maintain their spirits so they could lift the depression into which their boys could easily descend. They had a roster with regular activities to ensure a routine was adhered to, keeping everyone busy. The generic daily list, which would have specifics inserted at the beginning of each week covered various subjects:

- Breakfast 9:00 to 9:45 am
    - Preparation
    - Eat
    - Clean-up
- School work until 12:00 pm
- Exercise 12:00 to 1:00 pm
- Lunch 1:00 to 2:00 pm
    - Preparation
    - Eat
    - Clean-up
- Kids' schoolwork until 3:00 pm
  Adults' admin to 3:00 pm

- 3:00 to 4 :00 pm
  - o Boys TV
  - o Fran more admin
  - o Don maintenance
- School work from 4:00 to 6:00 pm
- Supper 6:00 to 7:00 pm
  - o Preparation
  - o Eat
  - o Clean-up
- Family games, TV, other. 7:00 to 8:30 pm
- Boys quiet time 8:30 to 9:00 pm
  - o Shower, etc.
  - o Bed – read 30 mins

With this routine, a sense of normalcy prevailed during an insane time giving the family some feeling of security and daily purpose. Once the boys had gone to sleep, friends and parents would occasionally visit if they had an appetite to walk down the tunnel that had proved to be an unbelievable asset.

The panic call came in at 11:17 am from Gabriella that Enrique was trapped outside. There had been a lull in the storm, perhaps like the eye of a hurricane. "Enrique is locked out. Help! He went out to fix an antenna or satellite dish when the storm subsided. But snow slid off the roof over the front door and he never took a spade. I cannot even open the door, which is frozen shut. And the wind is picking up again. Please hurry."

Fran grabbed the two-way radio as she heard the word 'Help!' and shouted "Emergency!" to Don as she held the instrument to her ear so she would not miss any details.

Don was running down the stairs "What's happened."

"Kit up. Enrique's locked out his house." Don ran passed her to the front entrance where his survival gear was ready for emergencies and started pulling on his thick artic clothing. Fran opened a trunk next to Don and pulled out a rope with harness. "If you have to go out, you are going to wear this" she said adamantly. She knew it would be futile to suggest Don ask for a volunteer to go outside in his stead. His commitment to helping or saving people even if it meant risking his own life, dictated his behavior in such situations. It was not that he did not deeply love his family and Fran knew this. She had the two-way radio headphones in her hand to pass him with the wire back to the set in an inner pocket, left there to already be in place for an emergency. He was about to pull on a Balaklava and Fran said sternly "Wait!" as she reached up to place the headphone around his head. Don bent down so she could reach while she quickly positioned it. "Just keep up a steady stream of talking so I know what is happening."

Don nodded and said, "I need to go out the Hernandez' house next door if Enrique's door is already blocked with snow." He was now pulling on his boots. "Radio to see if Miguel thinks I can get out through his front door and that their tunnel access is clear for me."

Gabriella's terrified voice came in over the radio. "Please hurry. What is happening. Who is doing what?"

Fran replied "Don has been kitting up. Miguel, can Don go out through your front door?" After a few moments of silence, she called again. "Miguel, Beatriz, are you receiving me? Can Don go out through either of your front door?"

"It's Miguel Fran. Sorry I ran to the door to see if Don could get out and yes he can. I am going down to the basement to open up for him."

Anxiously Fran called back. "Don will have a harness with security rope. You must play it out and manage it. You must get into your gear too as you will be at your open door. Please look after him."

"Of course. I am running back upstairs now and will dress up immediately. Anyone else nearby who can assist in case we have to try and pull back two people. I will then need extra muscle?"

Oliver replied. "Kitting up now and will be their asap."

The storm was picking up fast and there was no visibility through the windows. Suddenly Fran said "Don, I am going to get your infrared binoculars and see if I can get heat readings from your and Enrique's bodies through a side window in the Hernandez house. Gabriella, did Enrique take a radio with him by any chance."

"Yes" she called back. "But not the headphone with mic and earpiece. He just ran an earpiece to his ear and if conscious, should have heard all these transmissions."

"Enrique, this is Don. I am on my way and hope to be outside in about three minutes. If you can, move to the lee side in front of Miguel's house. Getting close to the stairs up to their front door will give you marginally more protection and I will know where to first look for you. If you do not know which direction to go, stay where you are."

Before stepping out into the roaring storm, Don thought: Why am I always the one to volunteer? This must be the last time. I cannot believe the force of the storm. I cannot see a thing. What if I cannot find him? If I trip will I be able to get up? Will I be able to get Enrique up and then back to the house? How did I get myself into this situation? Again!

Miguel had closed off the inside door to the entrance area and pulled on the front door to confirm it would open. The strength of the blast that came in took him by surprise but after the initial surge, it was bearable. He closed it and waited for Don who arrived about a half minute later. He handed Miguel the coiled rope attached to his shoulder harness then nodded at Miguel who opened the door again allowing another blast to fill the entrance hall with more, swirling snow. He pointed to the rope and over the radio said "Miguel, tie the end so it is secured in case it gets whipped out your hands by the wind."

Meanwhile Fran had put on her artic survival gear to go into the tunnel across to the Hernandez house. She had called Sean to bring down the infrared binoculars from Don's study upstairs and left a radio on for the boys to monitor, knowing they would be anxious and in case they needed to communicate anything. Fran went down to the basement to enter the tunnel. She had put on her headphones to be able to talk hands-free and called Beatriz. "I am on my way to you. Meet me at the entrance to your basement to take me quickly to your side window overlooking the front of the Rodriguez' house."

"Copy" said Beatriz.

They were soon running up the stairs with Fran pulling down her goggles then pulling off her hood so she could use the infrared binoculars. Fran powered them on and peered into the darkness praying the storm was not too thick to allow infrared rays from their body heat to reach her. "Bingo!" she said. "Don I can see your outline. You are just at the edge of

211

the house. Go right about five degrees or you will hit their stairs." She swept the glasses around looking for Enrique.

"Can you see him?" asked Don. I asked him to try and get to the lee side of the stairs for some wind protection."

"No!" said Fran. "I hope he is not on the other side of the house where the satellite dish is mounted. I should have rather gone the extra distance to William's house on the other side as it looks onto that side of the Hernandez house. Do you have any visibility?"

"Not really. I am shuffling forward by feel."

"Damn. I better rush around to … no, I see him. There must be a gap in the storm. He is lying about five meters from the stairs straight out towards the road. Move about forty-five degrees to your right. … A little more to your right. You must be only four or five paces from him now. Stop! Don't fall over him. Feel with your foot."

"Don inched forward pushing his boot out cautiously. "Found him."

"Thank God" said Beatriz quietly behind Fran as she crossed herself.

"Yes, but Don still has to get Enrique back inside, so it is far from over" responded Fran's concerned voice. "Don are you able to get Enrique up?"

"No, I think he must have tripped or been blown over by a gust and may have concussed himself when he landed on one of the rocks surrounding their flower bed. I will have to try and carry him."

"I am coming out to help" radioed Miguel. Oliver and Robert have arrived to help with the rope so I can leave my station. I will follow the rope to you. Fran keep an eye out for me too."

Fran radioed "You need to loosely tie yourself to the line Miguel so you do not get separated."

"Good idea Fran" said Robert. I am tying a short line around Miguel with a loop at the other end around Don's rope."

Miguel was shocked by the vicious force of the wind that threatened to push him over. He was smaller than Don and not as strong, but his determination to help his friend Enrique gave him the additional fortitude he needed to continue against the hostile elements. Their parents had immigrated from Brazil when they were nine years old and the pair had grown up together in the Toronto suburb of Downsview-Roding where many Hispanics lived. The boys had gone through school together and were inseparable. While their interests in most things were similar, fortunately their taste in girls was completely different so there was never any social conflict over girlfriends. Moving into the nIce Age development was a joint decision by the friends as much as by their wives. And Miguel was not about to lose his best friend Enrique who he considered more of a brother. "Fran, if you can see me, tell me how far I am, especially as I get close. I cannot see my hand in front of my face as this ice soup is so thick and I don't want to bump into Don or fall over them."

"You are about halfway" said Fran. "At least you have the rope to guide you directly to them. The infrared binocs are not that clear but Don, it looks like you have lifted up Enrique."

"Yes, he is across my shoulders in a fireman's lift. But I feel most unsteady being buffeted hard by the wind. Miguel you can stabilize me rather than try to help carry him. In this storm I don't see how we can share the load by carrying Enrique together."

Fran gasped while looking through the infrared binoculars. She covered the microphone with her finger and said to Beatriz "Don's fallen. Enrique is lying across his back and the image looks like a cross. He must be winded as he is neither moving nor talking." She then radioed "Miguel, Don has fallen, probably pushed over by the wind and I think he has been winded as he is not talking. You are now about three paces from Don and should feel the rope going down towards the ground. Roll Enrique off his back so he can get his breath back."

"Copy that. I am at Don. Feeling which way Enrique is lying. *Mia madre* this storm is thicker than pea soup. Okay I am sliding him sideways to lie next to Don. Don, if you are okay just squeeze my hand." After a few moments Miguel reported "Fran he squeezed."

Fran gave an audible sigh of relief and the tension of everyone monitoring the radio transmissions abated marginally. Don's rasping voice came in. "I'm alright. Was pushed over. Yes, winded but my diaphragm is finally relaxing. Miguel, help me up and then I will lift Enrique back up across my shoulders. You will need to support me against this blast."

Fran radioed "Miguel, go to Don's right side since that is the direction from which the wind is pushing him. Don, if he holds your right upper arm to support you, would that be best?"

"Yes, Miguel, lock your left arm through mine and with your right, feel the rope so we head in the right direction. Robert and Oliver, don't pull hard or I will fall over again. Just pull it in slowly at the rate we approach you so we can use the mild tension as a guide back to your stairs."

With Don carrying Enrique and Miguel helping him, they made their way slowly through the blizzard towards the house. Don said "Miguel, I counted forty-seven steps when I went out to Enrique and have counted forty-three now. You need to feel for the stairs before we fall onto them. The rope angle should be getting steeper as we approach the front door. From where Fran is upstairs on the other side, she can no longer see us and warn when we reach the steps."

Miguel found the bottom step by sliding each foot slowly forward. "Here is the bottom step Don. Can you get up the stairs with Enrique's weight. Maybe we can swing him off your shoulders and each take an arm between us."

"Too dangerous and the steps are not wide enough for three people abreast. Go behind me and push me gently on my lower back as I go up each step."

"We are coming out" announced Robert and reached Don when he was about three steps from the top. Oliver linked his arm into Don's one armpit to give him more lift and he reached the top stair quite exhausted from carrying and struggling against the pressure of the wind threatening to push him over. Between his three helpers, Enrique was lifted off his back and carried inside.

Everyone started converging on Miguel and Beatriz's house and as Fran ran downstairs, she suddenly called over the radio "Please everyone, do not come now to the Hernandez house as we need to focus on Enrique and not have a melee of well meant, concerned people in the way. Gabriel you must obviously come."

"I am already in Beatriz's basement running across to the stairs." Gabriel radioed back.

Fran spoke again into the two-way radio "We are waiting outside the lobby's inner door until you are all inside as five men will fill it leaving no more space. Please obviously bring Enrique straight into the lounge as soon as you can close the outer door."

Someone grunted a "Yes, of course" over the radio. But the men had already carried Enrique into the lobby and were closing the outside door against the wind so they could open the inner door. The inside door swung open and Enrique was quickly carried into the lounge. Miguel was still in the lobby scooping up snow that had blown in, into a bin before it all melted, and Don was pulling off his gloves and goggles so he could unbuckle the harness that he had not thought about using and would never have managed without. He reminded himself to praise his beloved wife who once again showed her mettle in an emergency by managing everyone and being creative in finding vital solutions including the harness, headphones with mic, and infrared binoculars. Without all these items he thought, this emergency probably would have ended quite differently, and he hurried inside to see and hear how Enrique was.

Gabriel was kneeling next to the couch where he had been lain with her head on his chest, arms around him and was sobbing. Beatriz had also arrived and put a towel under Enrique's head in case there was blood. She was bending over him so Don could not see his face. He immediately asked, "How is he?".

People moved apart as Don approached and he saw Enrique's glazed eyes looking at him. A wave of relief passed over him, but he was worried about concussion. Nurse Mary appeared and was pulling off her gear. She went up to Enrique, kneeled beside him and said "Enrique, do you know who I am?"

"Mary."

She held up a finger saying, "How many fingers do you see?"

"Uh, one."

"Now follow it moving" and she moved her index finger sideways to the left and right. Enrique's eyes followed her movement. She pulled out a penlight LED flashlight with a bright globe from her pocket that she waved slowly across both pupils to see if they responded, which they did. She then said, "We are going to roll you onto your side so I can look at the back of your head where you may have hit a rock." With Gabriel's help, Enrique turned onto his side facing away from them so Mary could inspect his head.

After a few seconds Mary announced "A slight cut but quite a big bump. I will clean it and cover the spot with a Bandaid. Enrique you will lie here for a while before going home slowly and have bed rest for 24 hours. I will check on you from time to time and we will decide whether you are able to move around after that. Gabriel, Enrique does not seem inclined to look after himself by taking such big risks and risking others. I am therefore relying on you to enforce strict rest and to remain quiet. Don, Fran, I think this is a good time to comment on the lesson we must all learn from this incident."

Enrique looked at Don and the other helpers standing around the couch. "Thank you, Don and everyone. I could still be lying out there freezing to death if the A-Team had not arrived to rescue me." He then choked up with tears in his eyes.

Gabriel's eyes were also full of tears and emotionally said "Our children nearly lost their father today and I nearly lost my husband. People risked their lives to save my Enrique. How do we thank you? Words are not enough but thank you, thank you, thank you everyone. Now does not feel like a good time for a lecture but yes Mary, we need to learn from this. Don, maybe a message for everyone?"

"Well, I do not intend lecturing Enrique as he took a calculated risk not realizing how viciously and quickly the storm could turn and build up again. We are all learning about the new climate conditions and have now learnt not to trust an apparent lull in a storm. We know that under full storm conditions we cannot go outside. This has now been extended to no outside activity during a lull unless it is already an emergency until a Polar

Vortex storm has completely subsided. That obviously includes repairs and maintenance unless there has been a serious breach of a house that can only be sealed from the outside."

Enrique announced "In the next few days when I know that I am fine, everyone here who helped is coming to our house for a thanks-giving dinner. It is the least we can do."

Later, after walking from the tunnel into their basement and closing the door, Don turned to Fran, held her arms and looked into her eyes. "You saved the day my darling. Lying in the snow, pinned down by Enrique's weight and winded, I thought how, between the harness and the infrared binocs, you were so amazing with your anticipation and cool control of the situation. I am in awe of the incredible women who happens to be my wife. How lucky can one man be?" He then pulled Fran into a tight embrace and gave her a long kiss brimming with love and relief that this incident ended without casualties or death.

PART 8

Phoenix rising

Phoenix: A bird that rejuvenates from death back into life, often depicted as emerging regenerated from fire.

From the Ancient Greek word φοῖνιξ. Originally attributed to Mycenaean Greece folklore, first mentioned the poem 'Precepts of Chiron' by 6th Century BC Greek poet Hesiod.

In the fragment, the wise centaur Chiron tells a young hero Achilles the following:

<blockquote>
A chattering crow
lives out nine generations of aged men,
but a stag's life is four time a crow's,
and a raven's life makes three stags old,
while the phoenix outlives nine ravens,
but we, the rich-haired Nymphs
daughters of Zeus the aegis-holder,
outlive ten phoenixes.
</blockquote>

Chapter 25   PLANNING THE FUTURE

If we could first know where we are,
and whither we are tending,
we could then better judge
what to do, and how to do it.
- **Abraham Lincoln**

Fran said "We need to talk about remaining in Toronto. Is it the best option now that ..."

Before she could finish, Don interrupted her. "DO you remember when we first discussed where we should live, you said you want to remain within a Canadian way of life and not in some foreign culture such as Kenya?"

Fran continued "Since then things have changed dramatically. We have been hit by the ice age and we now have two boys. We need to consider their future."

Don asked, "What about our future?"

"What do you mean?"

Don explained that "Any change to what we have built up here will undoubtedly fall on my shoulders. I just do not feel like the burden that I had when we originally started this development. We have secured our position, our homes work at minus fifty and we are more than surviving with the specialized homes we continue to sell."

Fran repeated "We have the boys to consider. Wherever we live they are likely to continue remaining when they grow up. Kids will not move around so much anymore because of the extreme climate change. Our lives have shrunk here because of the ice age. Summers are not much more than a mild winter and are short resulting in a way of life that has become far more difficult. Remember before the ice age struck, we superficially discussed moving south to San Diego or Miami. Those places are warmer than here, but we do not know what the trend will be as the ice age entrenches itself deeper each year. It would then become progressively worse in Toronto and we must consider where this could be heading."

Don said "You may consider me intransigent, but I just do not have the strength or motivation to uproot us and start all over again. Relocating to a warmer region means the work my dad and I have been doing will no longer be a potential source of income and what will we do to survive financially?"

Shrugging her shoulders, Fran needed to shift her argument with some other form of leverage. "This is going around in circles. We need to see what the general sentiment is and not just for us. For all you know others on Delaney Street are discussing this problem already and we may have a move thrust upon us."

"Well, I will not be attending" said a stubborn Don. "Enlist whoever you want. But count me out, not in."

For the next two days, the couple barely spoke, upsetting their sons with their standoff, especially as they did not know what it was about. Finally, Don capitulated, acknowledging that Toronto was nothing like it used to be, conditions were deteriorating progressively every winter, and there was no predicting how much more the city and the country would decline. With a lame excuse, Don said "Okay Fran, you win, and I am giving in for the boys' sake who are really upset at us fighting. I would have thought a mother would have been more sensitive but ... never mind, just call a meeting and put this on the table."

With an irritated glare, Fran said "It is because of how much I care for Sean and David that I am not prepared to compromise their future. Anyway, let us not start another round of arguing and justifications. I will call everyone to discuss it and we can decide from there depending on what the majority feel."

Fran convened everyone for a serious discussion about the near- and medium-term future.

Here I go again addressing the elephant in the room. I hope others feel the same way and this is not a one-person crusade. Other mothers, especially with young children should agree. Don has a point about how starting all over again will impose both responsibility and a severe workload on him. But it must be done. I cannot resign myself to incessant winter and such a constrained lifestyle. I would rather perish in one of the storms … perish the thought! Sean and David, will you ever realize what your parents have done for you to ensure you have a bearable life?

The group was squeezed into their open plan lounge, dining room, and kitchen area. Everyone had been told what the subject would be so Fran launched straight into it. "We were the ones who strayed from the herd. We did not accept mainstream beliefs. We had the courage to refute the overwhelming evidence and predictions of global warming continuing indefinitely. Having taken the plunge and been vindicated by the devasting advent of the ice age, I am going to appeal to you all to think laterally again. I want you to contemplate the short to medium term future of the ice age trend by considering where it is heading. As I said to you all prior to the first protracted Polar Vortex storms, it may or may not happen. Similarly, what I am going to say may or may not come to pass. But for me the probability is high enough to warrant a review of our current survival strategies. We are expecting or perhaps foolishly hoping that things will stabilize in this new paradigm and with the structure we have, that we will all continue to survive in a new environment in a tolerable way. Sorry, but I do not. I do not find the current situation acceptable and for my children, even less so. First, I do believe as the ice age continues to entrench itself deeper, our access to essentials will decrease. This includes food, other consumables, items necessary to maintain and repair our houses, access to decent medicine and medical facilities, clothing and who knows what else. Secondly in the medium term, this is no longer a world I would like my children to grow up in. We now have three seasons, short springs and short falls followed by protracted, extreme winters. Summer is a time that only grownups will recall and the lifestyle we enjoyed will not be one our children will experience or remember. With this bleak outlook, Don and I feel we need to head south. Move closer towards the equator.

"Over the years Don and I, and then with our parents, would discuss various scenarios, especially if the first extreme winter was not an exception but a progession that would change the nature of Western Civilization in the northern hemisphere. While we were building the first houses, Don and I did a reconnaissance trip to Kenya. Our objective was to investigate the feasibility of moving to the equator where temperatures on the planet would be warmest. We could not afford to emigrate then as we were living pretty much on our combined salaries. But we also decided that the way of life would have been so different that we felt we would rather take our chances in Canada. Included in this decision was the hope that civilization as we knew it would not collapse. We anticipated that our knowledge and technology would prevail in making appropriate adjustments to survive. But the devastation of the first winter virtually crippled the country and subsequent winters have put most survivors to ongoing, extreme survival tests. Over the next few years, will we either bounce back into some new paradigm or will we spiral downward as more and more aspects of our life degenerate, returning us to the Dark Ages? I feel the current trend is on a downward spiral."

Evan said "We have all read about and watched various doomsday science fiction stories and debates. More so now that we find ourselves inside one of the scenarios that these movies and books presented. I have also wondered what we should do if the situation continues to deteriorate and try to be proactive rather than be caught in intolerable circumstances. Buying one of these ice age houses is an example of how we were proactive."

"Do you have you any preemptive ideas then if you have given the matter serious thought?" asked Don.

"Absolutely!" said Evan. It aligns with your comments about moving to a warmer area on the planet Don, but not as far as Kenya. As Fran said, on this continent the furthest south we can go is San Diego on the west and Miami on the east if we wish to remain in an English-speaking country. Earthquakes on the west coast or cyclones in the east? It must be earthquakes. Why? As we have seen, the Polar Vortices come down from central to eastern North America with the west experiencing less extreme weather. But from Toronto it is over 4,000 km along either Interstate-40 or -80, which is a really long trip. We could encounter all sorts of problems during the journey but in a convoy, we would have safety and help in numbers."

"Sybil asked "What will we do there, wherever the final *there* is? We need homes, income and would probably find many others from both Canada and America have already made this pilgrimage, which would overburden local resources. Property prices here have plummeted and would be climbing there. Would we want agricultural land to be self-sufficient? So many questions and options?"

Fran said "When Don and I first considered where we would live and whether we would want to invest in an expensive home, we followed a decision tree in a way that reduced the process to a series of steps that eliminated many options as we progressed. For example, we considered whether we would be prepared to live in Kenya or rather try to remain within a North American way of life. Once we decided on the latter, all emigration options fell away. If we chose to move south, all the options of how best to remain here and survive are no longer relevant. As a matter of interest, how about a show of hands for the following three scenarios:

1. Remain here.

2. Go south.

3. Unsure.

"Show of hands for option one? One hand per couple please." Fran counted the hands and said "We are sixty-four adults and sixteen people want to stay. Hands for option two to move south?" Again, counting the hands, Fran said "Nineteen couples. I suppose there are ten people or five couples who are still undecided. Hands just to confirm. Yes, five couples undecided."

Accepting that the majority considered emigrating south was the most prudent strategy for them, Don said "I suggest we set up two think tanks. One with those wishing to stay and one to best plan how to go forward. The last group considering whether to stay or go, should sit in on both groups to help them decide."

Fran added "One group with those going, to plan the trip and another to plan what to do when we arrive. For the people wanting to remain, those departing will be looking for people to buy their homes so the ones staying must prepare for new partners. You may want to review applicants, especially expect more buyers than homes being offered. You should also prepare a homeowner's association agreement, which is common with housing complexes. We have the whole of winter to complete our plans but should not be complacent and procrastinate."

Chapter 26   TREK PREPARATION

> "The ability to tell a good route from a terrible one
> is a valuable skill when leading an expedition.
> **- Tahir Shah, House of the Tiger King:**
> **The Quest for a Lost City**

The emigrant group first had to choose a route. There were three options. The first option was through Chicago and then through the States of Iowa, Nebraska, Colorado, Nevada and into California. The second route was via Michigan, Ohio, Indiana, Missouri, Oklahoma, Texas, New Mexico, Arizona, and into California. The final option branched off the second route shortly before St. Louis and continued down into Arkansas, Texas, New Mexico, Arizona, and into California. A pragmatic Robert said "As we have always found, with everything there are pros and cons. The safer route would be one with fewer and smaller towns on route with fewer vultures happy to predate on passing prey. But if we have vehicle problems, being near a town would be more convenient. Also, in terms of 'trigger happy' populations, would it be better to avoid places like Texas when running this gauntlet? Are they as comfortable with guns as their reputation suggests or is that outdated from old Western cowboy days? Am I being paranoid as we can come across troublemakers anywhere?"

Simon said "I feel it is random luck. So whatever route we choose, a successful trip will depend on how our cards fall rather than clever planning."

Bill was more of a believer. "I believe in fate or destiny. If we have been saved so far, perhaps God or the gods will continue to smile on us."

Encouragingly Don said, "Apart from which route, although the property market has fallen, two of us were approached by random people asking whether any of our existing, specialized homes would be for sale at the 'right price' as we have a backlog of orders that cannot be satisfied during our short summer, if it can still be called that. Therefore, I am sure that we can easily sell our houses at good prices. Those that remain can continue with our housing project as a source of income for either those who want to or for the remaining group as a whole. I hope we can convert all our Canadian Dollars easily to US Dollars as we are planning a one-way trip."

The group decided on I-80 West with overnight reservations to be made in Chicago, Illinois; Omaha, Nebraska; Denver, Colorado; Las Vegas, Nevada; and on to San Diego, California. As seriously as the route planning exercise was, it was trivial compared to the challenge of deciding what to take in their cars and trailers. No trimming of lists could shrink them adequately. Finally, they decided to ship some large truck loads to San Diego. While whatever they needed could be bought in California, it was considered such a waste to try and sell any of their secondhand goods then replace them at full price with new ones. But sanity had to prevail, and a pragmatic solution was found, hence the trucking option. The one exception was Don and Jake's tools. There was little compromise acknowledging that on a farm, there would be even more need to be independent as they would not be in a city or large town for rapid back-up.

Those leaving Delaney Street put their houses up for sale and soon prospective buyers were filing through. Demand exceeded supply irrespective of the price and house sales went quite fast. Those that had chosen to remain in Toronto were concerned about the strangers who were becoming their new partners and even more concerned about their engineer partners leaving. Who would manage the systems once they left? Were there any engineers applying to buy a house that could replace Jake and Don? At least the two men had compiled extensive documentation, manuals, list of suppliers and service companies. The remaining people knew how to use their systems and were not unduly panicked. But in the long term, they would need the right people to rely on.

Who can hope to be safe?
Who sufficiently cautious?
Guard himself as he may,
every moment's an ambush.
                    - Horace

The convoy had driven about 50 kilometers along I-80 out of Omaha
when they came across a detour into the Eugene T. Mahoney State Park. As
it looked informal with a hand-painted sign, Don was immediately
suspicious and stopped everyone. The park's gate was wide open and
unmanned, probably another victim of the ice age with few people
interested in camping and other outdoor activities. They climbed out their
cars to debate what to do. Don felt two cars should drive a way down the
interstate to confirm there is some bona fide reason for the closure. But
Evan suggested they rather cut through the park than possibly waste time
on the I-80 and carefully proceed in a tight formation while being extra
vigilant. Simon sided with Evan adding that they need to be extra cautious
and not take risks. A vote was taken, and the majority agreed with Evan and
Simon, especially as there were numerous tread marks onto the dust road
indicating frequent, recent usage.

The park was deserted and over one of the hills they came to either a
wood or a forest as the end could not be seen. Don continued to be
uncomfortable and followed Evan who wanted to take the lead. It was an
ordinary right-hand bend with an embankment on the side and a ditch
below. As Evan drove onto the bend, it gave way at an angle down towards
the dry watercourse. Evan's car simply rolled down the embankment
landing upside down on its roof. Don braked hard and skidded to a stop with
his front right wheel over the edge of the collapsed road surface. As he

rushed to unbuckle his seatbelt to help Evan and Lily, Fran opened the glove compartment saying "You were worried about a trap. Take this!" and shoved Don's .357 Colt Python revolver into his hand with a two-way radio. He took them and reached for his sheath knife that was kept in the car door anticipating that he may have to cut seat belts with the occupants hanging upside down. As he was climbing out Fran then took her 9 mm Parabellum Glock pistol, slid a cartridge into the chamber and set the safety catch. Fran shouted after Don who was already clambering down the soft slope to the rolled car. "I will radio everyone to stay in their cars with firearms ready and keep a lookout on both sides of the road. We will standby for your instructions."

Evan's engine was still running, which could become a fire hazard if the fuel line had been damaged when the car rolled down the embankment. As Don ran and slid down, he saw where the road had collapsed, there was loose sand and some cardboard cartons sticking out. He radioed Fran and everyone who were now monitoring any and all transmissions. "The road was sabotaged by covering empty cardboard boxes with sand to look normal, and as planned, it collapsed under Evan's car weight. Be extremely vigilant!"

He kneeled next to Evan's window as Lily's side of the car was against the bank and looked in. They looked dazed and distressed. Don shouted through the closed window to Evan." Try to open your electric window. Press the button." In parallel, Don gestured by rotating his hand as though he was winding down a window. The window started opening and Don immediately said, "Cut the engine!" Evan, although still in shock and hanging upside down, stretched out his hand to the ignition key and turned off the engine. Don said, "I will try to open the back window and climb in so

I can help you out of your seat belts." He reached through Evan's open window and stretched to the back-window button, which he pushed up since the car was inverted. As it wound open, he called in on the radio. "Evan and Lily are fine. Quite shaken but unhurt and hanging upside down. I am going to crawl in a back window to release them and will call if I need help. Meanwhile stay in your cars, keep them locked and continue watching out for anyone sneaking up on us. The slope that collapsed under Evan's car weight was deliberately made that way so know we are in a trap."

Don slithered through the opened back window and wriggled himself to lie facing between the two front seats. "Evan I will need help to release you so hang on. Lily you are lighter, and I am going to push upwards on your thighs to release the tension on the seat belt. You must try to press the belt's catch and I will lower you, so you don't fall." Don put his hands flat on the top of Lily's thighs and pushed up. The seat belt loosened slightly, enough for Lily to press the catch for the buckle to slip out. Anticipating the sudden load, Don had locked his arms and took the weight quite easily, then lowered Lily until her arms touched the inverted car roof below her.

Lily said, "I can crawl out of your window Evan if I can get under you."

"Try!" said Evan. Lily leaned over Don then stretched out towards the window under Evan who was watching his wife being released. She slid under her husband and managed to wriggle passed the steering wheel and out the car window. When it was obvious that she would manage, Don radioed "Okay, Lily is free, but Evan weighs more than I can manage by myself. Dad come with someone and we will get him out of his seat belt."

Always the first to volunteer, Simon arrived with Jake at the overturned car where Lily was standing, and Jake gave her a reassuring hug. "I am so relieved that neither of you are hurt. Now let us get Evan out."

Don called out from inside the car, "I need you both to reach in through the window and place your palms on Evan's thigh closest to you. I will push from his other side from here so he can release his seat belt catch. When the clip pulls out, he will fall against our hands. We must support the load and lower him until his outstretched arms can support his weight by pressing on the roof." With the three men pushing to support Evan, he was able to release the seat belt buckle and was gently lowered. Don said to him "I will back out to make room for you to try and get yourself out your window. You need to roll either your legs or your torso to the passenger side so you can slide out through the window headfirst or legs first." With help from Jake and Simon, Evan half crawled and was half dragged out of the car. Mary and Emma were already there with a flask of hot coffee, pouring them mugs of caffeine and sugar with Evan and Lily's hearts still racing from all the adrenaline that had started pumping as the car flipped and rolled down the embankment.

Since they had not been attacked and everyone was curious, people were climbing out their cars to get down to Evan's car, see the damage and discuss the situation. The men were soon discussing whether the car could be rolled onto its wheels with the all the men pushing and pulling. And then how to get it back up onto the sand road. Sean and David had climbed out of the car and were standing on the road edge looking down, but Fran had not climbed out. She was still concerned about the trap and felt she should remain watchful on the road. Fran wondered whether the large convoy rather than a single car had kept the ambushers at bay. She looked towards the boys, away from the other side of the road, then felt something push against the back of her head and heard a voice quietly but firmly saying "Be quiet or I will shoot you. Open your door and slowly get out." Fran's heart started racing, and she wondered whether she would be able to use her Glock pistol. Out her window she saw a second man crouching with a revolver as a backup to the man who had slipped through the back door that had been left open when the boys had climbed out. As she slowly opened her door, she dropped the pistol between the seats where they could not see it. The crouching man held his revolver directly at her in case she tried to bolt. As she stepped clear of the car door, the man at the back grabbed her arm and hissed "Not a sound or it will be your last." With his compatriot, he ushered Fran across the road into the trees on the opposite side to where the car had rolled. They ran, pulling her along until they were about a hundred meters from the road and completely out of sight, hidden by the tree trunks.

Indignantly Fran then said "What do you expect to do against so many people? Securing only me hardly accomplishes anything."

"You are our hostage and if your group does not meet our demands, they will continue without you" said the one man smiling wickedly through narrowed eye slits.

He was tall, thin, unshaved, disheveled and smelled of stale sweat from obviously not having washed in a while. The man's greying hair was unkempt, his collar frayed, the sweater was so mired in grime that Fran could not identify its original color. His jeans were full of holes and muddied sneakers were coming apart. However, his shorter companion comported himself in a more gentlemanly fashion, was cleaner and although his clothes were not as old, they were still quite worn. This man evidently took more pride in how he conducted himself than the other one. Quietly in a more friendly voice, the second man said, "We will hold you deeper in the forest and await a call on the walkie-talkie I left on your car seat so we can tell them what we want."

Fran thought: Every step further away makes rescue less likely and whatever nightmare they may wish to inflict on me more possible. There is a limit to how much I can slow them down without some severe backlash or retribution. I must try some unarmed combat techniques. What? Which one?

David had seen his mother disappearing with the two men when he turned around to call her to come and see the car lying upside down. Initially not sure what was happening, as she disappeared, he called out "Dad, mom has gone with two men into the forest." But with the noisy chatter of everyone below, only Sean standing next to him could hear.

"What did you say?" asked Sean.

"Mom went that way with two men" he said pointing into the forest on the other side of the road. They were pulling her by her arms. What's happening?"

Sean called urgently "Dad, dad!" but he also was not heard above the chatter. He then let out a scream that immediately attracted everyone's attention. He shouted, "Mom's been taken by two men into the forest".

Don charged up the bank with some men following him and ran to her side of the car. He saw the walkie-talkie lying conspicuously on Fran's seat, which he knew was not one of theirs. His heart sank leaving him with a pit of fear in his stomach. He then saw the Glock between the seats and knew she was in serious trouble.

Fran was about to reply to her captors but considered it more prudent to remain silent. The other man had moved behind her and pulled her arms back to secure them. She wriggled vigorously so his one hand lost its grip, and the other man grabbed her other arm to help his accomplice.

235

Remembering one of the unarmed combat techniques that Don had taught her, she sagged so they men had to lift her and support her weight. Fran lifted her feet off the ground then brought them down hard hitting their kneecaps, then continued pushing her feet down to scrape their shins until she hit the bones of their feet hard. Both men cried out and dropped her arms. She spun around and ran back towards the cars, weaving to keep trees in the way in case they started shooting while screaming for help.

Don was already running in the direction that Sean had pointed when he heard Fran's screams and changed direction slightly to intercept her. His Colt revolver was cocked, and he was more than ready to shoot first and ask questions afterwards. A few moments later they saw each other and ran into a frantic embrace. "Are you alright? he asked, and she nodded affirmatively. "What happened?" he asked.

With panting breath, she explained that "A man sneaked up to the car, got in through the open back door and put his pistol against my head. A second armed man came to the front window with a revolver, crouching not to be seen and gestured for me to get out. I had no time to do anything and they threatened to shoot me if I made a sound. About a hundred meters into the woods, I used that unarmed combat technique you taught me of kicking down on their kneecaps and feet, which enabled me to escape."

"So are there only two of them?"

"If there are more, we never reached them."

Don immediately pointed Fran towards the cars, not wanting to be caught unawares by their assailants in case they were chasing after her. He said, "Go to the cars quickly while I cover your retreat. Here is your Glock and get out my rifle. By now other men were arriving. Simon and Miguel were brandishing pistols and Don said to them, "Stay with me. Everyone else, go back to protect the convoy and get your weapons out." Turning back to Miguel and Simon, Don said "We need to secure the area as we still must recover Evan's car before we can move on. There were two armed men that captured Fran, from whom she managed to escape. I think they may be injured and not able to move fast. Spread about five meters apart out so we are not a bunched target for the two men and any others who may have joined them."

The trio headed back along the direction that Fran had run towards Don and after about fifty meters Don said "Look here on the ground. Marks of a scuffle and some footsteps leading away. They are not uniformly spaced suggesting they are both limping."

Simon asked, "Don, if we catch up to them what do you intend doing? Have a shoot-out? Try to capture them? Do we want to end up risking our lives to make a citizen's arrest of a couple of outlaws? Then after extricating Evan's car, take them back to the police in town, be tied up with statements and effectively lose a day's travel. I think they will leave us alone and we can get word back to the police once we have a cell phone signal again. This is a police problem in their area of jurisdiction, not ours."

Miguel added, "I am sure we can return to the main road and find there is no damage for it to have needed the detour. This road may not lead to another park gate for us to exit back to the interstate highway."

Don said, "I must admit after having my wife threatened by these bastards, some revenge would be most satisfying. But the convoy and everyone's safety take precedent. Yes, we do not need to become involved in unnecessary risk situations and should just get back." They turned round and walked briskly back to the cars while frequently looking over their shoulders. When they reached everyone who were looking at them for a report, Don said "We decided not to pursue the men as Fran is safe."

Turning towards Fran with a reassuring smile, he said "Fran seems to have injured them, which enabled her to escape. Once we have cell phone signal, we will call 911 and let the local police look for these men. Meanwhile we need to sort out Evan's car urgently to minimize any more delays by being exposed here. Ladies you need to keep watch while the men work on getting Evan's car back onto the road. While we were in the woods has anyone come up with a plan?"

Robert answered for everyone. "I think together we can roll the car back onto its wheels as there are enough of us. There is insufficient space for us to push from the bank side, but with ropes we can pull from the opposite side of the car. Then using the winch on my Landcruiser, we should be able to haul the car back up the soft slope that it rolled down. The roof will probably be dented and scratched and hopefully the doors will still open and close. We will then be able to continue and worry about some panel beating and spray painting when we reach San Diego."

The car was rolled onto its wheels after much heaving, grunting and pulling with even two of the wives tugging on the ropes. To tow the vehicle up the slippery incline, some excavating and shaping of a path was necessary. Don took out a spade and the men took turns doing the laborious work to create a reasonably smooth ramp. It was then easy to winch Evan's car back up to the road. His car started first time and the convoy turned around to return to the main road having now changed their minds about the authenticity of this detour. At the turn-off, Don pulled down the detour sign and threw it into the back of car. Fran asked, "Why don't you just leave the sign at the side of the road?"

"These guys could simply set it up again so I will throw it out later. It Is not intended to be a souvenir reminding us of your ordeal. How are you feeling?"

"Relieved! Angry with myself for not being more observant and vigilant. Actually, quite good to think I may have really hurt those villains."

Don stretched out his hand to grasp Fran's and gave it a loving squeeze. "My best pupil. Although we tried to take your lessons seriously during the Covid lockdown, I felt it was more to increase your confidence and was good exercise whenever we practiced. I never thought you would ever need it. And you really did now. Look how well you applied what you learned and how successful it was. It continues to give me confidence that in a tight spot, you have skills that will see you in good stead."

"Thanks Don. My success was due to having a great teacher." Concerned about their delay, Fran changed then subject by asking "How much time did we lose? Our schedule is tight, and we still need to try and reach our destination before sunset. I see that my phone has a signal now that we are back on the highway, so I am going to call 911 to report the incident. I am extremely concerned that we will be targeted by desperate people again, trying to survive after the devastation of the Polar Vortex storms." Then quietly so their sons would not hear, "Oh Don, once again I am feeling terribly guilty about bringing our boys into this mad world."

"Never feel that darling. We have discussed before how humankind's history is full of wars, plagues, pestilence, oppression, and other tragedies. But people's resolute spirits have enabled us to survive and progress. You and I were fortunate to grow up in a time of relative harmony within our country and would have preferred our boys to enjoy similar lives of peace." Don glanced at Fran and saw tears running down her cheeks. He wanted to stop the car and hold her in a tight embrace to make her feel safe again.

Because he had the convoy behind him, instead he took her hand and said softly not wanting the boys to hear, "I am sorry you had this experience. I had a sick feeling in my stomach when Sean shouted you had been taken by two men. I hate to think how you must have felt."

After a few moments Fran regained her composure. "My mind was racing, looking for an opportunity to warn you or to escape from my captors. My heart was also racing, I suppose preparing my 'fight or flight' reflex, of which I did both. Only when I saw you while dashing back towards the cars did this immense emotional wave of relief and love for you come over me knowing you would do anything to protect and save me. But the danger was not yet over. I had to get to the cars to warn everyone and pass on your instructions. I wanted the boys to see I was safe and therefore had no time to indulge myself in any raw emotions." Fran stopped talking feeling quite weepy again. When she felt she could speak, she said to Don, "We need to still check for some road problem in case it was a *bona fide* detour that these villains were exploiting and that it was not a set-up as we have now assumed. So please remain alert and do the 911 call."

The rest of the trip to Denver, Colorado was uneventful. It was an 865-kilometer drive and only arrived about an hour later than planned. Everyone checked into their pre-booked accommodation, ate, showered and went straight to bed quite physically and emotionally exhausted from the day's events. Don was still concerned and asked Fran, "You must still be troubled by today's kidnapping incident, which is understandable. And the way you always get us to talk about something traumatic, I do not think you had enough catharsis in the car afterwards. Where are you at right now with it?"

240

After a brief pause she said "Of course I was terrified as they pulled me away from you. But what has bothered me more was my concern that you would continue after my abductors, blinded by some retribution rage, and could have run into a camp full of these desperados. A resulting shootout could have ended up with you, Miguel and Simon being injured, or worse, killed."

Fran became too emotional to speak again so Don spoke to ameliorate her intense feelings. "Would you believe it was Simon who persuaded me not to pursue them? He pointed out the danger of a shootout, that you were safe, and this matter should be passed on to the local police. Fortunately, sanity prevailed, and we returned as soon as we found their tracks showing they were injured and retreating."

Fran regained some composure and said, "I still have this concern for our boys in this changed and volatile world in which we now live."

"Well, they are here in a society that has changed dramatically. They need to develop different survival skills to those we had, and we need to help them learn another set of abilities to the ones we used to grow up. We also need to learn new talents for ourselves, to reinvent who we are to endure the different, more complex paradigm that humans have been thrust into with this extreme climate change across the planet. We are fortunate to have survived three winters and now to be able to relocate to a more temperate region. Compared to many, we are most fortunate and need to keep those thoughts going to ensure we create a positive reality for all of us. Never forgetting to count our blessings." Don kissed Fran, held her tightly and they eventually drifted off into an exhausted and dream troubled sleep.

Chapter 28   A NEW HOME

When the convoy finally arrived in San Diego, Fran insisted they celebrate. They drove to La Jolla and found a restaurant with a beautiful sea view where the relieved and happy contingent finally relaxed, enjoyed good food and chatted amicably after their long trek and ordeal on route. Sybil said, "A toast. We survived the Polar Vortex extreme winters, have made our way across North America to a new, safe haven that is more temperate. After all we have been through together, helping each other, you are now part of my family. Thank you all for coming into my life, into Robert and my lives, and we can now look forward to some normalcy returning once we re-establish ourselves on a self-sustainable farm. Cheers to an exciting future!" She raised her glass of wine and everyone followed with whatever they were drinking.

A brief silence followed as the group were all lost in their individual reveries about the events that brought them here. Fran broke the silence saying "Yesterday while on the road, I phoned some realtors and agents specializing in farm sales to make appointments with them. They have a list of some of the specs we agreed on and are expecting us tomorrow morning. We will see what they have and how much they cost, then decide which farms we would like to see."

Sybil again raised her glass saying, "And a toast to Fran and Don who have done so much to bring us to this point and continue to contribute so much towards us achieving our new life objectives. Cheers!"

The group's main criteria for a farm were plenty of water and primarily arable land. Southern California's decades of drought had denuded much of the soil of nutrients and the sparse vegetation that could endure arid conditions did not get recycled to return nutrition to the ground. But the vortex storms had changed the climate and rain was now becoming a more common winter occurrence. The biomes were changing because of the decrease in the average annual temperatures and the increase in the amount of rain. Farmers were building dams and the whole region was in a state of flux. New crops had to be introduced that needed more water and would grow in a cooler climate. These changes created both opportunity and risk. The demand for food had increased enormously as traditional areas were no longer productive or yields and seasons had shrunk dramatically. Although the large number of deaths from icy polar storms had reduced northern hemisphere populations, food demand still exceeded supply. Migrants were moving south in search of warmer climes, which increased the demand for farms resulting in substantial price increases. Fran anticipated difficulties in finding something suitable within their budget. She foresaw their numbers swelling with time and perhaps their chosen place becoming a village as its hub rather than a few scattered farmhouses. There needed to be sufficient land to accommodate this expansion as well as being reasonably developed so they would be able to live off the land quite soon and have sufficient surplus to sell to generate an income for the group. Profits would be ploughed back into expanding infrastructure, but they had to find the right piece of land at an affordable price.

That evening after dinner in their hotel, Fran told the group about a film she had watched with her boys called The Biggest Little Farm. She recommended that everyone watch it as it mirrored many of their dreams, aspirations, expectations, and possible challenges in creating a sustainable, working farm from land that is probably quite barren. Sean, do you remember any problems they had and what they did to fix it?"

Pleased at the attention, Sean said "I was impressed in how they handled the coyotes. They were killing chickens, but proper coops were then built, which the coyotes could not get into at night and instead they started eating gophers that were damaging crops."

"That is an excellent example Sean. Thanks. David or Don? Other examples?"

David said "I couldn't believe how snails climbed all over their fruit trees and the ducks ate them. Therefore, they did not need to use poison to kill the snails."

"I had forgotten about that one David. Thanks for reminding me and telling everyone. Don, your turn."

"Their mentor insisted on diversity and said that was the secret to being self-sustainable. It would lead to a balance that therefore did not require artificial fertilizers or insecticides. This policy extends to a farm also having livestock and fowl as well as a diversity of plants. They had cows, pigs, sheep, goats and of course a dog. They had chickens and ducks. And the plants ranged from cereal crops and fruit trees to vegetables ensuring sufficient variety to feed everyone a completely nutritious diet. The key point is that it should not be a specialized farm like a wine estate, grain farm, cattle ranch or some other dedicated plant or animal ranch."

After a short pause, Fran said "What else Don?" but continued, "They introduced bees to fertilize crops, droppings were collected to make natural fertilizer and waste plant matter was turned into compost. Boreholes were put down and a dam was restored to collect rainwater."

"Yes Mom" said Sean. "New wildlife came to the farm like eagles and owls which also helped with the gopher problem. New water birds arrived, fish were put in the dam, frogs appeared, and I loved how a desert became an oasis."

Fran glowed as only a proud mother can. "Sean, we are building this farm for you, your brother and all the other children that will be living on the farm." Then turning to the adults, added, "This is an overview of what I feel we should aspire to. A natural farm with almost everything we need."

Don said "My first choice is land with a river where we can harness hydro-electric power so we can be off the grid. It is more efficient than solar which does not work at night or windmills that do not generate electricity when there is no wind. But we have come to a traditionally dry region although the climate is changing here too. If we cannot find a farm with flowing water, I think we should look for a farm that has one or more dry gulleys that could start running again as weather patterns continue to shift."

Fran concluded, "Please all give this serious thought and watch the film. I will send you a link to stream it and I am sure you will feel inspired. It also helps in giving us direction and specifics to look for in a farm"

Lucas asked, "What size is their farm and was this one barren when they started?"

Fran answered, "Their farm was 200 acres which is about 80 hectares. It was barren, dry, the soil had no nutrition and in the early years it remained quite bleak. But they persevered and you will see what a Garden of Eden created when you watch the film. This is what we must aspire to."

Lily asked, "Fran please send the link this evening as I want to watch the film now so I can be better prepared to assess any land offered to us by the agents tomorrow. These snippets are exciting, and I am looking forward to a new phase in my life when I thought all I had left was boring retirement. I also want to tell you about another important documentary for us to watch. The film is called The Need to Grow and has won many international awards. The documentary is dedicated to understanding the health of natural soil full of compost and natural components such as microorganisms, fungal mycelia, algae, and worms. The quality, yields and speed of crop growth in such a natural environment far exceeds what the traditional intensive farming with artificial fertilizers and insecticides can produce. It complements everything you told us about The Biggest Little Farm and will expand our knowledge how to produce better quality foods with higher yields in line with our vision of being natural with the kind of farming we hope to practice. This is all fascinating and thrilling, and I feel like we are poised to create our own Fields of Elysium."

After everyone had previously watched the documentary of The Biggest Little Farm, Fran stood up to open some discussion while thoughts were still fresh about what crops and livestock they should farm. Fran said "In a 2020s book called *Wyoming: A History of the America West* by Sam Lightener Jr., he writes about the ending of the last ice age resulting in the death of mega mammals such as the Woolly Mammoth, giant bison, the giant sloth, and others. One reason was the change in the flora because of global warming and the other of course being the advent of the Clovis people, hunter gatherers who were the forerunners of the current Indigenous American Indians. The point is that any significant climate change has a major impact on flora and therefore the overall ecosystem. In North America where the weather trend has reversed back to an ice age, what impact will that have on the continent's flora? More specifically on the food crops we can grow. We have moved south to minimize the advent of this ice age, to an area that we hope will be far less cold than Toronto since we are closer to the equator. I did research to find the top five crops grown in cold climates and it does not include cereals like wheat or corn, which are the staples we enjoy in some form or another virtually every day."

"What are the five?" asked Lily.

"Kale, spinach, Collards such as broccoli, carrots, and broad beans." answered Fran.

Mary, wearing her nurse's hat asked, "Only beans in that list have significant starch and protein. Do you know what the nutritional quantity and quality of broad beans are?"

"Considering their essential amino acid profile, fava or broad beans are the worst of the common beans such as soya, kidney, black, navy, mung, and lentils. For an average person of seventy kilograms, the number of cups of most beans is one point something whereas broad beans need more than two cups to be eaten every day to satisfy a person's RDA or Recommended Daily Allowance of essential amino acids."

"And carbohydrates for energy?" asked Mary.

"Also, low. Only 110 calories per 100 grams."

Beatriz said "How can we decide what crops we should grow now, especially if the weather everywhere is becoming progressively colder? Surely we need an agronomist's expert advice regarding what crops will be suitable for the area, type of soils, amount of water and the climate change trend. If we are reduced to surviving on such a small variety of cold weather crops, things do look bleak. It seems everything else about life is becoming progressively depressing too. I left Toronto with this misguided sense of departing from the miserable existence that had descended upon our beloved city, but this forlorn way of life has blanketed the whole continent and therefore us too."

Continuing as not only a nurse, but as a mother and concerned member of the group, Mary felt she had to uplift people's spirits before Beatriz's downhearted sentiments infected everyone. "Do not forget to count your blessings dear. By joining us, you comfortably survived the first Polar Vortex onslaughts, became part of an extended family with all its love and support, and are making the most of living in a dramatically changed world. The farm will be transformed by us into a wonderful oasis and under the circumstances, you will be blessed with continued comfortable living. Naturally, there will be changes to what we were accustomed. Having moved from Brazil to Canada, you are accustomed to extensive change and therefore once we are more settled, I suspect you may be a role model for some of the other ladies who may struggle to adjust." Mary gave Beartiz a small smile and wink, deliberately imparting a sense of expectation for Beatriz to be a stalwart, supporting any of the other ladies who may find aspects of their *semigration* difficult.

Chapter 29   INCURSIONS

If your plan is for one year, plant rice.
If your plan is for ten years, plant trees.
If your plan if for 100 years, educate children.
- **Confucius**

Eventually a compromise farm that did not meet all the ideal criteria was found and the group's new life began. Although adequate in size, it had less water than hoped, was hardly developed and the ground was less fertile than they were led to expect. Initially they had an enormous list of tasks that appeared endless. But the pioneers poured their energy into manifesting their dream with relentless, hard work, commencing with bore holes that were sunk to increase the water supply. Fields were made arable by removing stones and boulders requiring back-breaking effort. Accommodation was built, they learned about agriculture, buying of suitable farming equipment, choosing of climate appropriate crops and what longer term trees to plant. Livestock was bought, fields were enclosed with wooden posts and wire, and an endless list of more things to do. Enthusiasm prevailed and each new milestone passed was celebrated. After the second year, the farm had taken shape, it was becoming productive, and the group were now confident in their abilities as farmers. By the fourth year they were completely sustainable with an infrastructure and development of which everyone was proud.

However, with the country's economy continuing to shrink partly as there was insufficient food production for the general population. Everyone was increasingly concerned about theft and worse, it could be accompanied by violence. Because of the size of the farm, it was not possible to monitor the whole area. As part of Don's general strategic planning with everyone to manage the ranch, spots for CCTV cameras were chosen that were within range of one of the repeater base stations so that video signals could be fed into the network they had installed. Anyone could then monitor the cameras since they were unable to station a dedicated person on a 24x7 basis. A radio call came in late one afternoon from Logan who glanced at the monitor in his home as he was walking passed. "Two men are in the potato field digging up potatoes and filling back packs. I am getting a rifle and will start moving to the area. Who can support me?"

Don came in first. "On my way. I will get my trailbike to get there faster. Fran, are you there?"

"Yes, standing by."

"I have my handgun, but a rifle may be necessary as it we may need a longer range. Is there anyone else responding?"

A few voices called in affirmatively. Don ran home where Sean was waiting with the 7mm Remington and .300 H&H Magnum rifles, ammunition for both and a pair of binoculars. Sean said, "I loaded both magazines and the chambers are empty. Which rifle do you want?"

Fran added, "Should I call the sheriff?"

"No, rather stand by. It is probably starving people again and we do not need to manage desperate people with too heavy a hand so I will take the Remington. But if they are armed or resist, I will let you know. Apart from Logan, who else is responding?"

Just then James called in. "I have arrived home. Should I get a rifle, shotgun, handgun?"

"Just your rifle. Leave the handgun for Amelia" replied Don over the radio.

"Noah here. I am nearly home and will do the same as James."

"I think five of us for two of them is more than enough." replied Don. "But in case there are more of them that we have not picked up on the security cameras, please will others be on standby. And also monitor the CCTV cameras for any other intruders. Logan, meet me in the orange grove's northeast corner since it is the closest covered point to the potato field. James and Noah cut across to the bull field and be ready to approach west into the potato field. Since you will be exposed for a longer distance in the open, we will go out first. If they bolt when they see us, it will be towards you. We will respond according to how they react and radio you if they head in your direction." Turning to Sean, Don quickly said "Let's go!"

The five were in position in about nine minutes and Don radioed James and Noah. "Logan and I will move out now. If the two men stealing potatoes remain there rather than flee and we get within talking distance, come and join us as a show of force. If they bolt, make yourselves visible and head towards them conspicuously. But if they pull weapons, immediately retreat. We will rather let them escape than start a shootout." Turning to Sean and Logan, Don said "We will walk abreast about two meters apart, so we are not a single target. Keep your rifle over your shoulder so it does not look blatantly aggressive." Don then stepped out the tree line into the field and started walking briskly towards the two men who were about a hundred meters away. They were busy digging with their heads down and backs towards Don and Logan but periodically looked up from side to side. When they were ten meters away Don called out "Hey! You two. You are trespassing."

The men jumped up, swung around, saw the rifles, and stood there unarmed and subdued knowing they had been caught. "I am sorry sir," said the taller, older man in his late forties. His clothes were old, worn, dirty from digging and his lean, unshaven face looked dejected and defeated. "We are famished. I know this is theft, but we are desperate with families who are starving to death. Desperate times have forced us to take desperate measures. Here are your potatoes. Please do not hand us in to the authorities as my wife and two young children have no one to care for them or to try and find them food. Regretfully, I have not done a good job in looking after them." Tears well up in his eyes and he looked down embarrassed.

The second, younger man had been looking down submissively, lifted his head slightly to see what Don, Logan and Sean were going to do. Meanwhile James and Noah had been rushing across once they saw the two men were not going to fight. After a moment Don said, "What are your names? And no, I don't think we will report you, but I need to know more."

The taller, older man said "I am John Connaught and this is my brother-in-law Ari, Aristotle. We live about thirty miles from here on a small holding that is dry, has neither water nor crops and our borehole dried up about six months ago. We have had virtually no food for the last ten days. My daughter of eight and son of three cry all the time from hunger. Some neighbors have tried to help but they are also struggling and do not have enough food for themselves. Your farm is considered an oasis in this arid region because of what you have accomplished here. We felt that not only would you have food, but you would be in a better position to manage the relatively small amount of produce we proposed stealing. Potatoes were selected as they have plenty of calories although they are not very nutritious. We also proposed giving some to those neighbors who have helped us. What else can I tell you?"

Logan had been feeling responsible being the one to have spotted them. Although Don had always been their informal leader, Logan felt so emotional about their plight that he answered first. "I am really upset to hear about your situation and as Don said, we will not report you. In fact, I will help you irrespective of what my compatriots may feel. Are you unarmed?"

"Yes!" said Connaught.

"Come with me. We are going to my home. I will call my wife on the radio to prepare some food for you to eat. I will then give you some provisions and a ride home. But this is a once off."

Don added "We are sympathetic to the plight of people around here. We feed any needy people coming to our gate and are involved in some feeding schemes. But as we are a fairly large community, we need to look after each other first and then sell off any surplus to help keep the farm going. We are not a charitable institution to feed everyone but do have compassionate values and do what we can. Logan is entitled to make his decision to assist you in his personal capacity and others will probably want to reach out and help as well. I am so sorry you are going through this ordeal and we do pray for respite so the region can regenerate."

The two men went to Logan's house where Isabelle had quickly laid a spread of a whole wheat seed loaf she had baked earlier, cheeses, jelly, salad and some pies were being heated in the oven. John and Ari climbed into the bread and cheese, but John asked if Logan and Isabelle would mind if they took the pies home for the children. Isabelle eyes filled with tears. "No, please eat your pies and I will give you more. How many people are in your families and who are they?"

John Connaught answered with a mouth half full of food. "Thank you for something I do not feel we deserve. You are both so kind, and it makes me feel all the more guilty. My parents, my wife's parents, her brother Ari here and my two daughters represent our extended family. Seven adults and two children."

Isabelle said, "Others have brought or are bringing personal provisions to donate to you too. I have prepared a hamper with more bread, cheese, some vegetables, fruit, ham, and I will add pies and some candies for the girls. How old are they and what are their names?"

John answered, "Tammy is eight and Olivia is almost six."

"And your wife's name? "

"Ava."

"I do hope things improve for all of you." said Isabelle. "These are terrible times for so many ordinary folks, most of whom are good people."

Chapter 30   CONFRONTATION PLANNING

"What road do I take?" (asked Alice.)
"Well where are you going?"
(asked the Cheshire cat.)
"I don't know" (said Alice.)
"Then it doesn't matter.
If you don't know where you are going,
any road will get you there"
(replied the Cheshire cat.)
- Alice in Wonderland
by Lewis Carroll

The next Sunday Don called everyone for an urgent planning meeting. "We have never strategized on how to handle incursions seriously and fortunately this recent one was almost a nonevent. But it clearly shows that there is much suffering outside that makes us vulnerable to not only more infiltration but potentially violent ones as well. We need to formulate a portfolio of strategies on how to handle different situations ranging from passive to wild shooting. Without any pre-planning, our ability to manage more serious incursions will be uncoordinated and inefficient. We cannot be unprepared for life-threatening stand-offs."

"Does this include fully automatic weapons?" asked Javier.

"We need to include that scenario too as there is no way to know who may come, how determined they may be and what armament they may have" answered Don.

Hannah spoke up. "As a mother with young children, you are making me scared. We left Canada to seek a better life and this is all sounding like anarchy."

Fran tried to pacify her. "I am also a mother with children. I find this discussion frightening too. But the world has changed, and we face situations that we never even vaguely considered before the Polar Vortex

255

storms tipped us into an ice age. We survived the first three years of extreme arctic blizzards, the trek across a continent to Southern California, have built an incredible farm and are therefore survivors. This discussion is to prepare ourselves so that we will continue to survive. By considering scary situations, it does not make them real or inevitable. But if we find ourselves in one of these circumstances and we know what to do, everyone will pull together, there will be limited surprises and hopefully we will prevail. This is not merely a good idea. It could be life or death for any one of us and even though the idea is may be terrifying, we must do the exercise."

"Okay" mumbled Hannah. "I understand why we are doing this. But I am just telling you how I feel about all of it."

After a silence with no one quite sure whether to commiserate with Hannah or get down to business, Don spoke up. "Hannah, this exercise is to protect you and your girls, my boys and everyone else here. We are pacifists but not everyone out there is" he said as he swept his arm in a gesture representing the outside world. "I suggest we form groups to discuss various scenarios and write down plans on how to respond to them. The men will work in four groups. We will divide up alphabetically and the ladies are welcome to join the teams if they wish. In fact, they must so they know what to do back in our homes if we ever must engage trespassers. This has to be a combined effort pulling together on many fronts using all our personnel resources."

Jake called in over the radio shortly after five in the morning. It was first light and evidently timed for the intruders to be able to see, commit whatever they intended to perpetrate and leave before people were up and about. Jake was only up as he had gone for a pee and from habit, pressed on the TV's remote power button as he went to the bathroom. On his way back to bed, he picked up the remote to turn off the TV and glanced sleepily at the screen. What he saw woke him fully in an instant. He called in over the radio "Alarm. Alarm. Alarm. Armed intruders on quad bikes. In the southern cattle field. Not rustlers. Looks like they are after meat. Is anyone hearing me?"

"It's Michael. I am getting up. Get Mary to call people on cell phones to wake them and I will tell Ella to do the same. You say they are armed. I don't suppose you saw with what?"

"They all had rifles across their backs, and one looked like an automatic rifle. But the image was poor because of the distance and wan dawn light." said Jake. "Still, we need to go fully armed."

Don was woken by the alarm call and already his mind was working fast to assess the risk, threats and what their response had to be. 'Since these intruders were armed, brazen, and have transport to remove a potentially large quantity of meat, they are undoubtedly prepared to engage us. Therefore, they must be treated as potential murderers dictating Plan Kappa Omicron, our Plan for *Killers Onsite*. Ideally, they need to be contained until the sheriff and deputies arrive and not chased away to prevent any reoccurrences. This will send out a strong message to the district as well. There is definitely a high probability of a shootout. I am responsible for everyone since this is my and Fran's dream. I will have to fire the first response shots if these thieves do not capitulate immediately and start shooting at us. I need to identify either the leader or the one with the most lethal weapon, which would be the semiautomatic that Jake saw. Then the shotguns.'

Don called in "This is the worst-case scenario plan. We are implementing Plan Kappa Omicron to make sure we all know how we are responding to these intruders. We will form a semicircle on the south side from behind the low ridge for protection and not be facing each other. We do not want to be firing towards one another.

Michael and Jacob go to the wood on the East side of the field and remain just inside the tree line out of sight. If they come towards you, fire shots over their heads to send them back. We want them to be pinned down where they are until the sheriff and his deputies arrive."

"Copy" called in Michael.

Don continued "Similarly Enrique and Miguel go to the north side of the field, watching from behind the hill. Also fire if anyone tries to escape towards you."

"Copy" replied Miguel.

Finally, Don radioed "Robert and Jake, stay here at the houses to help and protect the women and children in case any intruder slips through our net. And those ladies comfortable in using a firearm, stay armed and vigilant. Women and children please go to my house so you are all together. Apart from Michael, Jacob, Enrique and Miguel, everyone come to my house. We will drive together in the electric truck as it is silent and go to the field's south side ridge."

As Don stepped out the door, he heard Sean behind him. "I am coming too Dad."

Don's usual first thought was to protect Sean and say no. But he knew that the teenager required real experiences and said, "Okay but listen and instantly obey any orders I give as this will be more serious than the potato thieves. I see you have already taken the 7mm Remington rifle. Jump into the truck."

Fran thought: A machine gun! And my men are off to engage them. Why aren't they prepared to wait for the sheriff? And if these intruders out-shoot our novices, will they come for the women and our resources? Just try and I will be the first to shoot whoever is in front. I need a live video feed of what is happening with the men like the police or military. How do I just sit here, especially if I hear gunfire? This is terrifying – like a war. We need to leave this place. It is too attractive, enticing desperate people to come and plunder our food. We have created something fantastic that everyone wants. Our farm is now too appealing for hopeless and wretched people who will do anything to survive. I suppose I would too. Change my thoughts. This is too dangerous a road to go down right now.

As Don drove towards the field where the cattle were being slaughtered, he glanced up at the sky in the east. The sun had not yet risen but the scattered dawn clouds were daubed with reds, yellows and pinks floating under the dark blue canopy of the sky that was slowly brightening. He thought 'Nature in all its beauty, oblivious to men's dramas unfolding below.' At the field's fence they came across a truck and three quad bikes. Don left Oliver to disable all the vehicles to prevent them being used to escape. Soon everyone was in position. Don put down the bean bag that Fran had thoughtfully given him, laid his .300 H&H Magnum rifle on it pointing towards the group, then peered through binoculars to examine the group of intruders and whatever armament was visible. Sean was about two meters to his left, protectively behind a boulder. Cuts of meat were placed in large, black plastic bags and into backpacks to carry the meat back to the truck. After confirming that everyone had settled in position, Don raised his megaphone towards the men who were butchering two more cow carcasses. "You are surrounded by armed men. Put down your weapons and place your hands behind your heads."

Don anticipated them adopting a defiant stance and was not surprised as the group dropped down behind carcasses or flat on the ground in the open. They started shooting and the man with the semiautomatic rifle being more aggressive, only dropping to one knee to spray the general area with bullets from where Don's voice had come from. There was shout of pain on Don's right and alarmed, he shouted "Has someone been hit?"

"It's me, Mason. One of the bullets shattered the rock next to me and a chip went into my arm. I am pulling it out as it is not big or deep."

Don shouted "Javier, you are next to Mason. Help him and ensure you stem any bleeding." Returning his attention to their assailants, Don moved into position behind his rifle. He had chosen the .300 H&H Magnum caliber as the bullet could travel accurately for nearly a mile and was used by hunters trying to shoot mountain goats and eagles at long distances where they would be exposed or could not get close enough to their prey easily without being seen. The prestigious British company Holland & Holland or H&H had necked down their larger .375" caliber to .30" resulting in a disproportionately large cartridge case for the smaller .30 caliber bullet. The additional charge therefore propelled the bullet faster and further than most other rifles. At 1,250 meters the 150-grain bullet still travels at supersonic speed. Don's rationale in choosing it was its long-distance accuracy giving him the ability of a sniper when using its telescopic sight. Not for hunting but for protection. How to respond to the automatic fire was a simple decision. He knew who had the most dangerous weapon and would shoot to injure the man, not kill him by using the accuracy of the .300 H&H to merely wound him. Then hope that the others will capitulate. Don looked through the rifle's scope but from his position he was unable to see the men including the man with the automatic rifle. Sean had crawled up to Don and said "Dad, I can see them from behind my boulder. Give me the three hundred rifle.

Don thought 'Sean is as accurate a shooter as I am, but do I want him wounding and possibly killing someone? He is asking me to enable him to shoot a person, a human being – or an apology for one! Would Fran agree with his request …'

Knowing what his father was thinking, Sean said "Dad you must let go and not try to protect me forever. Anyway, we do not have time to debate this. Just give the three hundred."

They exchanged rifles and Sean crawled back to his boulder. He looked through the telescope and saw the man was wearing a bullet-proof vest. Not a problem as he was not planning to shoot any vital organ, just his exposed shoulder. Sean moved the crosshairs of the scope to the man's right shoulder, and as the rifle was sighted to 200 meters, to compensate for the bullet's curved trajectory at half that distance, he dropped the rifle about seven centimeters below the position he wanted to hit. Sean squeezed the trigger and the man fell backwards. He knew it was a hit but could not see whether he was on or off the spot at which he had aimed.

Sean felt no elation, but some of the others cheered, which had a frightening effect on the other men who were pinned down. Three of them jumped up and started running. Two headed for the wood on the east side of the field where Michael and Jacob were concealed. Don radioed to them "Start shooting over the heads of the two men running in your direction and let's see if they stop or turn back." Shots rang out from the wood and the men did stop. Don called over the megaphone "Drop your weapons, place

your hands on your heads and come back before we have to shoot you too."
Watching through his telescopic sight, Don saw them slowly lowering a rifle,
shotgun and two handguns as instructed, then walked back toward the
butchered cows with their hands on their heads. Meanwhile Don had
radioed Enrique and Miguel with similar instructions. When shots were fired
towards the single man running their way, the man stopped, raised his rifle
but could barely make out Enrique and Miguel lying flat, mainly concealed
by the curve of the hilltop where they were lying. Realizing that he could not
engage them and seeing the other two on his far-right surrender, he did
likewise. He dropped his rifle, a handgun, put his hands on his head and
started walking back.

> Don had a dilemma. 'If we approached from our cover, these men could grab
> their weapons and start firing at us. There was no guaranty they would remain
> submissive. They are apparently accustomed to violence and are confronted
> with jail sentences at a time when men are struggling to provide for their
> families. Desperate times encourage desperate actions. What about the
> wounded man who may be in urgent need of attention? How long is it still for
> the sheriff to arrive? Until they were completely disabled, there is a chance of
> them trying something stupid. Decision made. We must secure them and
> assist the wounded man now.'

Don said to everyone, "We need to immobilize them, and I am concerned as
we approach, they may do something reckless. I am going forward with a
shotgun and I want two volunteers to accompany me" and looked at Sean
shaking his head slightly so he would not volunteer. "We will approach from
the left while the rest of you cover us from the right along the ridge where
we will be out of your line of fire. Fran gave me cable ties to use as
handcuffs and once they are secured, the rest of you can come forward."

Simon and William who were closest to Don said they would accompany him. Don swapped his rifle for Logan's shotgun, being the better weapon for close quarters work. His strap over the .357 Colt Python in its holster was unclipped. He instructed Lucas, "Once we start putting on the cable ties without a problem, radio Fran, give her an update to reassure everyone that we are fine, and that the situation has been successfully contained. She needs to call and tell the sheriff that one of them was shot. I will call in what the extent of his wound is to determine whether he can be transported by the police, needs an ambulance or perhaps a helicopter if it is a mortal wound, which I doubt."

Over the megaphone Don said, "We are coming across to you now. Everyone has instructions to fire if any of you try to shoot or resist." He immediately stood up as a leader should to present the first target, but the intruders remained submissive. With his heart pounding, Don walked determinedly forward with Simon and William running up to walk parallel to him. Don said to them, "Keep about two meters apart so we are not a bunched target. Shoot first if you see any hostile activity. I will put on the cable ties. Simon you cover me, remove each person's weapons once fastened and William, you maintain watch over the others. Only once they are all restrained, we will check the man who is wounded." Just before they arrived, Don clipped the strap back on his Colt so no one could suddenly grab it out of his holster. With his police training, Don knew exactly how to wind and strap the cable ties around both their wrists and ankles, so they moved through the group quickly.

The wounded man was lying near the middle of the group with his bloodied hand on his shoulder, glaring at his captors. Simon moved the semiautomatic rifle away with his foot, which was an AK-47. Don wondered where he obtained the Russian or Chinese weapon. Don thought 'Maybe it was in someone's collection before the climate change. I must tell the sheriff to interrogate him about it.' Don tied the last two men and they returned to the wounded man. "Looks like you took the bullet in your shoulder. Can I look?" Still glaring, the man moved his hand away. "You were lucky" said Don pleased to see the bullet was where he wanted Sean to place it. The bullet went right through you, missed the shoulder joint and the hole is just below your subclavian artery. If it was slightly off target, you would have had to replace your shoulder joint or worse, bled to death."

Gritting his teeth, the man said, "My definition of luck would be escaping with the meat from at least a half a dozen cows."

"I am not going to respond to that statement. I will leave our sheriff to determine who each of you are, whether you are the gang of marauders who have been preying on farms in this and perhaps other areas, and have the appropriate charges laid against you. There would have been more casualties if your men had kept up firing at us as we were under cover, excellent shots and determined to protect our property. Do you need something for pain? You will have surgery to clean the wound and stitch it up so you should have minimal fluids."

"I will just have a bit of water."

Don took his radio and made a general call. "The intruders are all bound other than the wounded man. The shot went cleanly through the shoulder, so it is a relatively small wound. Everyone in and around the field can come forward now. Logan, please bring a canteen of water. Six cows were killed and four were roughly quartered. We need to complete the job to avoid wasting any of the precious meat. What has been crudely butchered in a hurry will need to be cut further into reasonable sizes and frozen. Ladies, please prepare yourselves to assist including making space in your freezers. Fran do you have an ETA on the sheriff."

Fran responded speaking rapidly indicating her anxiety while waiting for a reassuring report. "Thank goodness you are all fine. We were so anxious just waiting and hearing gunfire. The sheriff is about a half hour out. I did advise him that one of the intruders was shot. I will call again to report on the nature of the injury. I assume no helicopter, but do we need an ambulance?"

"Yes. The paramedics will drip him, give him some intravenous analgesic and maybe antibiotic. He will then arrive at the hospital in a suitable condition to go straight into surgery."

It was a long day with the meat being cut up, vacuum packed and placed in people's freezers. Hides would be stretched and tanned from the following day. The distraction meant that people did not have much time to dwell on the events although everyone was pensive while they worked on prepping the meat. Mary and Sybil announced that they would make pizzas and salad for everyone's supper and took off midafternoon to prepare bases, toppings and enough salad to feed an army. Finally, when everyone had eaten and were lounging about lethargically from an exhausting and eventful day, Sybil stood up and said "Again I want to say that am proud to be member of this awesome team. No, not just a team but my extended family. We all pulled together and no one shirked the dangerous interaction with these armed invaders. Thanks to our forward planning we all knew what to do and our strategy, planned to anticipate such an incursion, worked extremely well. As Don is my son-in-law any praise I feel that I should be lavishing on him may sound biased. So, I call on anyone to say a few words of thanks."

While the men all held Don in high esteem and appreciated his limitless contributions, there was an uncomfortable silence. Women are more comfortable in expressing their feelings and none of the men considered themselves much of an orator. Fran jumped up to break the developing tension. "Of course, I am biased but I can be objective too. One of the important traits Don has that I have tried to imbibe into who I am is his engineering ability to anticipate. Or maybe it is the other way round where his ability to anticipate many things took him into engineering. This is not restricted to technical situations but reflects Don's general thought processes. How he anticipated the intruders could and did behave is the most recent example of this. As a result, there was minimal injury, which was also carefully inflicted on the most dangerous of the individuals and the situation worked out as well as could have been possible under the circumstances." Don tugged gently and imperceptibly on Frans sleeve. She glanced down and he gave her a feint shake of the head implying, 'No more please.' She paused then said to everyone "We are all tired after an eventful day and I am not going to carry on with my favorite subject. But I do think Don should end the day with a few words." and promptly sat down.

Don slowly rose to his feet and with a wry smile towards Fran said, "You are going to pay for this later! Okay, a big thank you to everyone. This was a joint effort, we all pulled together, the outcome was positive considering some of the alternate, possible scenarios, and instead we are almost celebrating how we successfully pulled through this armed raid. Sean tipped the aggressive and defensive stance of the intruders into surrender with his excellent shot into the shoulder of the man with the automatic rifle. And Mason received the only injury, which he insists was trivial. Tonight is not the time for any autopsies but we need to analyze the events and see

266

where we can enhance our response options. In particular, we need to devise some better way of being alerted to intruders. We were lucky that Jake noticed them on his monitor so early in the morning and that these guys happened to choose a location where a camera picked them up. Considering the size of our land, we are a soft target, which means there are many places where people can easily enter. Our perimeter is too long for continuous camera coverage and we are not able to have people monitoring screens on a 24x7 basis. But there are systems that respond electronically to movement that can trigger an alarm. It does mean more investment in surveillance systems and may be difficult to justify. I suppose if these guys slaughtered say ten cows valued at around $2,500 each, the total loss of $25,000 would have cost us more than additional components to our existing surveillance system. But that is not a decision to make now. Instead, I suggest an early night for everyone and let us make tomorrow another great day." Don sat down to spontaneous clapping, which is how everyone felt comfortable in expressing their thanks and appreciation for all he had done for them.

When the Whitelys finally returned home, Fran immediately convened a family gathering. "Sean, your shot ended the stand-off, but I want to know how you feel about shooting someone." As with Sean's bear shooting, she wanted Sean to express his feelings and not end up with sentiments that may become detrimental in the future.

"At the time, we were under fire and Dad could not see the guy with the machine gun, I could. It therefore seemed to be the best and only option. As with the bear incident, I functioned automatically without inviting in any analysis paralysis. I was congratulated by many people and have been too occupied by the goings on since then to adequately consider on it."

Fran continued to press him. "I accept that and now that you have a moment to think about it, how do you feel about shooting a person?"

"Well, I do not feel guilty as we had to end the shoot-out and capture these men. Obviously, it was not first prize to retaliate by shooting back, and my shot was not with the intent of killing him. Contrasting this, the man was trying to injure and possibly kill some of us as his bullets were not shot into the air over our heads as shown by Mason's injury. How should I feel? Dad as an ex-policeman, how do people tend to feel after shooting someone?"

Don replied "There is no single answer as each situation is different. If you are being shot at, if you shoot an innocent person, if they are wounded or killed. Each circumstance results in a different response, which is also dependent on the personality of the person and perhaps the quality of the psychologist assisting with the compulsory post-traumatic stress counselling."

"How should I feel?" asked Sean.

"I cannot tell you how to feel. You need to look within and if necessary, modify your beliefs about the situation so it does not become a problem. That is why talking about the incident helps one get in touch with these feelings and beliefs. When you asked to shoot because you were in a better position, my first thought was how you could subsequently feel about having shot someone, especially if your bullet was off target and seriously injured or killed the man. I knew you would shoot accurately and that by being the one to take the shot, it could help you in various ways such as developing further self-confidence, reassuring you in the future if confronted with a similar situation that you have the mettle to do what is necessary, and to simply experience the feeling that *I shot someone*. The world has become a more dangerous place than the one your mother and I grew up in and this was a form of training to help be prepared for what life may still decide to throw at you. Let us have a chat tomorrow evening by which time you will have had more time to reflect on it."

Chapter 31   WHITHER TO NEXT?

The man who has bread to eat does not
appreciate the severity of a famine
- **Nigerian Yoruba Proverb**

Soon after the shooting incident, Fran assembled everyone after a brief discussion with Don. She decided as the Sunday was to be warmish, they should have a debate followed by a barbeque. Everyone prepared salads, bread and rolls were baked, desserts were made, drinks set out and a variety of meat prepared to satisfy everyone's palate. However, as there were now two vegans and four vegetarians in the group, they added to the variety of salads plus some plant protein dishes appropriate for their respective diets. Kids ran around playing, people lazed about, good food was enjoyed, and everyone felt quite relaxed. The weather was bearable, a few wispy clouds in the sky, no breeze, and a teasing sun suggesting but not delivering much heat. Days were far cooler than they were at this time of year because of the planet's climate cooling down.

Finally, Fran decided it was time to address the serious matter that was bothering her more and more. She was not comfortable with the subject and had some misgivings.

Fran's thoughts: Déja vu. Me addressing the elephant in the room again. First why we should not be assisting everyone in Toronto after the first storm. Then if we should even continue living in Toronto. And now if we should move to somewhere like Kenya. Always me broaching difficult issues and always Don taking the risks in dangerous situations. All we did was have a vision and a business, and now we are unofficially the alpha male and female of this group. Please will someone else step up and lead. I am tired of it. Oh well …

270

She summonsed all the adults together and opened the subject saying, "The last time I requested a meeting on this topic, we were still in Toronto, I was concerned about what the future held for us and more so for our children. We have developed this beautiful farm, but sadly, after the recent shootings, I am troubled by our ongoing safety and again what kind of our world we will be leaving our children to grow up in? I therefore want to initiate the following for discussion.

"When Don and I originally started working on the Polar Vortex survival project, one option we considered was if the impending ice age became too severe to live in, whether we should consider moving to the tropics. We then visited Kenya on a fact-finding trip as it lies on the equator and is a country where they speak English. Uganda and Tanzania were other options in the area. While our relocation south has resulted in weather that is warmer than Toronto, it is still fickle and its summers have also shortened, limiting our ability to enjoy adequate farming seasons. But with the shootout and the surrounding region struggling to survive, I am concerned that in both the short and medium term, we will continue to be threatened with incursions. Summers may shrink further and become colder as the ice age progresses. Having shown our strength to the outside world with a willingness to face armed intruders, any future ones will be with even more determined men. This is not a life I want for myself, my family and all of you who are my extended family. I therefore want to debate whether we should all emigrate to Africa or elsewhere on the equator and invite everyone's thoughts on this suggestion."

Fran's thoughts: An unsurprising silence as our concerns are constantly being discussed by everyone anyway. In Toronto I also had a stunned response despite people talking about the problems of survival there all the time. I suppose this is another wedge like the one that split our original group and will probably divide this one as well. At least relocating to America was a familiar environment but Africa! Why does this type of responsibility always seem to fall on my shoulders? Does no one else want to address these controversial issues? Why am I the pariah who always disrupts the status quo?

Finally, Amelia broke the silence. "We have young children and have had the same concerns. During the Covid-19 virus pandemic lockdown, in Kenya there was enormous loss of income when the tourist trade died, and people resorted to poaching wild animals to survive. Not only did they eat the meat, but animals like giraffes were hunted so the surplus could be sold for income. Butchers were then selling it to replace beef. I believe despite international food demand far exceeding Kenya's agricultural capacity, a decline in mainly tourism has put the Kenyan economy under severe pressure, and it is apparently in a state of collapse. The American President tried negotiating with their Prime Minister to allow American farmers to start a Green Revolution and turn Kenya into a breadbasket to feed itself and other nations. But they were concerned an American invasion would eventually take over the country. Now on American TV, political and economic commentaries are suggesting a colonization of the East African English-speaking countries, and some South American countries too. If the Kenyans rise up and resist, there could be another Mau Mau revolt against whites living there. But I suppose the problems I have mentioned with Kenya are applicable to virtually all Third World countries in warmer areas."

Jake said "I am reluctant to contemplate another move, especially at Mary and my age. And this would be a far greater move than the last one. Fran is right that the region is becoming increasingly dangerous. We struggle with the weather and the short summer seasons to grow sufficient crops. While we are in a better position than Toronto, if we are brutally honest, we are not far enough south. I do speak some Spanish, so I am more flexible than needing an English-speaking country. Central America is around the equator that passes through Panama. The other countries in the region are Costa Rica, Belize, Guatemala, Nicaragua, Honduras, and El Salvador. However, my first prize is not to leave the USA."

Gradually people wanted to voice their opinions. Miguel said, "Enrique and my families know Portuguese and if not Brazil, the leap to Spanish would be easier for us than those who are unfamiliar with the structure of a Latin language. Central America is also within driving distance whereas East Africa requires us to fly there. That would represent far more difficult logistics for the type of things we were able to pack into a car and trailer when we left Toronto. But we are in a minority and suspect an English-speaking country would be more appealing to everyone else."

As suspected, Fran's suggestion was a wedge with about half interested in change and a new adventure and the balance more conservative wishing to maintain the status quo. Michael raised a point about the farm's shareholding and their value. "If we go, those that wish to make the move will want to realize their equity to help fund emigration costs. Assuming the number will be around 50% of us, those remaining will be too few to farm the ranch and should therefore seek new shareholders. They could buy out those who decide to go, which is the money needed to travel and establish us elsewhere."

Mason said "I am one who wants to stay. This is my home. I love what we have built here, and I do not think it will be any safer in Africa. The problem with Michael's suggestion is that we may end up with one or more undesirable families as new shareholders and during any interviews, may not pick this up until some stressful event occurs, when they show their true colors."

"Easy to manage." said Don. "Put them on a six-month probationary period. If a committee of the original people do not unanimously approve their tenure, sell their shares to someone new and reimburse them."

Fran added "Applicants must sign a blank share transfer form and the committee holds the share certificate. If they pass the suggested six-month period, the transfer form is torn up and the share certificate is given to the family. If not, they are given notice, the name of the new applicant is entered on the share transfer form and a new share certificate issued. It is a common business practice and easy to do." While Fran had maintained an upbeat and positive demeanor to everyone, she had this pit in her stomach having to consider abandoning their dream farm and emigrating to a Third World country. But if they needed to be on or near the equator, there was no other choice.

Finally, everyone fell silent considering the serious ramifications of Fran's suggestion that no one had wanted to address. Sybil eventually spoke. "Irrespective of what I want, being with my children and grandchildren will take precedent. If they leave, we will accompany them, and I am sure Robert agrees." She looked towards him and he nodded back. "As we will not reach a decision now, I suggest we enjoy the rest of the barbeque and have a follow up next Sunday. During the week we will all be discussing this proposal between us and will have better ideas about what we each want to do. And if enough of us agree that we should go, what our preferred destination should be. Fran and Don, we will need you to give us a presentation say on Wednesday evening about your trip to Kenya with your observations and photographs. That will help everyone get a better feel for what life in a Third World country entails. I can't believe it, another big adventure at my age!"